LONG JOURNEY HOME

Jackie Smith, Ph.D

To order additional copies of this book, contact:
Bookwhip
1-855-339-3589
https://www.bookwhip.com

Dedicated to:

Laurie Rudig

This one's for you!

…because you loved the autobiography trilogy

Chapter

ONE

Yes, I admit it-I'm an old lady now but that doesn't mean I can't remember my youth as well as anyone. As a child I used to hate it when some adult would start out with "In my day...". I lived in the present, as do most of the young. As a matter of fact, I still do. As a youth, my past was not yet as exciting as I longed for it to be and I had difficulty in even attempting to imagine what my own future held for me. No one was really aware of the backpack of issues I carried within as I made the crossover from childhood into being an adult. Although I failed to understand how and why some people commit atrocious acts and attempt to blame it on the same acts being done to them as children, I believe, as I grow older and watch the world evolve around me, that William Earnest Henley had it right in his poem, "Invictus". We are all responsible for our own choices, good and bad. We cannot blame others. I find it inspiring to feel I am in control of my choices when for so many years I allowed others to totally control me. It is easier and understandably more human to blame our mistakes on others.

The older I grow, the more I notice that the young either pity me and act as though I am a child again (at least in my mental capacities) and my opinions don't really count for much *or* they dismiss me entirely as being senile. Shakespeare's seven stages of life do not ring true to me or perhaps he had a handle on the answers because it often seems as we age, we *do* become more child-like. My childhood was not one which would

1

encourage any longing on my part to return there. For a great portion of it, my main desire was how to escape it.

When I read for pleasure, I enjoy non-fiction. I get hooked by the words, "This is a true story". Well, this story is a true one and though I do realize that other characters in this book may have different perceptions as to the people and events, this recitation is how *I* remember it.

In my youth there was no such thing as video games; I didn't even see my first television until I was seventeen and while no man had stepped on the moon as yet at that time, most families didn't have to walk anywhere because all had at least one automobile.

I have often heard people say that God puts certain people in our way at exactly the right time and I can certainly agree with this. Of course, people also say, "There but for the Grace of God go I" when we see misfortune fall on someone other than ourselves. I do, however, believe that certain people for whatever reason have an impact on us that make them unforgettable; whether in a good or bad way. I do not believe in my fate being already decided before I was even born; what enjoyment would such a life bring if everything was already decided from start to finish and couldn't be changed or affected from any choices we made as individuals? Therefore, I would rather accept the blame for any mistakes I make with my choices and feel proud of the successful ones I made on purpose *or* by chance.

I have always been an avid reader and while that can be a good thing, it also has its downsides as well. I did use reading as an escape from my own environment, however, reading also gave me some very unrealistic expectations about what *I* could expect from life.

If the girl in the story ended up with a handsome knight someday to live happily ever air hereafter, why shouldn't I expect the same? Let's be fair about it, right? When I hear youngsters arguing about who should be leader with the old; "Who died and made you king?" argument I think, who, indeed?

Long before all the psychoanalytical babble became a part of everyday conversation, I knew my family was different from most of my friends'.

My family was, in today's grossly overused terms, very dysfunctional. My father was an alcoholic and a committed gambler and my mother was somewhere between an undiagnosed bipolar individual with perhaps additional schizophrenic tendencies. Her quick flare up temper and love of drama made my three brothers and myself live between a fear of her reprisal for some real (or imagined) transgression we had committed and a desperate longing for her approval.

Our home eventually looked like one which belonged on the "Hoarders" program on television. Except for the forays I made to clean it up myself; no one else minded stepping over or around any obstacles which lay in their way. Dishes piled up in the sink, clothes piled up on the floor, excrement and urine from our long list of pets was the norm and not the exception. At various times in our lives while I still lived at home, we had at least two dogs, cats, hamsters, goldfish, a spider-monkey, parakeets, full sized parrot, Guinea pig, ant-farms, canaries, boa-constrictor, and probably others I have forgotten. All these pets were not from shelters or the "pound". No, while we didn't always have what we (the humans in the house) needed, these were always American Kennel Club registered (or other kinds of proof) with pages of birth certificates to prove it their lineage.

It was not always like this. I have vague memories of what it was once upon a time. Prior to this time, we had a lady who came to our home to do the laundry and house cleaning but suddenly she disappeared from our lives.

I remember my mother didn't work outside the home then and my father was a lithographer. I really wasn't sure what that was, but he left each morning wearing a suit and tie. I vividly remember the onset of the great depression although I didn't understand what it meant. As a child I do remember gas rationing, tinfoil and rubber band saving and hearing a lot about the "war effort" and savings bonds.

Things changed in many ways, not the least of which was my mother's loss of interest or motivation for her homemaker role.

Time stands still for no man, but the dramatic changes in my mother between my youngest years and the end of my elementary school journey were almost unbelievable. In a novel they would have been unrealistic and shout for a better storyline. First, her personality and character traits were so different as to belie she was the same person. When I was very young, she was fastidious in her personal care. She dyed her hair an auburn shade and kept it up so well, even my brother and I thought it was her real color. Her manners were impeccable, and she never used obscenities in her speech. She was slim and had beautiful legs; think (Betty Grable here). She had good taste in clothing. She had a varied selection of aprons, which she always wore in the kitchen and for any meal preparation. Even now, thinking back I can see her in her ruffled apron, tied around her waist to protect her dress from splatters and spills.

I never ever saw my mother in pants of any kind; just as the familiar commercials would later show women, she wore dresses and aprons as she went about her housework. This even included sleep-wear. She had nightgowns and robes, but never pajamas. Her manner was such that when around the outside world she was considered friendly, charming and attractive. I was in awe as I watched her beguile outsiders with her charming persona. Who could have guessed this was the same woman who beat her children and was such a shrew in her own home?

The other side of her was related to her housewifery duties. At first, she believed completely with "a place for everything and everything in its place". Woe be the child who left their toys in the living room at night, who forgot to make their bed in the mornings, who didn't take their plate and silver to the sink when excused from the dinner table. Children were required to ask permission to be excused from the table prior to leaving after they had finished their meal. I prayed for small portions on my plate when filled by my mother or father because children were required to "clean your plate", before being excused. So, you didn't like liver and onions? Too bad. Eat what was on your plate or sit at the table until bedtime and eat nothing until morning. Or peas and carrots? Same rule.

My father was not exempt from being derided for not putting his soiled clothes in the hamper or cleaning the tub out when done with his bath. But it was much worse for my brother and I. How about not being allowed to go outside on a balmy spring afternoon to play because you left dirty clothes on the bathroom floor? My mother was the queen of "No second chances. Ever.

She had a daily schedule early in my memories. Monday was laundry day. Soiled bedding and clothing were washed, hung out on the clothesline, brought in, folded and returned to their proper place long before my father came home each day. Pillow cases, table cloths, table scarves, were starched and ironed with my father's and brother's shirts; and this ironing was done on Tuesdays. Wednesdays were thorough cleaning of bathrooms and all the floors in the house. Sweeping, mopping and waxing with my brother and I regulated to our bedrooms until all floors were dry and clean enough to eat from. If we missed the call to come into our rooms while floors were drying, then we weren't allowed in the house until she gave the okay. You could get a drink from the water hose outside but the worst thing was the "no bathroom breaks" until the floors were all dry and her "all dry" signal was given. Our friends on the block were sympatric to some extent and sometimes when a "bathroom code red" was given they would let us go in their houses and use their bathroom.

Thursdays, which my brother and I loved best, were for baking. Homemade bread and sometimes cookies, a pie, cake, turn-overs or cinnamon rolls. The sweet smell permeated the house and made your mouth water with saliva.

Fridays were venetian blinds, windows, sometimes the ice-box (and later, a refrigerator) oven, and inspection of our rooms by my mother. My father took care of the yard. They had purchased this brand-new little tract house, but that was considered quite an accomplishment for a young couple and the fact that we had "help" who came in regularly gave the family a certain status they were never to achieve again. After my father's enlistment into the Air Force and our first military transfer, the house was sold and the family was never to own another home but always rented housing.

I don't remember being really, really hungry during *this* time but I do know that we often depended on financial assistance from my maternal grandmother.

The earliest I can remember anything about my childhood is about age six. I knew my father lost his job and was hunting everywhere for a new one. I cannot erase from my mind the image of him cutting out cardboard to insert inside his shoes because he had holes in the soles and couldn't afford a new pair.

But now, my father's *real* job was the Air Force, but drinking and gambling ran a close second. My mother was forced to get a job and for many years worked two full time jobs at the same time. This was something I took for granted and never fully appreciated this sacrifice on her part to feed and clothe us. I never really gave her credit for this until I was grown with a family of my own.

Our father may have earned our admiration with his wonderful stories and many different talents (like the magic tricks he taught us and his dramatic way to tell stories about mythology and how to catch fish with just a little piece of baloney.) She was a licensed practical nurse and a telephone switchboard operator for "Ma-Bell" when that was the only phone service in town.

My father was very, very attractive (especially to women) with dark curly hair and sparkling dark eyes and a real talent for what we called "Texas bull-shit". The reader might remember the old saying that some people could sell refrigerators to Eskimos; he was charming to women and extremely respected and likeable to men. From childhood onward I have watched him beguile everyone from babies in their mother's arms to the teachers and principal at my school.

Since I was an Air Force military brat now, we moved frequently. For some unknown and obscure reason each time we moved, I made friends easily and did better in my scholastic endeavors, at least until the newness wore off. It was as though I knew that others would be watching me and I had to prove myself before I would be accepted. It was just the opposite for my siblings. They hated the moving.

Because our family was limited in funds, both due to military pay being extremely low and because of my father's propensity for the cards and the Jack Daniels, there was never any to spare. I saved babysitting money all one summer to be able to afford one name brand sweater like my friends had. Then I had to be careful I didn't wear it too often for fear they might realize it was the only one I had. I was wonderfully adept at the fences I built in my character; the ones where I told myself I didn't care; I considered myself lucky to get many of my clothes from the Sears and Roebuck catalog, at least they were new and not from the Woolworth five and dime store which would equate to the current dollar stores.

When I was in the eighth grade, I shared with my favorite teachers that one day I was going to be a famous writer. Several of my teachers agreed with my goal. I loved writing and enjoyed being allowed to read my work to the class. I wove my stories between truth and fiction, often taking the most mundane outing with my father and brothers into a wildly imaginative maneuver barely escaping a grizzly bear in the national park campgrounds.

A setting like these camping trips were the ideal surroundings for my father. We sat around a campfire, marshmallows and wieners roasting while he told us magical stories with a twinge of ghosts and goblins to make it dreadfully difficult to sleep. His favorite story, which caused nightmares occasionally, but also delighted us and gave us those little hair-raising chills up and down our spines was one about a man who had lost one of his arms in an accident. The man was named one-arm Jake. The story deliciously explained that the arm had been lost after surgery, and the man was doomed forever to roam the forests searching for the missing arm. The story further emphasized that if an individual slept on his back with his arms crossed all night, the man would not bother him but leave him in safe peace. I often woke up in the middle of the night, found my own arms uncrossed, and quickly crossed them. Trying to stay awake to guarantee the man wouldn't accost the sleeper was almost impossible. Fighting sleep was so difficult after a day of fishing and hiking, but otherwise he would cut one of our arms off and take it with him.

How horrified today's parents would be to realize this was story-time fare on the camping trips or perhaps not, when I see some of the T.V. or movies available to today's youth.

Truthfully, I never got less than a top grade on any writing I did. Some of my closest friends would come to be helped with their assignments which I felt proud to give.

English was my favorite subject and when I entered high school and a creative writing class was offered, it became another favorite.

Many of the books we were to read for class I had already read on my own. I could list my favorite writers and why I enjoyed their works. When teachers assigned essays and the rest of the class moaned, I got excited and usually finished the assignment many days early. Once I even asked my teacher if I could turn in more than one. She thought I was angling for extra credit, actually I just wanted her to read it.

For a while my father was assigned for duty at the base service club. He scheduled entertainment for the young airman on Friday evenings and often bands for a dance on Saturday. My brothers and I thought it was a wonderful job for him; he could watch all the movies free; he could select plays for the airmen who could audition for parts, and then perform the plays. He was very gifted himself and very appreciated for his acting abilities.

Just as some children will choose to the clown in class, rather than be ignored or because they knew they would not be recognized as the smartest, most attractive, or blessed with an unusual sports ability which insured them a place and sense of identity within their peers, *I* was very good at telling stories, embellishing them with, twists at the end or comical explanations of cause and effect of specific action or behaviors of my characters. The characters I wrote about were very real to me. For years, the story I told the world about my family and home-life was very different from the one I pretended to have at school. I was wise enough to carefully select what I volunteered for, making sure I matched my abilities to the task. Failure was not an option for me. I always was on the fringes of the popular clichés; not in the center, but enough to keep me from being delegated to the indivisible ones who envied even my somewhat "barely in" status of this special group. Therefore, I was on the debate team where my unusually large vocabulary and aptitude for creating good arguments for either side made me a successful member.

As is said, "The spirit may be willing but the flesh is weak"; I desperately wanted to play on the volleyball team or basketball but I was barely five-feet- two, even with tennis shoes on, my legs were curvy and attractive but short.

However, I did find a niche on the newspaper and yearbook staff. Once, while in fourth grade, I wrote a one-character play and presented it to the class where it was warmly received. The satisfaction I felt from this triumph carried me for months afterwards. Even some students who didn't actually know me prior to this experiment found time to congratulate me and tell me they envied me my courage to perform before others.

Until I started school and at that time, a child was required to be six years of age by September first, my brother, ten months younger than me and I were left pretty much to our own devices with the exception of few rules set by our mother. It didn't matter if we broke one of these rules early in the day, my mother would bring my father up to date on my transgression and a complete report when he arrived home each day. He was obligated to then administer the consequences even if we had been punished by our mother earlier for the same offense.

These offenses were not always consistent but would depend entirely on the whims of my mother. What warranted a severe "attitude adjustment" as my mother titled it or a mere mild admonishment varied from day to day. I can remember being slapped, open palm, in the face or on the buttocks by my mother, shook by the shoulders or dragged about by the arm or shoved into my room with the door slammed behind me, there to remain until my father arrived home or she came and released me. It wasn't, as today's saying goes, to be taken personally, my brother received his share as well. If my mother was significantly angered by the transgression, she would nag or goad my father until he punished us according to her satisfaction, usually with his belt. I never got angry at my father, wrongly or rightly, I held my mother responsible for these punishments and chose to feel sorry my father was being pushed into his actions in order to buy himself some peace.

I do not remember ever being hugged or kissed or even praised by my mother. Neither was my brother, Jary. I found it extremely difficult to express my emotions to others even after I was grown and had children of my own. It was completely foreign for my mother to offer sympathy for a bruised knee or a tumble from tree-climbing. Today, were she here, I am sure she would have employed the "Suck it Up" so commonly used by some parents today instead of her favorite labels of being a "sissy" or a "suck-tittie baby" she applied to us in derisive labeling. I believe I was so conscious of the lack of affection in my childhood, it resulted in me trying to mete out love and kindness to my own children so often it resulted in less discipline than they probably deserved or needed. Showing affection often felt fake or as though it were a pretense I was trying to learn how to use. How I learned to cherish memories of touches, pats, squeezes and closeness between my children and myself. How different, I now wonder, would my life had been had it included these signs of loving attention and affection for myself?

It was a cold, strict, and almost impersonal environment. Even between my parents there was a shortage of emotional expressions of affection or kindness. I never saw my father or mother hug or kiss each and the once-in- a- while-time when my father seemed to reach out for such he was immediately rebuffed by my mother.

Of course, it was natural then, that I perceived my father as the "good parent" notwithstanding the role forced on him as disciplinarian by my mother. At one point in my childhood, I pretended to myself that she wasn't really my biological mother and this was reinforced when I saw my parents' marriage license certificate the first time. The names were what should have been expected. My mother's maiden name was there, on the correct space and my father's was on the line for his signature; but the date was over a year past my birth. Was I adopted? My imagination ran wild with theories. I preferred the one I liked best: my father had me with some other woman, who didn't want me, so he brought me to his marriage with this woman who pretended to be my mother. I liked this explanation. No wonder she had no love or patience with me. She resented me. How did I explain my birth certificate? Well, first of all, when I later compared the two documents, the marriage license was dated a full year after my birth. Who had me that first year? Where did I live, and with whom? Did they go through any kind of formal adoption legality to get her name on the birth certificate? At least I felt secure in my bloodline to my father after all, I never found any paperwork giving my last name as different from his.

This satisfied me so well, I often told my friends that she wasn't my *real* mother but my adopted one but he *was* my real father.

I was a year old when World War Two began, and though I can't be sure, I credit effects of the Great Depression (1929-1941) with my father's enlistment into the Air Force. The depression had its disastrous world-wide economic crises and left many without jobs and homeless. This was both a way to serve his country and to provide for his family. Of course, I was very young during this time and the bulk of my memories come from others. My maternal grandmother counted ration stamps to purchase gas, classroom students salvaged tin-foil and rubber bands to help the country. Ration books for food purchases such as meats, sugar, and others were zealously counted and used sparingly. My father was to spend twenty years in the military and being caught in the middle of the depression and the war was to set the foundation for the future path for many people. Basically, our family went from being "well-to-do" to a life of continual financial struggle and the life of displacement with no real roots as we moved from one military assignment to another.

There's the old "twenty-twenty" vision which could be applied here. Many people had their lives changed from these tumultuous events. No matter how we justify the changes in our lives there can be no argument that like many other Americans, our family was changed by events we, as families or individuals, had no control over. These two events changed lives; some were made richer, some were made poorer, but all were changed.

Had we been born in a different generation or if these two dramatic events had not taken place, who knows how different our paths would have gone?

I don't know what job responsibility my father had during the war, but I do know he wasn't deployed overseas. Even considerable years later he did not see overseas action in the Korean conflict. This in itself almost didn't happen because my mother had just had a miscarriage which ended up with very serious complications and her doctor wrote a letter which basically changed the orders he had received to go to Korea because the doctor did not feel she could take care of herself and four children without his help. There was relief on her part and though I may have misinterpreted his true feelings about it, I always felt my father had a sense of shame that others served overseas, and he had some guilt about having been excused from serving there. At various periods during his military career he served in special services, then went through training and became a radiologist, a staff photographer and probably some I have long forgotten. He dressed every day in his blue uniform and I never saw him in anything but that or the scrubs he wore after becoming a radiologist.

He was a very good-looking man, as I noted before, but was also viewed as charming and charismatic. He loved hunting and fishing, playing the guitar and harmonica as well as singing his own accompaniment. He was often compared to Frank Sinatra in his looks with that glossy, wavy black hair and dark, flashing eyes. Very late in life, during his sixties, (and after his release from the military he took advantage of the G.I. bill to go back to school at Abilene Christian College in Abilene, Texas and achieved his B.A. in Creative Writing.

Many of us have known couples who as individuals, might lead very successful lives but as a partnership were totally toxic. My parents were perfect examples of this although growing up I saw my father as almost perfect and my mother as wicked and evil beyond belief.

Early in the military lifestyle my father began his love affair with the bottle and gambling. This duel commitment on his part placed the greatest hardship on the financial health of the family and did two other things: drove my mother into getting employment outside the home to support the family and changed the dynamics within the members of the home. My mother began to view him as the anchor dragging the family down and her constant criticism and disrespect for him only served to alienate my brothers and I from her, and made us secret allies of my father. Everything he did wrong we blamed on her; she "made" him the way he was. My brother and I read "Call of the Wild" by Jack London once and thereafter to each other referred to her as the "Alpha Male" in our pack.

This new life also meant that my mother was rarely home. Her schedule took her from a working the 11:00 p.m.-7:00 a.m. shift as a switch-board operator straight to her second job as a practical nurse in training at a senior citizen home from 8:00 a.m. to 4:00 p.m. She made arrangements with her supervisor to not take a lunch or eat it "on the run" as she called it so she could leave at 3:00 p.m. She got home about 3:15, bathed or took a shower and went in her room, closed the door and slept until she had to get ready and leave for her shift at the switchboard. When I look at this now, I feel the shame and lack of understanding I had for her and this enormous sacrifice she made. This wasn't a temporary "fix" for the family's financial survival, she did it for years. And all this time I acted as though she *chose* to do this, to get out of her role as mother and homemaker. It forced me into doing her work. I would come home from school, do my own homework and make sure my brothers did theirs', then figure out something to feed us for supper, enlist my brother's aide in feeding whatever pets we had; throw a load of laundry in the washer, and before we got a clothes dryer, either hang it outside on the clothesline, or a folding clothes dryer rack to dry indoors in relays. Then fold the clothes and put them away. I wasn't assigned these duties because I was the oldest or because I was the only one who knew how but strictly because of my gender which meant it was all considered women's work.

My brother's one and only assigned chore was to take the trash out each day.

No dishwashers at that day in time, so dishes and cleaning up the kitchen before I bathed and went to be. I can close my eyes and remember being woke up when she arrived home so after she grabbed something to eat, and before she went to bed, she made sure we were up and getting ready for breakfast and the school bus.

I guess in today's world, a therapist would tell her it was all her fault because of her *enabling* my father to live a free spirit caused all the trouble. He couldn't have kept his daytime work in order and his evening playtime with his friends, the cards, and the alcohol if she had just stayed home and forced him to "shape up" and do his share.

Be that as it may, my father was my brother's and my hero. Late one night I was in bed asleep when I began to hear shouting and felt the stings of being hit time after time. By the time I realized what was happening and sat up, trying to get oriented, the hits stopped and I began to make sense of the shouting. My mother had found that I had left supper dishes in the sink and went to bed, planning on doing them before school the next day. I knew all along that this wasn't going to be acceptable to her, but had foolishly believed by some chance she wouldn't find them. She pulled me by my hair, finished her blows with the hairbrush, and told me in no uncertain to get my butt downstairs and do those dishes. I remember now I hurried to get them done and escape back to bed before she got out of her shower. As I stood there, washing and rinsing the dishes and then placing them in the rack, I was crying and letting my tears fall down in the dishwater. I heard something and realized Jary had heard all the ruckus and he picked up the dishtowel and began to dry the dishes and put them away as I finished washing and rinsing them.

"You don't have to help me," I said, blubbering in my tears.

"I don't mind. You should have known better than to try and skip the dishes. If you had told me, I would have helped you earlier."

"I know. I know it's my own fault. It was just plain stupid of me. But she will be even madder if she finds you helping me."

"I can take it," he said, though his expression belied the fact.

Luckily, we finished and were both back in our beds when she went to her bedroom and shut the door. After this incident I found myself always sleeping on my side, with my back to the wall where I would more easily wake up if someone approached my bed while I slept.

As I look back on this exchange the thought comes to me that herein began my almost lifelong willingness to accept blame (and punishment) so easily. Perhaps the helplessness my brothers and I felt with absolutely no resource or champion to side for our defense (of course my father was absolutely invisible in such a role) set a pattern which was difficult to break. For many years, I fought very hard to convince myself I was worth fighting for. Unfortunately, my eldest brother never got there and his entire life he asked the question, "Why do people see me as helpless and vulnerable?"

He not only accepted his unworthiness of help, but used pity as his strongest communication skill. Later, much later in life, this attitude in him caused an estrangement with me which never got resolved. It was the constant "Poor me" and "How could they treat me like this?" negatively which caused me to sever ties with him. He was married almost 30 years and eventually she left him. He never got over it. The energy it took to listen to him bemoan the fact of their treatment of him after all those years was a daily complaint and had a draining effect on my own perception of the world around me. His acceptance of his role in life had the effect of making me more independent as well as giving me my refusal to fall back on excuses or blame others when things didn't go my way.

There was another lesson I learned *the night of the dishes*, as I dubbed it forever in my mind, the rest of my life I never, ever, not once, leave dirty dishes in my sink overnight. Every piece of silver, every glass or cup, they are rinsed and put away (in most cases currently, the dishwasher) until morning. I hate dishes in the sink. Even my friends go down a notch in my estimation, if I see their dirty dishes in the sink. Does this make me a "neat-freak"? No, because it doesn't apply to other housekeeping chores. I can leave clothing hanging on the stationery exercise bike and though I most often *do* make my bed when I get out of it, it won't disturb me if I neglect to do so every now and then. Besides, I read somewhere that a study was done and statistics show a dramatic difference in success rates for people who make their beds each morning and those who do not.

Another evening; a week-end when she was home and my father was getting ready to go out; to a poker game with his friends, the two of them got into an argument. It was a familiar argument; primarily about money or the lack of it to pay bills because of my father's gambling.

My brother and I weren't paying much attention, after all, this was not unusual and then my mother turned to me and she said, "I'm right about this one. Jacquolin was with me when I had to go in person to the light company to pay the fee so the lights wouldn't be turned off. Tell him, Jacquolin. You remember that, don't you?"

Actually, I didn't remember anything about it because she usually left us in the car when she went somewhere with us.

Tentatively I answered, "I remember we did go to the light company once but I didn't go inside. I stayed in the car and so did Jary."

She snorted and gave my father a sneer. "There," she said, "Even your own children have to suffer because you chose to spend give your pay away to those drunken friends of yours. It's bad enough to play but you're not even good at it. You never even win."

When my father had had enough of the argument and dealing with her sarcasm, he left the house. As soon as he left, she turned to me and slapped me cutting my lip. Both Jary and I were completely surprised by the act. I reached up and felt the blood on my lip and as she said, "That's what you get for standing up for his lies and stories. Maybe next time you will not defend him but tell the truth." Jary went to get a wet wash cloth for me.

My mother was an extremely jealous woman and frequently accused my father of cheating on her. I didn't know if her accusations were based on fact or just her intense jealous, but I found myself silently cheering him; if he were, I hope the woman was sweet and caring to him. He certainly, in my mind, deserved it. I never spoke about these things to my brother but I am sure he would have felt the same way I did. I never saw my father physically abuse my mother but they were both masters of emotional and verbal abuse.

It's strange how often and how early children from abused households began to develop methods to hide their situations from the outside world. This has different effects on different children. In some, as in my own case, I believe it made me strong and more resilient even up to and through adulthood.

Another effect it had on me was to make me vulnerable to other abusers. When I was about nine or ten years of age my parents were friends with another couple who lived next door to the small house we rented when my father was transferred to Colorado. They had no children but were expecting a baby shortly after we moved next door. They were friendly and were often at our house, sitting in the kitchen, playing hours of card games with my parents, such as gin or cribbage.

At first, I really liked both of them. The young woman was pretty and would talk to me like an equal sharing her movie magazines with me and teasing me about boyfriends at school. Her husband was a nice-looking man, tall, dark hair and an easy grin. Often he would come outside and join our sandlot baseball game in the empty lot across the street. Sometimes we would play a game of Kick-the-Can or Hide and Seek as well. Just as most children do, we were thrilled to have any adult showing interest in us and willing to play our games.

All this changed however, when we were playing Hide and Seek and I chose to hide under a neighbor's house which was built up on high stilts which allowed us to duck under and then stand fully up and hide behind some of the big pylons. I was still breathing hard from running away from home base; my brother was "it" for this turn.

All of a sudden, with no real warning, I felt a warm breath on the back of my neck and two large arms encircled both me and the pylon I was holding on to. It was Jeff, our neighbor and he whispered in my ear, "Can I hide with you? This is a great place. They will never find us here."

I was suddenly uncomfortable and there was a sense of real fear there as well. I was too timid and too shocked to say anything. He stood there for a few seconds and then he pulled my dress up and stuck his hand down inside the front of my panties. I was so shocked I did the only thing I could think of and that was to take both of my hands and try to pull his hand from my panties.

"Wait, wait a minute. Doesn't that feel good?"

"No, no, it doesn't," I said, still trying to pull his hand out. When I realized he wasn't going to pull his hands out, I called out to my brother, "Coming in free," I yelled, for the game rule about coming in before the "it" person called out "Ollie, Ollie, Oxen Free."

This wasn't the end of this story, though. I did not tell my parents or even my brother then. It was to be many years before I finally shared this with my father, years after I was married and had children of my own. And yet, the memory is as sharp and clear today as it was then. If ever I needed proof of the lasting effects such an incident has in an individual's mind, I just have to examine my own experience. As is often usual with children and such incidents, I felt ashamed and blamed myself. What had I done for my father's friend to do such a thing? I was on my guard after that to stay away from him unless I was with my parents, his wife or my siblings. I realize now I must have imagined it, but I often wondered if his wife knew of this dreadful thing, he had done to me and if he had done it to others. I wondered if she knew about it, and was thereby somehow condoning it? What a dark secret for her to share with him. After that, I viewed her with suspicion and dislike just as I did him.

It was about two weeks later and my mother went into labor with my brother, Sam. Until this stage in our family, it had been my brother Jary and myself. Now we were excited about this new baby coming to our family. I was especially looking forward to it because my mother had given her assurances that I would have a great deal of responsibly in taking care of the baby, especially after she went back to work. Jary went along with my father to pick my mother and the new baby up from the hospital when they were to be discharged. I was allowed to stay home, clean up the kitchen, change the linens on my parent's bed, and just tidy everything up for their homecoming.

I even went out back where there was a small creek which crossed this property, and I picked some of the wild-flowers growing there and brought them in to put in an empty mayonnaise jar on the kitchen table to surprise my mother.

Last thing on my list was to change the bedding on my parents' bed and I had stripped it down and was putting the fresh sheets from the clothesline. I held them to my nose for a few seconds, enjoying the fresh sunshine smell. As I spread the bottom sheet, I heard a knock on the front door. Thinking I was just imagining it, I paused and when I heard nothing else, I re-started my bed-making chores. Suddenly I heard footsteps and then I looked up to see Jeff, from next door. He smiled really big and asked me, "Hi, princess. Where's your father?"

Stunned, I replied, "He's not here."

"Well, where is he? I'll just wait for him."

"Oh, no, I wouldn't. It may be some time. He went to the hospital to get my new baby brother and my mother."

"Where's Jary?"

Without considering the harm I was putting myself in, I answered truthfully, "He went with them. I stayed home to clean house for my mother."

He walked on in the room and said, "Well, that's alright. I was really coming to see my little princess."

"Me? What for?"

"I have a new little game to play. You didn't tell anyone about our little hide-and-seek game, did you, princess?"

I shook my head negatively and he walked around the bed and putting his arms under my arms, he lifted me and laid me down on my back on the bed.

He pulled my dress up, and my panties down and as I stiffened and tried to pull my panties and dress back up, he took hold of both my wrists and held them above my head. Then he took his free hand and saying, "Don't worry, princess, this isn't going to hurt. I would never in this world hurt you. He rubbed my private parts and inserted a finger inside. I started crying and asking him to "Stop. Please stop."

As if I hadn't been shocked and scared up to this point, he bent his head down and began to lick me. I could feel his scratchy whiskers and was conscious of his rapid and quickening breath on me and then suddenly he was still. I was still crying. He released my wrists and as though suddenly aware of what he was doing, he pulled my panties up and my dress down.

"See, that didn't hurt, did it, princess?"

I began to gain control of my tears but still couldn't speak.

"It's like a downstairs kiss, isn't it?

When I did not reply he said softly, "You know this has to be our little secret, don't you princess?"

When I still did not reply he added, "You don't want your daddy to know what a bad little girl you have been, playing games with his best friend, and without asking permission either."

"Your father would lose his best friend and you wouldn't want that, would you? He would blame you. After all, there's no harm done, is there? I didn't hurt you, did I?"

I was still mute, but I thought, *you did so…hurt me. You hurt me down there…and you hurt my heart, too. I thought you were my friend.*

There was to be no repetition of the episodes; Jeff and his family moved a few weeks later, to my great relief. One effect the entire incident left me with was a suspicious nature of any adult who eagerly tried to engage my brothers and I in our activities. Later in life, with my own children and my students I did not easily choose to let my guard down with adults I didn't know well or trust. I viewed adults as the enemy or at the least, unworthy of my trust. I was often suspicious of adults paying what I considered and inordinate attention to my own children or the children in my care.

I never told Jary. There was this overwhelming sense of shame I felt. I did tell my father, a few years before his death when we sat on his back porch one summer visit and watched the hummingbirds he cared so much about. I don't know how the subject came up but I do remember the sweet feeling of relief (even all these years after it had happened) to be able to tell someone. I didn't know then and still don't know all these many years later when he had passed *why* I finally told him the story He was shocked, and though it had been so very long ago, he did not doubt the story, and the anger he clearly felt towards his friend and the mixture of guilt and sorrow he felt for failing to be there for me and protect me when I had been so young.

I think, as well, he wondered at his failure to recognize the character of his friend so completely. I do not think he was a good judge of people, especially in his later years. He was a creative, empathic and charming man but was taken advantage several times in his life by stronger personalities he trusted.

Chapter

TWO

When sober my father was the story-teller, the one who took us to purchase and set off firecrackers on the Fourth of July, taught us how to bait our hook to fish, how to go rabbit hunting and frog-gigging and told the best jokes to our friends who loved him.

He started giving us an allowance, but forced it on my mother when he spent his entire paycheck on poker games and couldn't pay us. When it first began, it was wonderful. We would wait for the weekend and take our booty, go to the civilian guard post, catch the city bus downtown and see a movie. There would always be the movie itself, like the entrée of a wonderful meal, a cartoon (the appetizer), the news of the day (veggies, or something good for you), and a tantalizing peek into the future with the previews of coming attractions. This was the day of the Saturday serial chapter. Each week you got a selected "cliff-hanger" chapter of the current adventure to ensure you would return next week to discover if you had guessed right on what would happen next. These were mostly adventure, action type abbreviated versions of a story which had cleverly spaced cut offs: Superman, Flash Gordon, and the old Batman and Robin thrillers. The boring part was all the credits you had to watch until the main feature began and I very rapidly understood when the words, "Directed by" came on, next was the actual main course. The worst thing was that when my father began by giving us our weekly allowance, we grew to expect it each week and it was never consistent. Some weeks we got it and some weeks we didn't. How resentful I felt when I knew a special musical was scheduled and my brother and I didn't get our allowance that week so therefore were forced to miss the movie. I felt we were entitled to it; once it was started, my father should have followed through. In later years, I would try to keep this in mind when dealing with my own children and grandchildren.

One week my brother was especially looking forward to the Red Ryder chapter and he spouted off to me, "How unfair is that? He (my father) doesn't have to miss his card games, he should have set aside our allowance before he spent it."

"Well, look at it this way. Would you rather get to go to the movies or have them get groceries for the week?"

Rapidly he answered, "The movies!"

We had been studying the French Revolution that week and I said, "Kind of 'Let them eat cake', not movie popcorn, huh?"

He laughed and replied, "I don't particularly like cake, anyway. I like the popcorn."

Which brings another memory floating to the top...When sober, and home, a combination which wasn't common, sometimes my father would fix popcorn for us to eat while he read the current choice for our reading. He had a special talent for his popcorn recipe and all these years later I can remember the smell as he cooked it. He used a black cast-iron skillet, put oil in, the corn kernels, and the lid with the sound of the popping corn inside. If he had any, he added pecans to the corn and roasted them as well. The smell of popcorn to this day brings back such a strong visual of my father standing at the stove shaking that big black cast iron skillet I can almost smell it.

It's strange how sounds, smells, touches can trigger memories which mere words cannot.

The smell of the popcorn, the smell of his pipe tobacco, which was always a can of Sir Walter Raleigh brand into which he had quartered an apple. You smelled the apple when he opened the can and when he smoked the pipe as well. We never had soft drinks at our house, but the delicious smell of the flavored Kool Aid as we mixed it (no sugar free at that time, the more sugar the better it tasted to us). Even today I can bring my father's memory to mind when I smell *Old Spice*, his choice of after-shave or cologne.

Once in a while my father let my brother and I have a half cup of what he termed "children's coffee"; a mixture of milk and coffee, mostly milk. We had milk delivered to our house when we lived in that first little cracker-box sub division, but once the financial logistics of our family went down, my mother bought boxes of powdered milk which we mixed with water. It wasn't too bad, if you made it ahead of time and it could get really cold in the refrigerator. I remember the taste of the "Post-Toasties" cereal we ate on a regular basis. No sugar-coated cereal had been put on the market yet so we would liberally spoon more sugar than we needed on the cereal before we added the milk—and eat it in a hurry before the cereal got all soggy (like mush).

This was a glorious time for the cinema. My very favorite movies of the time were the colorful musicals and I could rattle off the stars with their remarkable talent: Betty Grable, Fred Astaire, Gene Kelly, Debbie Reynolds, Marge and Gower Champion, Julie Andrews, Judy Garland, Margaret O'Brian and many others. How I sat in that movie seat, entranced with the music, the costumes, the happy endings and the not so subtle messages I took away from the storyline. Who could ever forget Ava Gardner's sad life in the fabulous "Showboat" all because she had even a drop of Negro blood?

Or course, there were some non-musicals which have made their mark on me as a child and which I still remember fondly; the tears I shed for little "Bambi" when hunters shot and killed his mother. Who can forget the classic "Old Yeller"?

Somewhere along this time I didn't realize it, but writing had become my life-focus. I wanted to write like Betty Smith with her story of poverty as a child in Brooklyn ("A Tree Grows in Brooklyn"). I wanted to be able to write like Harper Lee and her moving story of the old south in "To Kill a Mockingbird". I wanted to be able to write well enough to bring a reader to tears or out-loud laughter. Never did I entertain the idea of becoming a nurse, movie-star, popular and glamorous singer or model like a lot of my peers. Even when I was reporting something I had seen or heard about I almost found it impossible to "stick" to the truth. I always wanted to exaggerate and embellish it to make it more exciting and interesting.

I read about famous authors and this helped me feel less disappointment and despair when I received those infamous (to a writer) usually pink rejection slips. Some were kind and gave helpful tips and most said, "Keep writing". I learned what writer's block was and what it meant to be writing and have the words just flow out in an endless stream of wonderful meaning.

I completely and totally believe had I not been in the cage of my first marriage I might have ended up as one of those writers I so enjoy reading about today. Would I have been a Stephen King; A John Grisom? Maybe a Nicholas Sparks? I loved words, especially the ones children make up to express something when they don't know the correct one. Too, children aren't intimidated and will often try out words because they enjoy specific sounds and facial expressions needed for those private words.

My life was filled with survival and fear but sometimes late at night I would lie sleepless and imagine the books I would write someday.

When I was about twelve, I could tell you what the term "pay-day poker" meant. It meant playing poker when you have no money, with promise of paying for your losses out of your next paycheck. Which meant you often barely broke even. I even once told my brother that in a former life our father must have been a river-boat gambler who traveled up and down the Mississippi river, gambling and flirting with the women.

We never blamed him for having to eat corn-meal must for breakfast and fry the same mush in deep fat for supper when there was no grocery money. Our diet during these often-hard times primarily existed of pinto beans cooked with fat-back, fried potatoes, biscuits and gravy, occasional meat-loaf and once in a while, a wonderful pot roast with potatoes and carrots on Sunday when my mother was home. I learned early how to cook almost everything; though I never ate a steak until long after I married and left home. Often when I would go baby-sit, I would look at these well stocked refrigerators and pantries and long to have these goodies at our house.

I have thought about it a lot, but have very, very few memories of things I learned from my mother, except for her recriminations on my mistakes. It didn't occur to me until long after she had passed that I owed anything of me to her influence. I can remember so many things I can lay at my father's feet. He taught me not to quit—anything. He stressed that giving up when things got difficult served no purpose except to accelerate the downward spiral. He gave me an everlasting and marvelous gift with his love of reading and appreciation for the past writers which helped shape our culture and country. He never was good with money but he was imaginative and creative when it came to building models or inventing specific small gadgets for certain needs. He could build a good campfire, could play his guitar and sing "Rambling Rose" like a professional country-western star. He was quite aware of the fascination with which women held him. The way he told a good story, remembered names and faces and details, kept a repertoire of jokes (good ones, truly funny) and talked with his hands along with the curly black hair and flashing hazel eyes could (and did) hold listeners spellbound in anticipation of the ending. He was never overweight, even in his later years and always dressed in impeccable taste. I was proud of him when he was sober and stood, surrounded by a court of admirers immersing them into his story and gaining appreciative ears for his tales. My brothers and I used to say he was a man of all trades, but master of none. He could do a dab of this and a dab of that but was prone to start a project and never finish it. I think mundane tasks bored him and he needed the stimulation of admirers to bring him to life. Flattery came easily to his lips but those who grew to love him or truly become his friend knew better than to accept his flattery at face value but to weigh it carefully.

After years of psychology classes, trying to understand what makes people "tick" I have concluded that part of my mother's personality came from something very simple: her lack of self-esteem. She forced my father to marry her when she found herself pregnant and thrown out of her parents' house in disgrace. He wasn't ready to get married but did not shirk what he considered his responsibility, however, it came at a price. H did move my pregnant mother into his mother's home where they lived, unmarried, for a little over a year when she gave birth to my brother. So, while he did eventually give her status as a married woman, she felt the shame of his waiting to do this until she gave birth to her second child. I believe she always felt it wasn't his wish to get married (to anyone at that particular time) but reluctantly felt obligated to do so. She was an attractive woman, but was always jealous of the attention other women gave him and never felt secure in their commitment to one another. She disappeared from my life after I had ended my marriage to my first husband and I don't think she ever realized I had four children or how my life had turned out. I don't know when or where she eventually died. After she divorced my father, she married a full-bloodied Native American who came from an Oklahoma reservation. I was notified by my brother when her husband went in their kitchen one evening and using a shotgun, committed suicide. She did call him (my brother) with this news, but I never heard from her. It has been difficult at some times, living without any real knowledge of her medical background. On the forms an individual has to fill out with background history of their parents' medical history I have to either put "not applicable" or "unknown". I don't even know when she died. Another sign, of her low self-esteem was her hesitancy in meeting new people or even socializing with other couples or neighbors, or even appearing at her children's school functions. My father was "hit or miss" with these, but when he did show up, he was very social and people responded to him immediately in a positive way. On the rare occasion, she did show up, she stood, practically mute as far into the background or sidelines as she possibly could. No one knew who she was or which child might be hers. She had a difficult time deciding what would be appropriate dress for any occasion and looked to my father for his advice. Then, when she came home, she would be full of things she felt she had said wrong, ways she should have dressed and extremely jealous of any conversation she had seen him have with a woman, or the amount of time he didn't remain right at her side, but wandered off to talk to others.

I wondered at their toxic relationship as I grew older and wondered at their inability to let go of one another. Of course, divorce was frowned on but I had friends whose parents had done it and I felt the entire family would be better off. Naturally, in my mind they would part and I (and maybe my eldest brother) would get to live with my father. I could visualize myself keeping house for him, cooking and making sure he had freshly laundered clothes neatly put away in his chest. I never (at that time) wondered why my mother stayed there, working two jobs and being miserable but I did wonder at my father's inability to leave my mother until basically, she was the one who left. It was after he got out of the Air Force. He was not employed at a regular job then and she was still working two jobs.

This was nothing like I had pictured it. He just disappeared. From everyone. I learned many years later, when he reappeared in our lives, that he had gone with friends to Florida and worked on a shrimp boat for a while. This, course, is heresy so I am not sure of the validity. She left him but then forever blamed him for her loneliness and jealousy when he found someone else to marry. Was his eventual return part of his "never quit" philosophy?

Years later when he had met and married his last wife (probably the best relationship he had ever had in his lifetime, they eventually celebrated fifty years together) they went on a trip out of town. My mother found out where they lived and she broke into their house, not to steal, but to cut up every picture she found of my father and his new wife on display.

During my parents' entire marriage there were accusations of infidelity from both sides. At one point she had (in my belief, totally fictious) convinced my father that one of my brothers was not his. She presented as proof that because three of us were little towheads with very blond (nearly white) hair, green or blue eyes and this one brother had brown eyes and brown hair. We did have cousins and past relatives (I thought my maternal grandfather looked exactly this brother of ours). She thought my father had been unfaithful with so many women it was hard to keep up with the stories.

My escape from not merely my home environment but the world at large was, from my earliest age, books. I read far beyond my years. I was only five years of age when Betty Smith's "A Tree Grows in Brooklyn" was published but by the time I was ten years old I had read it three times. This was only replaced as my all-time favorite novel when Nellie Harper's "To Kill A Mockingbird" was published in 1960. By Middle-school I had moved on to even *meatier* books, such as Dante Alighieri's "The Devine Comedy: Inferno, Purgatory, Paradise."

My father encouraged these reading "binges". Often some of his stories would nudge me into a period of specific genres and I would read a specified author until my interest was sated or I had read all their works. One of my biggest disappointments was to find out I had read all the novels written by Betty Smith. When Valerie Raleigh Yow wrote Betty Smith's autobiography, I checked my mailbox every single day until my order arrived and read the book in two days.

I never saw my mother reading anything; book, magazine, nursing journals (even after she became a licensed practical nurse).

This love of reading was something my father shared with me and my siblings, to some lesser extent. One of my grandsons has been given this gift of literature and I cherish the conversations we have had about certain books and poems. I wonder if the reason he hasn't pursued this talent could be that he doesn't want to take my own specialty and intrude. He allows me to be the writer in the family when he is every bit as gifted in this area as myself and perhaps even more.

I find it rather ironic that as of eighth grade, I visualized myself as a writer; and at the age of sixty-three my father went back to college (Abilene Christian College) for a degree in Creative writing. Not that I was much quicker in my writing endeavors; I sought my escape from the abusive, neglectful and hopeless childhood home by marrying at age sixteen. My life took many twists and turns before I allowed my mind to believe I *could* somehow, become a writer. When I was in elementary school or junior-high, I felt anything really *might* be possible and I could bravely announce to friends, family, and teachers that I *would* be an author when I grew up. I deliberately chose "author" instead of writer because I wanted no misunderstanding. Writers could do correspondence, newspaper ads, letters and such but an author wrote stories.

In his defense, my father did try to talk me out of it. By this time, though, the years of being one of the "have-nots" in my academic and social world had left me in a deep and dark depression, during an age when many such children "fall through the cracks", it is often literature which saves them. To find similarities among oneself and others, even in fiction, can often swing hopelessness into a possible happier future. If an individual can see others in the same kind of situation, the possibility therefore for themselves seems not just possible, but probable.

It is only when a child gets old enough to realize that seeing others overcome much the same difficulties doesn't necessarily mean time will make the same difference for themselves as well. Still it does ring true that seeing others facing the same, often grim future, does not guarantee they will or will not find their way out. If a child goes hungry often enough, hunger may become the expected norm and having something to eat becomes the unexpected miracle.

Sometimes it is not food which is the obvious differences.

As a child, I wondered at the unfairness (especially on holidays) when some children rode the shiny new bicycles or perhaps pushed lovely doll carriages with dolls and I received new underwear or school shoes which I so desperately needed. Often children are not as interested in having the necessities as they are the luxuries. Sometimes when my mother would be sleeping after her midnight shift, when we (my brothers and I) got ready for school and I would frantically scrounge around, trying to find something we could pack in our paper sacks for lunch. If I were lucky, perhaps there would be some eggs I could boil; one in each sack. Assuming there was peanut butter (with or without jelly) it was a great back-up plan. It was always welcome and though it got repetitious and tiresome, by the time lunchtime at school arrived, it was welcomed. Learning how to make a believable show of being happy and not lacking anything was, at times, difficult. Pretending I didn't want to join everyone to go to the drugstore to get sodas was because I was way too full, or because I had to hurry home for something, not because I did not have the dime it would cost. Pretending I preferred to pack my lunch instead of purchase the school lunch was another example. During the fifties when the poodle hairdo became briefly popular, I wore mine up in a ponytail, pretending I thought the poodle cut too masculine for me. Like many abused or neglected children, I did not want pity and would never accept anything, no matter how desperately I wanted it, if it were seen as charity or pity on the giver's part.

The smell of the cafeteria food which other students griped about smelled so good that my mouth would fill with saliva long before I reached the cafeteria. We never got to buy our lunches and thus, I pretended to hate the food offered there and griped about such gross offerings; claiming that was the reason I brought something from home. Occasionally, I brought wrapped cornbread or biscuits but I would usually make excuses for not eating with friends and hide in the bathroom to eat.

I loved success stories about writers. To read that Margaret Mitchell had her awesome "Gone with the Wind" rejected an unbelievable forty times before being accepted or that Emily Stockton's "The Help" was turned down sixty times until number sixty-one took pity on her and bought it. It has sold millions of copies to date. I did not have the courage (or fortitude) to keep sending any of my own off that many times, but this reminds me of the many, many times my father was unsuccessful in any of his attempts to get rich on his varied attempts at starting new, unorthodox (half-baked) careers, His familiar excuse was always the same, "If I had only had a father to guide and help me, I could have been rich and famous." This reminds me of Marlon Brandon in one of his signature roles as the boxer, Terry Malloy, in "On the Waterfront" with his "I coulda' been a contender."

There was a half-price bookstore in our neighborhood and this was a wonderous place to me. It wasn't just the smorgasbord of books available there, but the opportunity to purchase books, take them home and read them, and sell them back. Of course, I realized the bookstore didn't pay as much when the customer resold them back but I convinced myself the store had to pay salaries, for the utilities, and for the new books they also offered. Even so, I did not often have the extra money to purchase even a second hand book.

There was a shame about being poor. Along with the shame was a genuine lack of understanding the "why me?" At some level I could blame my father for his gambling and alcoholism but this did not completely satisfy me.

As I grew older, it seemed that the differences between people got larger. One afternoon, my oldest brother asked me "Wouldn't it be wonderful if before we were born, we could choose the parents we wanted?"

"That's really stupid, Jary. If you are going to wish something you should wish for something you might have a chance of getting. We're stuck with the parents we have."

"But does God just draw numbers or how does he decide who gets who? Why couldn't we get someone like Ronnie's Dad?"

"What's so great about his dad?"

"Well, he plays catch with him a lot and he take him fishing and teaches him how to work on his bike, lots of stuff like that."

I thought for a minute and then I said, "Yeah, I see how that's good. I would settle for his mom."

"Yeah, she's great, too. She bakes cookies for when he gets off the bus and when he gets ready for school, he has all his clothes clean, ironed and hanging in his closet. He doesn't have to wash them himself or iron them."

"Hey, sometimes I iron your shirts for you."

He laughed and said, "Yeah and I appreciate it, too, but wouldn't it be nice to have a mother who did it?"

"I'm not sticking up for her, Jary, but she would have to give up sleeping to do that, with her two jobs."

"That's another thing. She works two jobs and yet we never have any money. Where does it all go?"

"Well, let's see...the light bill, gas and water bill, gas for the cars, food—"

"What food? There's food here? Where?"

We laughed together and then he said, "Oh, yeah, and then there's that dye stuff she uses on her hair and her nurses' uniforms and shoes."

"Well, let's not forget Dad's booze and his card playing."

As I got a little older, I began to get several referrals for baby-sitting jobs but all these had to be worked out in conjunction with Jary's cooperation. My first responsibility was to do my chores at home and to make sure our two younger brothers were not left alone. Sometimes I resented this because I wanted to earn the money. One lady even paid me to come over on Saturday mornings and do her ironing for her. It wasn't anything fancy, mostly pillow-cases, sheets, scarves, and the children's clothing. I bought me a huge plastic piggy-bank, slot in the top and a round lid on the bottom. I would keep a running total on what I put in there each time I earned some money, and also when I took some out. This was my money; I had worked hard for it. Sometimes I would spend some of it on my brothers or save for clothes for school but when I came home after babysitting all one Saturday, I paid Jary for his share for his watching our two younger brothers so I could take the job, I went to my bedroom and got down the huge smiling piggy-bank, pulled the small paper out, and went to make a note of my earnings that particular day. My bank was empty of the currency usually folded and inside. Where was my money? Who had taken my money? First, I thought it had been my brother, but when I confronted him, I could tell by his expression and his words he was not guilty. My younger brothers couldn't reach the top closet shelf where

I kept it. My father had not been at home all day. That left one person...
My mother. Surely not, I told myself, all the while knowing she knew
where it was kept.

When I got up the courage to tell her someone had taken my money
from the piggy bank, she suggested the little boys had done it. She even
added, as though it made it more believable, "Don't be too angry at them"
she said, "They don't get any allowance and rarely any kind of sweet treats.
They probably didn't even think you would really mind."

"They can't reach it that high," I said. I thought to myself, and how
would they get anywhere to spend it? They didn't even have bicycles, much
less a way to get to the store in a car.

"Have you asked Jary about it?"

"Yes, and I could tell by his expression and his denial that he was
telling the truth, he didn't take it."

"Well, then. That narrows it down to one person left, doesn't it?"

I almost couldn't believe it, was she confessing she had taken it?"

Before I could say anything, she said, turning to go to her room, "Your
father must have needed some poker money or maybe some of his friend,
old Jack Daniels."

One of the surprising things about this conversation was it even took
place. For me to be able to start it asking my questions, and her not to do as
I had expected, and come on with her outraged expressions of innocence.
She didn't yell, she didn't show her anger at me asking her about it at all.
To me this was almost an admission of guilt. If she hadn't taken it, she
would have probably been howling at the injustice of me even accusing her.

She went in her bedroom and closed the door and I stood, considering
the way she blamed it on him and with no wiggle room for me to argue
about it. Usually my father was drunk when he came in from his poker
sessions but it was ridiculous to even consider he knew where I kept my
baby-sitting and household chore money, much less that he would take it.
I knew he wouldn't. I could count the times on one hand my father had
ever invaded the sanctity of my personal space and room. I knew also, that
Jary believed she had taken it. I sat on my bed and cried with frustration at
first, then anger seeped in; the only thing I could do was to find a better
hiding place. Jary and I discussed it together and his sympathy hung heavy
between us. He felt bad for me.

Finally, we thought we found what was the perfect place. We left some of the coins in the plastic piggy bank, but never again would I accumulate any sizeable amount of coins and never again would I put *any* paper currency in there.

My father had given each of us one of those small, purple, trimmed with gold drawstring bags in which Crown Royal Whiskey was sold. My father had gotten these bags with purchases of the whiskey he made in Canada after its release in the late 1930's. He brought them back (minus the whiskey, of course) from a training six weeks his Air Force squadron participated with the Canadians. It was released in the 1960's in the United States so we treasured ours. We used them for our marble collections and our friends were envious of the rich looking small bags.

We all received one because I, too, had a marble collection. I placed my currency from that day forward inside my little purple pouch and then shoved the pouch way down inside one of a pair of boxing gloves in my brothers' closet. We both felt even though it made it take longer to do my banking transactions, it would withstand any curiosity or search of my mother's. She would never look inside the boxing gloves.

We weren't worried about the boxing glove as being a secure place. My father had given my brother two sets one Christmas, with the promise of teaching him to box. This promise didn't last long after one such bout with my drunken father bloodied my brother's nose (supposedly by accident). They never boxed again, but my brother kept the gloves.

Being the oldest and the only girl in the family it was only natural that I was drawn into the rough-housing and activities usually reserved for the male gender. I played a lot of sand-lot baseball and though not the best player, I had a fair amount of talent. Enough so that no one objected to my presence on the team(s). I was a fast runner and was not afraid of going aggressively after the fly balls. One game though, at school during a P.E. class, I must have misjudged the ball or not being paying close attention because the ball smacked me straight in the forehead. I immediately fell unconscious to the ground. The resulting hub-bub was immediate. My brother thought I was dead since I didn't respond to all the fuss going on. Later, I was very moved when his friends told me he had even cried at first and he *never* cried. Of course, he denied this to me and insisted he knew I was alright. Teachers took me to the nurse's office where I regained consciousness, staff tried unsuccessfully to reach my parents and I was given an aspirin and cold rag for the rapidly rising bump on my head. The next day, I was somewhat a hero with my double black eyes and swollen nose, by everyone except the P.E. teacher who said it was all my own fault—my glove should have been in front of my face.

Later, I was to learn that the school nurse had said she thought it was disgraceful they were unable to reach either of my parents for this emergency. She had little use or respect for my mother; she was one of those parents who didn't get immunization records turned in on time or signed report cards and field trip permission slips. The school nurse, Mrs. Nelson, did like me and I could feel her efforts to make things a little easier for me. Once, when our class was going on a field trip to a local dairy farm, we had been told repeatedly that if we did not have our signed permission slip, we would not be allowed to go and would spend the day in the library doing extra homework. I nagged both my mother and father, leaving the form on the kitchen table, then next to the coffee pot, handing it directly to my mother who promised she would "get to it and stop nagging" and finally taping it to their bedroom door the night before the field trip. First thing the next morning, both of them were gone to work; mother having accepted a double shift for the extra money and my father to his usual radiology clinic on the base. Though I tried to reach him by phone, I was unsuccessful and left for school with the despair of knowing I would probably be the only one who wasn't going to be allowed to go. When I got to my homeroom class, there was the buzz of excitement about the upcoming trip and talk of free ice cream at the dairy as well.

My teacher received a note and she called me to her desk and gave me a pass to go to the office.

"What do they want?" I asked here, meanwhile mentally deciding I was going to be sent to the library. I took my books with me, to save another trip back. I even felt a little bit of relief I wouldn't have to return and feel like the lone wolf, unable to participate in this rare, exciting event.

"I'm not sure, Dear. It just says you are to go to the office."

I slowly made my way to the office and was surprised when they directed me to the nurse's office.

"Why?" I asked. "I'm not sick."

"I don't know," the harried and busy desk administrator said. "You know where her office is, don't you?"

"Yes 'mam," I said and when I got to the nurse's office, she was alone behind her desk. She looked up at me and smiled.

"Did you send for me, Mrs. Nelson?"

"Yes, I did, Sweet-Pea."

I waited and then she held out a paper towards me. She said, still smiling, "I noticed you were the only student who forgot their field trip permission slip, so I took the liberty of trying to reach your parents. I never reached your mother but I did reach your father."

"But he can't leave work and come sign it in time for me to go. They are lining up for the bus right now."

"Oh, your father and I figured that out. He gave me permission to sign for his permission and then witness it by my own signature. Easy solution."

I believe my hand trembled when I reached out for the permission slip. I felt like crying.

Mrs. Nelson could tell I was emotionally moved so she got up, bustled around the desk and gave me a little push towards the door.

"Go along, now You give this to your teacher for her records, and you have a good time and enjoy the field-trip, you hear?"

I broke the rule against running in the halls as I hurried back to my class.

Then, and in later years, I would acknowledge to myself that Mrs. Nelson had made a special effort on that day and many others. Every time I hear the country music song, "Angels Among Us" by Scotty McCreery I see Mrs. Nelson's face and remember her kindness towards me and others. I also give credit to her kindness in this incidence of the field trip for something I did for someone else, much, much later in my life. It is a common saying now, this "play it forward" people talk about when passing on a good deed to another. Many years later, I supervised a group of dancers on a special field trip and when I noticed that one of them (one of my favorites, though I tried not to show it) had very rapidly run out of spending money given her by her parent Her mother was a single parent and working hard to provide for her children; even to paying for the dance lessons which were her daughter's love. Since I was supervising several dancers, we had paid for two adjoining rooms with double beds, and had gotten roll-a-way beds as well. The two rooms had an adjoining door between them which we left open so I could keep track of all *my* girls. Some had even brought sleeping bags which actually added to the fun. Anyway, when I noticed this particular girl was out of spending money, I knew I couldn't offer her replacement money (even taking her aside to do it) because she would be extremely humiliated and embarrassed. She was proud and independent. So, one morning, as we rolled up sleeping bags and got prepared to go to breakfast, I took a folded-up fifty-dollar bill and snuck it right under her sleeping bag; between the bag and the floor. I was helping clean up and I called her over and said, "You really should be more careful with your money, sweetheart. Put this up and keep it either in your pocket or let me hold on to it."

She looked at the money, then raised the bag and looked under it and said, "Ms. Jackie, I don't think this money is mine."

"Well, you silly, of course it is." Then I looked around the group and asked, "Anyone else misplace their spending money? Tell me how much to identify it."

When no one else spoke up about having lost any, I told her, "There, you see it *is* yours. Now be more careful in taking care of it."

It wasn't until many, many years later when this group of dancers held a reunion party and this girl was a married woman with her own daughter that she came to me and when we were alone she said, "You know, Ms. Jackie, I always knew that fifty dollars was from you."

I blustered around and never outright admitted it, but said, "I believe it came from someone named Mrs. Nelson."

When she said she didn't know a Mrs. Nelson and never remembered knowing someone by that name I merely hugged her and said, "Maybe you can be a Mrs. Nelson to someone else someday, she grinned at me and said, "You think?"

I have always thought of the military life for families as being the closest to gypsies. Though many people are born to be risk takers and easily bored without the stimulation of new adventures and experiences, there is also some of us with a longing for "home" which is impossible within the military method of moving their personnel often to fit the mission and not the family. Often within short periods of time, especially if viewed in the fact all families only have a limited amount of time to be a family, family life may be disrupted by divorces, deployments, wars, serious or terminal illnesses, and how rapidly children grow all pay a part in the sanctity of a family. Marriage, birth of new offspring, milestones slipping by, barely noticed in their speed until children are grown, retirement looms, almost as a surprise. Putting down roots is very hard for military families, especially the children.

I have come to believe there are certain personalities in which both adventure and security have equal places. Perhaps Shakespeare had it right; we do have stages in common with one another; but just not at the same age(s).

Along with these stages are bulwarks in our memories which mark a certain period. One might say, "Oh, yes. I remember, that is when we were living on the lake."

"Oh, that was the year Louise got married."

I believe without our method of marking memory with these "hints", our memories would not be nearly so effective at keeping and noting time. The links with which our amazing minds connect the dots cannot be completely explained away by the experiments or trial and errors of the psychological and psychiatric experts and centuries of theories and research on the human as a species.

In examining some of the people who have had either long-term or short-term effects on my life, I vacillate between thinking they were, indeed, "put" in my life for a purpose or that as luck or fate would have it, I stumbled onto them or they into me. I only know people are often the links between our memory just as events and experiences can be. I also know that regardless of the research done on the human mind and brain, there are almost as many exceptions to the rule as there are rules themselves. These exceptions "pop-up" very regularly. As sure as we think we know how someone will react to a given situation, they will surprise us and do the opposite.

In my effort to escape my childhood, I unwittingly picked up some extra baggage of guilt for my feeling of having abandoned my siblings. In my heart they had been my sacrificial lambs. I spent many years feeling this guilt and no amount of justification on my part ever completely erased it. When I left home and married my first husband, I worried who would laundry my siblings' clothes, pack their lunches, clean the kitchen and bathrooms, make sure the pets got food and water? All the duties I had taken upon myself as their substitute mother?

When at sixteen, I met and rather quickly married my first husband, I saw him as I wanted him to be; not as any semblance of what he truly was. Physically, he had all the necessary requirements. He was well-built and put together like an athlete. He was a modern rendition of one of the then current movie-star heart-throbs: just like Troy Donahue in "A Summer Place", blond, blue eyed, charismatic and innocently sexual. He had come to the United States from Germany when he was a very young teenager. He had a very slight accent (really attractive) however; his English was just as fluent and perfect as his native German. The first time he murmured "Ich Liebe Dich" (I love you) in my ears I was swept away. His voice was strong and authoritative except for these special moments and then it would send chills up and down my spine and raise my pulse by several beats. He could have been a real Rudolph Valentino with almost any woman. He responded to flirting exactly as my father had; he enjoyed the game.

Before I married, I had such an idealized picture of what my life was going to be; now that I had found my knight, I would become the perfect wife for my him and perfect mother for my children. My best friend at high school had wanted to give me a bridal shower but when my mother gave her permission it was conditioned with the understanding that Renate (my friend) and I would have to do all the work. We were responsible for planning and preparing the refreshments, cleaning the house and especially the bathroom, living-room, and kitchen. We sent out the invitations I bought with my babysitting money, decorated the living-room and arranged for my father to take the boys to the movies and for hamburgers afterwards. I prayed he would stay sober and not forget about it completely or mess it up in some way. Conversely, I sensed my mother was hoping for a disaster.

I was excited, but even though it was a small gathering; no more than ten friends, I received some very nice gifts. Unlike current bridal showers, I was on no "list" or registry with any department stores or bridal specialty stores, but I received an inexpensive set of silverware from Renate's family, some new towel sets, a service for four of the then popular Melmac dishes, a set of sheets and chenille bedspread for a double sized bed. I even got a set of linens with a cloth tablecloth and napkins and strange as it seems, this thrilled me. I could easily imagine myself in a charming little ruffled apron, (like my mother used to wear in a dim and distant memory) setting my table and laying the silver on these colorful napkins and matching tablecloth. Ah, such beautiful dreams I had!

Here was my knight in shining armor, my Sir Lancelot, and we would ride off together into the beautiful sunset in order to live happily ever-after.

Not.

There were a few beautiful weeks, perhaps even months but they ended the first time his anger exploded and he physically attacked me. What followed before and after the attack was to set the rules for the next eighteen years of the marriage from hell. First came the recriminations from him on something I had done or failed to do which he would claim I did on purpose, just to aggravate him. There was no modern day "Me, too" movement about women being abused physically, mentally and emotionally then. I, as most women, was isolated and was filled with shame, guilt, despair and hopelessness. Even if we (as in all women) noticed black eyes, bruises, or other signs of abuse on a woman, we did not comment on it, ask questions or offer any assistance. We ducked our head and pretended to see nothing.

I also lacked any support system or resources. I hate the way women of today let the question "Why didn't she just leave him?" roll so glibly off their tongues as if most of these women really had a choice. The moment I got married, my family stopped being any kind of resource or assistance for me. As my new mother-in-law was fond of saying, "You chose to make that bed, now you lie in it." My family (especially my mother) felt the same way. It did not help that within two months of my having married, my father and the entire family were sent on a three-year assignment to England. Across the ocean and out of reach, even if they *had* been loving and caring. I had my new husband and his family lived in Florida while my we were assigned to a base in Albuquerque, New Mexico.

Talk about being isolated... I knew no one. I spent the days cleaning a two-room furnished efficiency apartment. The only thing I had with me from my former life were the clothes in the suitcase I had arrived with, having put my household items (for an example) from the shower put in storage, separate from my family's thins.

The pattern which developed early on was first, the unrealistic and unexpected accusations on whatever it was I was supposed to have done; secondly, the actual meting out of consequences or punishment (and this could be a beating or verbal ridicule and humiliation), next would be forced sex and or rape which he equated as "making up" or the ending of the incident, and finally what I termed as acknowledgement on his part that he may have had some part in causing the confrontation.

After a particularly violent attack which resulted in physical signs proving his part (black-eyes, bruises, bloodied nose or lips, bumps or lumps or even fingerprints on my neck or shoulders) he would sometimes cry (yes, real tears) with promises it would never happen again. There would perhaps be one final step and it was that I must show him I accepted his apology and forgave him (after all, I was still basically responsible for driving him to this, wasn't I?) This last step often became the hardest for me to fulfill. He never beat me without the necessary (to him) sexual act afterwards. For me to pretend forgiveness when most likely to be feeling pain from the beating and hatred in my heart for this man turned monster was the most difficult thing I have ever had to do. Later in life, when I would hear of some parents who may have lost their loved ones to vicious predators, yet could meet with them face to face and offer forgiveness I simply could not believe it. I knew I could never do that. I believe I have a strong faith and yet, I have my doubts as a Christian in my ability to do this.

Each time we had one of these brutal encounters, I felt that any love or tenderness I had for this man when I married him was being chopped away like an ice sculptor with his pick. Soon there would be nothing left; no feeling at all. I wondered if hate would replace it or if I would simply be like an empty container with nothing but despair and hopelessness.

Any woman who has not gone through this kind of abuse, especially over such an extended period of time totally misunderstands the psychology behind such overwhelming feeling and acceptance of helplessness. The possibility these victims could possibly choose this existence is ludicrous. No victim, child or adult, ever enjoys being dominated and living in fear or choses this life for herself or her children. Any woman who makes such a faulty assessment and opinion needs a psychiatric evaluation of her own.

These victims are right smack-dab in the middle of Post-Traumatic Stress Disorder long before it became a "condition" caused by trauma. Further, there isn't a woman who has been through such a lifestyle who wouldn't grab any escape route they could visualize as having the slightest possibility of success. At the height of my eighteen-year sentence, I had no high school diploma, no work experience (except for unrelated and short stints at babysitting), no money, no safe shelter, no family support and only transit friendships which changed every time my husband got reassigned.

The best years of this life were when he was deployed to a combat zone and my children and I had a brief respite. How different it was when he was gone! No more running to hide when the clock warned it was time for him to come home from work There was no rise in the level of anxiety if dinner wasn't ready to go on the table by 5:30 p.m. so that he could watch his special Huntly-Brinkley newscast. We could eat what and when we wanted and by majority rule; not dictatorship. The well-known (and hated) regimentation of our lives was totally different. I could take long, soaking baths and not dread the necessary relinquishment of my body to satisfy his sexual desires; even when so worn out by the tension and stress of the daily struggle to please him. I have to admit in all honesty, at these times, it did occur to me that if I was no longer married to him, the children and I would not just be better off emotionally, mentally and physically, but happier. Financially, I would have to get some work skills and work to help support my children. The children were growing up all this time, and instead of counting the days until he returned to our lives, we were counting the days we had left of our freedom from fear and our joy in just being alive. When he was there, we existed and survived. When he was gone, we exulted in life itself. It sounds almost foolish, looking back, how willing I was to submit to the two different lives.

He had told me many times (over and over for eighteen long years of my life) that no one else would have such a worthless and stupid individual such as myself, especially saddled with four children. Many years later when I sought help for a severe period of depression, the therapist I was seeing told me I was suffering from PTSD. Not that it really matters, but between my first marriage and my last, and even with four children I had three proposals of marriage. How surprised I was when I realized how wrong he was about no one else ever wanting me.

"But how can that be?" I asked the therapist, "When it was so many years ago and meanwhile, I had gone on with my life, even finding the man who really was my hero and who showered me with love and understanding? So many years between then and the present. How could she tell me this?"

"Yes, but you had eighteen years of a life filled with the constant brainwashing. Just like prisoners of war or kidnappings it is like even only one drop of water, if constantly and consistently dripping on a rock can destroy it. You think you could escape from such a circumstance and snap your fingers and it's gone and erased?"

As I considered her words, I realized I had merely escaped his physical presence, but meanwhile he lay inside my subconsciousness, ready for any new trauma to set him free again. It did not matter that it had been years in-between his violence and control, it could be triggered again by other traumatic events.

I remember how after once rather severe physical beating his mother came to visit and when he was at work, she hesitantly asked about the bruises and other signs. When for the first time, I dared to share my life with someone else, her response hardened my sense of isolation and hopelessness. We were never to become even remotely close. She thought my behavior and attitude accounted for way he responded to me. I was to blame for not doing what I knew I should.

"Maybe you could talk to him," I said softly, looking into her eyes as she sat at the kitchen table drinking her coffee.

"What did you do to cause him to get so angry?" she asked me.

I was stunned, even though I was expecting no real solution, I wasn't expecting her immediate condemnation and for her to blame me for causing such treatment from him.

"Nothing. Nothing. Most of the time it is something so little no one else even notices."

Then she gave her stock advice; "Well, all I can say is you made your bed, now you lie in it. It takes two people to argue. I was against your marriage from the very beginning, if you remember. That's why you two did it so secretly and didn't tell anyone until it was done." This would become such a familiar refrain from her, I could repeat it verbatim or ignore it completely. There was never any help from her for me and our children hated going to her house. It was a constant, "No, no, don't touch that. Be quiet. Sit still. Clean your plate," or other such admonishments about their behavior.

For the very first time I said what I felt, "But what if the same one always resorts to violence and never believes he could possibly be responsible?"

"You think you have it so bad," she said, with a snort of disgust, "During the war when his father died on the Russian front, I had to try and raise his brother and him on my own. If it hadn't been for his stepfather adopting the two boys and marrying me while he was stationed in Germany, I don't know what I would have done."

This would the appropriate time to share a little background and even speculation on what gave my husband his view of life and family. He was born in Germany and for a time, lived a rather typical life of a normal, upper middle-class German family. His father was a Calvary officer in the German Army. Not to be at all confused with the Nazi Party and the rise of Hitler during those years prior to the United States entering the war.

Once, when he tried to explain his past to me, he told me, "You, or no one in this country could possibly understand the upheaval of Germany. Though Hitler finally showed his true colors eventually, the majority of the German people thought he would be good for our country. Hitler got no credit for his part in pushing forward in his plans for the Autobahn, which is one of the finest highway structures in the world."

"What about the way he treated all the Jewish people? "I was emboldened to ask since he was in such a mild, yet expansive mood."

"He might have gone a little too far with that, but he had to have the entire country behind him to accomplish what he wanted."

"And that was," I said (remember, this was early in our marriage. We didn't even have children then) I paused before completing my thought, "What?"

'A return to a pure, white, Aryan race for Germany. A chance for Germany to emerge as a true world leader. The Germans, as a race, *are* superior to most others."

I looked at him in surprise. "You don't really believe that, do you?"

Rather vehemently he replied, "Yes! Yes, I do believe it. There are more scientists, engineers, shakers and movers in the German population than in any other and countries like Germany are drawn in to support and pull these others up by their bootstraps"

"And yet your mother chose to marry an American soldier from the occupation army, and come live in the United States…"

Heatedly he answered defensively, "Not my choice, but my mother's. Remember, my brother was only fifteen and I was fourteen. We went and did what we were told."

I realized this was probably a topic I should not bring up again. He was obviously agitated at me for my failure to understand his explanation of his past history, and his family.

One final query (which I realized almost immediately I should not have brought up) presented a dichogamy he could not reconcile to me, but more importantly to himself: "But how does the way Hitler tried to eradicate Jewish and other races mesh with *your* own religion? Weren't you raised as a Catholic? Before the war your mother said you even attended private Catholic school."

"I did, but where the classrooms used to have crosses on the walls, they took them down and put huge pictures of the Hitler. He gave himself the title of Oberbefehlshaber (commander). He was to be addressed as "Fuhrër". This was one of the ways they had of trying to focus the German youth on the leader instead of Christ. At a certain age, boys were required to serve in the Hitler-Jugend (Hitler Youth) the purpose was to begin training German boys for eventual membership in Hitler's elite storm-trooper organization. When Hitler won the election, he taught us we must start realizing that if Germany were to reach the high goals, he had set for her, all Germans would have to put their country first, not their religion."

"So, kind of like the Boy Scouts in this country??" I asked.

He laughed uproariously at this and said, "It was not to learn survival or camping skills. There was no game to this. It was serious business and believe you me, everyone took it seriously. Not that the boys didn't want to join. What young boy doesn't want a chance to not just play soldier, but *be* a real soldier?"

"So," I asked him, "You were a member of this youth group?"

"Yes, and my brother as well."

"So, using nouns, describe yourself as an individual to me," I asked.

"Okay. Human, Male, German, Catholic, husband, son, brother, soldier…"

Dryly I said, "I'm glad I at least made the list."

Suddenly, perhaps tiring of the subject himself, or because he could sometimes change subjects when he was finished and not interested in someone else's viewpoint or his chance of persuading them to his way of thinking, he said, "And of course, future father."

He got up from the recliner where he had been holding court, and came to put his arms around me and kiss me.

"Are we starting on the fatherhood bit tonight?" I asked mischievously, thrilled to see him at his rare, but totally captivating charming side.

Make no mistake, he could be charming, clever, manipulative and persuasive when he wanted something. As long as he was in charge and got what he wanted from everyone else…

If you could catch him in this kind of mood, you could occasionally learn more about him or his past than usual. Now, with the peace of his seemingly willingness to have a "normal" conversation with me, he still had his arms around me and he said,

"Yes, but only if we are ordering boys."

I pulled my head back and said, "Boys only? What if we have girls?"

"We won't. I won't allow that. I want only sons."

I laughed at him but later was to realize not only did he mean this, and would always demonstrate his obvious favoritism on our two boys' gender, but he expected them immerge from the safety of my body as little solders. They could never display any kind of gentleness or tenderness or need for sympathy. If they fell down or suffered even the smallest scrape which go along with childhood, they weren't allowed any tears, but were told, "Suck it up and act like a man." Once, when one was injured in a wreck on his bicycle and was required to have stitches at the base emergency room, my husband refused to allow the physical to numb the site before stitching it up. I wasn't there, but had stayed home to watch the other children and I didn't learn about this until they returned and my husband was full of praises for his "little man" and the way he accepted his pain without tears. I was horrified not only by this rendition of the incident, but in the pride, I began to see reflected in my son's eyes as he basked in his father's approval. He obviously thought the pain and fear had been worth it to see that he had pleased his father by his shown bravery.

I had to push down the anger I felt in his treatment of his son, and even for the doctor who allowed such a thing. When he said, "Yessir, that's my boy-no coddling for him. He's not a mama's boy; he's my big soldier."

He was looking at me when he said this and I knew it was advice intended for me.

Often when I hear the children who have suffered abuse from their fathers and watched it be meted out to their mothers, I cringe when they ask, truthfully and with genuine anguish of their mothers, "Why didn't you stop him? Why didn't you do something?"

I *did* try. Unsuccessfully most of the time, but I fought my small battles and have to believe in my heart that I did make *some* difference. To believe otherwise would break my heart and destroy the deep love I felt for each of them.

The eldest of my children was so resistant to potty-training and simply wet her underwear and her bed long after the average. Yet, she was bright, inquisitive and very neat and tidy about her other personal growth and hygiene. She was constantly getting kidney infections, would be taken to the doctor and given antibiotics to clear the infection only for it to reoccur a few weeks later. The doctor was reassuring but not much help, merely telling me that when she was ready, she would accomplish this task as well as others children master. My husband's cure was to administer the belt to punish her when we found her bed wet. I tried to set my mental clock and get up before he did in the mornings so that if her bedding and pajamas were wet, I could strip and remake the bed and put her in fresh pajamas. This was not always successful and very often I stood between her and his belt taking her beating with her sobbing and holding on to me to try to avoid the whipping. He didn't forbid this shouting, "Well, maybe if you take her punishment, you'll do your job as her mother and break her of this habit."

Even if she begged for a drink before bed, he insisted on limiting her intake of fluids after dinner each time. It didn't seem to help, except to make her urine smell stronger and give her an almost desperate longing for more to drink.

Finally, the doctor accepted that something was wrong and out of any childhood stubbornness or reluctance to "waste" time, holding her urge to go to the bathroom so not to miss out on any playtime. He sent us to a urologist which began a regular and lengthy schedule of dialysis. I'm sure that by this time, methods and treatments have changed tremendously but at that time, even the doctor said he hated to be into this kind of painful but necessary steps to try to help her.

Finally, after over a year of these measures, he suggested she be put in the hospital to allow him to perform exploratory surgery to try and pinpoint the problem. (C-Scans were far into the future at that time). I hated to put her through this but knew we had to do something. My husband still insisted it was psychological and plain old stubbornness but I agreed with the urologist. When he came from the operating room, he was smiling and so optimistic I immediately began to feel hope.

"The good news is she is fine. The more good news," he said, still smiling, "is that it is fixable. The opening to her bladder is too small. It has been like this since birth and can be a simple fix. Right now, her bladder and kidneys are working hard but each time she urinates, she is unable to completely empty her bladder. There remains a residue and this is what causes all the infections."

"And you can fix this?" I asked him, almost in tears.

He reached out and patted my arm. "That's what I came to tell you. I already did, while I was in there. She is going to have to stay in the hospital for a few days while we keep tabs on her urine amounts and she will be on some mild pain meds to keep her comfortable and antibiotics to prevent any infections. We don't want any signs of fever or unforeseen problems cropping up."

"Can I see her?"

"She's in recovery ICU, but yes, you can. Please—when she regains consciousness, no tears. It will frighten her and we want to accent the positive to her. She's going to have some pain, and she will want to go home but just keep emphasizing how wonderful it's going to be not to wet the bed, no more accidents and how brave she was, and what a big girl she is, okay?"

I nodded as he patted my arm.

"Can her siblings come visit?"

"No, unfortunately we don't allow children visitors on this floor but I will make sure they put her in a bed by the window right above the little park and you can bring them to look up here and they can wave to each other."

Such a simple solution, not without some worry attached, but he was right and the problem was fixed. The only thing remaining was this huge sense of guilt at what she had suffered since birth with something that was never her fault. My husband never seemed to either accept or feel any guilt about his (or our) dealing so unfairly with something this child had absolutely no control over.

It is fairly well accepted in today's age, but still difficult at times to put in action that the best way for children to learn is though the examples they have before them. Verbal understanding and acceptance of reasonable communication seem often to be slow in development. Thus, we accept when children of drug users or abuse of alcohol often follow the leader. You cannot tell a child to "Do as I say, not as I do" and fully expect them to follow your instructions. In their minds it is often "What is sauce for the goose is also sauce for the gander". And yet, professionals talk of the need to "break the cycle" from generation to generation. My husband used violence to enforce his rules—wasn't it to be expected his children would think this was the way other fathers kept their own households in order? Leading a child towards violence can be as simple as correcting their behavior with physical or verbal abuse. If a child hits his sibling and his father hits him in punishment, does this serve as a deterrent or encouragement towards using violence?

Or

Does it give them a total abhorrence of any kind of violence? To this day I get physically ill just seeing a violent act. I don't like horror movies or any movie with lots of gory details. Stephen King is not a favorite of mine, but Nicholas Sparks is. It doesn't have to be a sugary, perfect and happy ending, but it must be believable and entertaining. The best compliment

I ever received was when an editor told me I was his John Grisham. If only I were!

The largest underlying emotion in our home was fear. Fear of doing something which would bring either physical or violent verbal abuse. I fully understand the harm of no structure or of failing to teach the consequences of unacceptable behavior thereby allowing the child to be spoiled and selfish making them miserable companions.

Part of the problem I had, aside from the terrible misjudgment of the man I chose to marry was with a mother like mine, I had no self-esteem before my marriage, and my husband sensed and fed upon this, reinforcing my feeling of no value and hopelessness in ever bettering my situation. Hell, he may have even chosen me because he recognized the probable victim in me.

I looked with envy on the few friends and couples we associated socially with when I saw some of their tenderness or gentleness in their relationships and couldn't help but feel cheated.

The first time he cheated on me with an underage girl he had met working a part-time job to supplement our income, I shared the heartache I felt with my friend in a rare moment of honesty. Her response was this: "Men are like that. You think your father hasn't cheated on your mother, not just once but over and over? If they don't get what they need at home, they will go outside the home to get it. You must make them feel like a king in the bedroom, you can't be too tired for sex, you must be a chef in the kitchen, have yourself clean, in makeup, cheerful and welcoming when they come home. They really should feel their home is their castle and you are their slave. You can't let yourself go or the house and children, ether. You can't stand by the door ready to unload your miserable day or the list of the children's bad behavior. That's another must for the wife; handle the children and make them perfect representatives of your family, yet give him all the credit for achieving this."

This was not the response I expected from her. I felt defeated and lost with her willingness to place the state of my marriage on me. It was as though she was encouraging me to just accept the status-quo and become a slave.

Once when she came over to have a cup of coffee and allow our children to play together, I was on my hands and knees with a brush and bucket of mop-water, cleaning the floor.

"Hey, what are you doing?"

"What does it look like? Cleaning the floor. Did you come to help or watch?"

She laughed. "Why not use a mop and save the knees?"

"My husband doesn't believe you can get the floor really clean unless you do it on your hands and knees." I said this rather shame-facedly and didn't meet her eyes of disbelief.

She started to laugh but abruptly stopped when she realized I was serious.

"You're kidding, right?" she asked me.

I got up, emptied the bucket and wrung out the rag and put it and the brush in the bucket.

Then I poured us coffee and sat down where we could see the children in the living room playing with blocks and other toys.

"Nope. Not kidding. Wanna hear something else you won't believe?"

She nodded her head.

"How would you like to have Dan come home each day and check under the bed to see if there was any dust-bunnies under there, and check the closet to see if the clothes faced the right way and the shoes were all lined up?"

"What's a dust-bunny?"

"You know the little lint and fuzz that develops now and then in places where you don't mop or clean regularly."

"Ah," she said, "I had never heard it had a name. Kind of cute... dust-bunnies."

I knew she was trying to get me to laugh and cheer me up.

"And is that another reason you do your hair and put makeup every day before he comes home?"

"Well, yes, but two different things, one is keeping the house up to his mother's standards, you could eat off her floor and I mean literally, not just figuratively."

"How do you put up with it?"

"How could I not? To keep the peace, that's how."

"Maybe he gets that from the military. You know, like what they say is a white glove inspection, isn't that what it is called? The guy who runs around inspecting anything amiss on the base?"

"The office of the Inspector-general."

"And would that be the person to go to report an abusive husband and father?"

That conversation let the cat out of the bag and for the first time I had someone I could talk honestly to about my situation. I felt a huge sense of relief in having an ally, even a silent and secret one. Someone I could go to in safety and receive comfort and understanding without condemnation or accusatory advice about how I must do something and get out of this hopeless and senseless trap of a marriage with a real-life monster.

A bond was formed that day and even many, many years later I can feel the warm feeling of not being alone in my misery and fear but having someone who cared about me to talk to and try to instill some hope on an escape someday. What is it they say? Misery loves company? I didn't wish that my friend would be in the same situation but I did mean was that it lessoned the feelings of fear and inferiority I felt about my situation. Just to be able to talk to someone *does* help.

When I called her one morning and told her he had forgotten his wallet at home and I had looked in it and found a photo of a sexy blond in shorts. It was signed with love and her name. I stood there, big and eight months pregnant with another child, feeling big and clumsy and ugly. At that moment I also felt worthless and stupid and helpless.

When I called my girlfriend she said, "Grab your children and come over here. I'm making Mickey Mouse pancakes. We'll feed them and talk this out."

After the kids were seated in the appropriate seating arrangements, highchair, some at the little child-size table and chairs and the remaining two at the counter on stools, she and I sat down at the table with coffee and I showed her the photo.

She began with, "He's the lowest of the low. What a no-good S.O.B. First of all, he's breaking the law, the girl is underage. She's just a baby." Then she looked at me and said, "Strictly speaking, so are you; still in your early twenties and having your third child. Can you imagine what his first sergeant or commander would say if he knew what was going on? Second, you have already had two children (I was yet to have the final two) and are expecting another. What does that say about any love or trust he has for you? Third, from what you tell me, and I believe you, he is still having regular sex with you. So, he's having sex with two women at the same time. Having his cake and eating it too, so to speak."

"Has Dan (her husband) ever cheated on you?" I asked her.

With a wry laugh she said, "Yes, more than once."

"What did you do? How did it get resolved?"

"Sweetie, it never got resolved. I forgave him. Or pretended to. Remember I have seven children."

"I don't know if I can ever do that," I said.

"What else could I do? We have seven children. You're about to have your third. I had no job, no family support."

"Do you think you still love him?"

"I don't know. Sometimes, somethings I think I hate him."

Later when I had my cry and she cried with me, we cleaned up the kitchen and before I took my children and went back home, she said, "Sit down and make you a "stay or go list" listing the pros and cons on each side."

I later did as she suggested. On the "stay" list I had:

No job or job skills

No car or means of transportation (and with three children that means strollers diaper bags and all the required equipment)

No babysitter, even if I had a job.

No money of my own.

No family support or resources to call on. In fact, this took place during the time my family was in England on a three-year assignment.

No education to really consider; I didn't even have a G.E.D or high school diploma.

No driver's license, even if I had a car.

No place to live and he sure wasn't going to move out.

I was terrified, truly terrified of him and I fully believed he might kill or harm me or and the children.

Then on the to "go" list:

I simply could not continue to live in this kind of madness and fear.

My children were living in the same fear and uncertainty and it was escalating.

The possibility of going to his commander or first Sargent came to mind, but I ruled it out. Unless I went in with obvious proof of injuries,

51

what would keep him from lying and if they did believe me and threw him in the guard house for any amount of time, two things were likely to happen: They might demote him, reducing our already limited pay, and with such a thing on his file, it is unlikely he would ever get promoted again. Finally, no matter what their intervention was, he had such a violent streak when he was thwarted, what would he do to me when he got out? While he sat in the guardhouse, his feeling of being the victim would fester and grow out of all rational proportion. He wouldn't be looking at the trouble he was in, because he would never see this as being a deterrent to keep him from repeating it. No, he would look at it as my betrayal of him and our family. He would start planning some grand revenge.

"Let's face it", I told my friend, "I'm stuck here."

"Well, temporarily," she said, "But that doesn't mean there's no hope. We'll pray on it. Something will happen. Something good."

She always made me feel better, but this time I felt a finality about my situation. It was hard for me to feel hopeful.

Our family financial situation was a constant struggle and yet, though he allowed me to pay the bills, and we worked hard to stay current for our utilities, we also had a car payment, car insurance payments, monthly payments on the little nineteen-inch Motorola television we bought. I think he allowed me the bookkeeping responsibility because he wanted to blame me when there wasn't enough money to go around or any bill was paid late. He kept a modest amount from each paycheck for his cigarettes and lunches, but then he decided he wanted to take flying lessons. I, in my constant efforts to find the man I had married hidden in this violent and aggressive person. I compared him to my father, and he did not drink to excess. At first, I counted this as a plus in his favor; but at least some men who were abusive could blame it on the beer; he was just mean, and the booze did not have an effect on his brutality. He had always wanted to get his pilot's license, but at sixty dollars an hour it was very hard for us. Then he decided to trade the car in for a newer and nicer one. Of course, the payment was higher, as well. I dared not complain. It was my job to smile and not complain, just reassure him we could afford to do whatever he wanted, it was up to me to stretch our pay to meet the obligations.

Still, to be fair, he was working his military job on the Flight Line at the base, and about four hours several nights a week at the hamburger joint. I would later find out that's where he met the high school girl, he had the affair with. He wasn't one to sit around, even on the weekends and do nothing productive. He washed the car and vacuumed it regularly, he took care its maintenance, and a certain amount of repair on it when it needed it and it was something, he felt he could do proficiently.

When trying to assess any good points fairly, I told myself I was lucky he didn't gamble. Not at all. I tried to budget what he gave me, but each month it was tight and we barely made it, payday to payday. I always did my grocery shopping at the base commissary because it was so much cheaper. It was operated kind of like the current wholesale stores of today. I made sure I bought the children's necessities, such as diapers, pull-ups, baby food, formula, vitamins, then next priority on the list was a couple of six packs of his favorite beer. He was never really an alcoholic and I could never tie his violent personality to the beer he drank. I don't believe I saw him really drunk more than once or twice in our entire marriage. I sometimes wished I could blame his meanness on that. I would always purchase a carton of cigarettes for him and a six pack of beer when I went to the store for groceries; always looking for ways to appease him.

We did purchase a freezer (payments to the bank; financing of fourteen dollars and thirty-two cents monthly) and this helped. On payday I could purchase several gallons of milk as long as I remembered to defrost them as I needed them, we saved money on that; ditto the bread. I purchased ten l loaves each payday and took one out as a time as needed. Our diet didn't have much in the way of fresh vegetables or fruits, except the week of payday, but we managed.

I had offered many times to get a job, at least part time but I know now he wanted to keep me isolated. He also did believe women should stay home and raise the children, clean the house and make sure all of her husband's needs met. In his mind he should be able to come home, take a shower, have a beer, watch his newscast, have sex and sleep peacefully. The children were conditioned to play in their room and to pick up after themselves when it was time for me to bathe them and get them settled in bed. We certainly could use the extra money but I think there were several reasons he didn't allow me to even consider working outside the home. He was proud and did not want anyone to think he could not support his family. He was afraid deep inside that allowing me to move in the outer world might give me some strength and change me from the docile and compliant wife he had. Regardless of the things he did to humiliate, ridicule and tear down any self-esteem I might have simmering below the surface, he wanted to keep me from gaining some confidence from any interactions with outsiders. Sometimes told myself probably a lot of his co-workers didn't even know he was married or had a family.

He would occasionally throw me what I considered a "scrap of" affection or approval. Usually this was in the manner of a compliment on something special I had cooked for him, or how well I had laundered, starched, and ironed his fatigues.

There were exceptions I could not explain where I could almost believe he did, in some very controlled and warped way, love me.

He brought me flowers or candy some valentine days or anniversaries and once he even made arrangements with a neighborhood teen to watch our children and he set it up to meet with my friend and her husband at the non-commissioned officers club to go dancing.

Of course, I was told the rules before we arrived there. I wasn't to dance with anyone else, even if they asked him first if it was okay. I knew he would tell them, "Yes, of course, go right ahead." But he wanted me to say "No" and there was a threat implicit in his warning as to what would happen when we arrived home if I did not do as he ordered.

Some Christmas, he would ask what I wished for and he would take the kids to purchase it, then he helped them wrap it under the tree. It was always something useful; a new mixer, pressure cooker, vacuum, never anything frivolous or silly in his mind, a waste of good money One year I did ask for a sewing machine and when I got it, I began making the girls' dresses and some shirts for the boys. This was a wonderful way to show my creativity and the girls loved having new dresses different from their friends made especially for them.

I made sure to display my appreciation for these times of tranquility and for the semblance of a "normal" family.

Often, just when things seemed to have been running smoothly, he would deal a particularly harsh blow to the children.

One such incident occurred when he finally changed his mind about allowing the children to have a dog. He had allowed the children to have a dog. We got it from the pound and it was a beautiful little beagle. He set the rule; this was to be an outside dog and it was the children's job to water and feed it. Since there were no fenced in yards on the base housing, he built a dog house, allowed the children to paint it. I donated a warm quilt for inside and the kids designed and painted a sign, "Snoopy" for the front opening. There was no problem getting the children to care for the dog. They loved her dearly. She had gotten her immunizations at the pound. Generally, the kids would get off the school bus, come and take her off the long chain she was on, and because the back of our house faced a huge retention pond-grassy area, they would romp and play with her. Both the children and the dog looked forward each day to this "free play time".

She was not neutered when we got her and when she came into heat for the first time, my husband warned us that we must keep other dogs away from her because they would smell her and come around and if they managed to "hook" up she would get pregnant and he wasn't going to have to deal with a bunch of little puppies. I know that the children had a brief moment to wishing they *could* have some puppies but they did not want to lose Snoopy at all so they tried very hard to protect her. Even sneaking her in when he gone or not expected home for any length of time.

Well, as expected, it happened. Nature, being what it is, called and a canine boyfriend came calling. The very day, before he could even wait until it could be determined a pregnancy had happened resulted and she was pregnant, he took off from work and took her back to the pound and left her there with some excuse or another.

The children came home from school, the doghouse was gone, the chain, water and food bowl were gone and most importantly, the dog was gone.

The story from him was early that morning she had somehow gotten loose from the collar and chain. He supposedly looked for hours, having no luck and finally took the dog house, chain, food and water bowls to donate them at the pound, after checking that no one had turned Snoopy in as a lost dog.

They were heart-broken and lots of tears were shed. He tolerated a little of this but when asked if they could get another one bluntly said, "No, not until move somewhere with a fenced in yard. Get over it. It was just a dog."

This callowness was another trademark. I fully believed if I were to pass on, he would move along with his life without even a break in his step. Probably have another timid, fearful little housfrau to take care of his needs and the children.

I don't think he fully realized the depth of love the children had for that dog. He had never been allowed a dog when he was growing up; he was one of two boys, several years apart, and very independent and self-sufficient. Outsiders would surely have viewed him as a good father. He did try to attend some of their ball games when they played, but ruined this gesture when he then gave a searing and ugly critique of what they had done wrong in the game.

Truth is, he demanded perfection and no matter what they did, they would never be able to satisfy that demand.

Another thing which began to raise the level of my fear of him was when he began to collect guns. He had a couple of shotguns, a silver colt patterned after the old west revolvers, an Italian Garibaldi rifle, a twenty-two Remington rifle, a twenty-two pistol and he acquired various other makes and models. In fact, if I wanted to get on "his good side" for a while, all I had to do was save some money from the household budget and buy him some sort of gun for his birthday or Christmas or other holiday gift. Do not be mistaken. I saw the irony in supplying him even more weapons of choice when I was fully aware that his propensity for violence might someday cause him to use them against me. He did build a gun cabinet with a lock on it; but it had a glass front door and even a child could have broken it easily.

We had a matched set of swords hanging crossed on our wall and once when a little field mouse came across the floor, (our house at that time backed up to a large field where a development was going to be and we had at several times had little mice looking for new homes come in our house) he leaped up, grabbed one of those swords and pursued the mouse while the rest of us stood on couches and chairs screaming. He eventually cornered the mouse under the couch and impaled him with a sword. He was very proud of this kill.

Chapter

THREE

The night I found out about my husband's affair with the high school student I waited for him to arrive home with no real plan of action. I just knew I could not hide my knowledge and pretend nothing was wrong. Of course, when he did come home that night, I had to use every bit of restraint I had to not say anything until I had put the children to bed and closed the door to their bedroom. His evening probably seemed normal (or what was normal for us) to him. I had supper ready on time, he watched his special newscast and settled with a can of beer into his recliner. This was one of those nights he was not scheduled for his part-time job.

I was determined not to show fear; but realistically I knew he would instantly take the offensive, knowing my fear of him.

When I had found the photo and showed it to my friend, I had kept it; not replacing it in his wallet where I had found it.

I had it in my apron pocket and I stood in front of him in his recliner and I said, "I need to ask you something."

"What about?"

"This," I said, holding the photo out to him.

I did see a flicker cross his face and he said, "Where did you get that?"

"From your wallet you forgot this morning."

He stood up, anger filling his face.

"You looked in my wallet?"

"Yes," I said, trying to keep my voice steady.

He stood up, and walked over and slapped me, splitting my bottom lip. "You had absolutely no right going through my wallet."

I wiped my mouth on my apron and I said, "And what right did you to cheat on me, with me standing here with my big belly, pregnant with our third child?"

"I'll teach you to bother my things", he said and he slapped me again. This time I had difficulty in keeping my balance and when I reached out to steady myself, I foolishly grabbed hold of the standing floor lamp. It gave way and plunged down to the floor, breaking the glass bowl and light bulb. He reached down and grabbed a handful of my hair and attempted to drag me to my feet. I locked my hands around his, trying to relieve the pressure of my hair and scalp.

As he pulled me to my feet, I fell back to my knees and we both landed on some of the broken glass. I don't believe I even felt the glass.

He did succeed in getting me to my feet and he let go of my hair and grabbed me by my shoulders. He began to shake me back and forth yelling the entire time, "See what you make me do? See what you caused? Don't you *ever* touch my things again," he yells. My two children had run to their bedroom when the incident had begun and I prayed they stayed there.

He gave a last big shake and then released me, making me land on my backside on the floor some distance away from the glass.

I hadn't realized it before, but my nose was bleeding along with my lip and there was some glass embedded in each knee. Looking down, I was distracted by the photo of the girl lying bent in the middle of the glass from the lamp. Later I thought how ridiculous it was that I was hurting and yet, there was somehow a sense of real satisfaction that her photo was ruined. By now our fight had taken us to the hallway and I saw blood dripping down, I lay for a minute begging God to "Help me," but no one came to my aide that night. One of my fingers had a severe cut, and probably would have healed better if I had gotten a few stitches but even then, I knew he would never allow me to go to the base dispensary to tend to it.

I know that he kicked me, how many times I couldn't say, but finally he said, "Get up and clean your mess up. I am going to take a shower and when I get out, you better have this mess all cleaned up."

When he had gotten himself some clean clothing from the bedroom and gone into the bathroom and locked the door behind him, I managed, despite my pain to get to my feet. Bracing myself with one hand on the wall, I went to the kitchen and sat in a chair while I pulled out the pieces of glass embedded in my knees, and gently washed them with a soft hand towel from the rack by the sink. I would probably have to look at them each again later to check for any pieces too small to see without a closer examination. I took rolled up tissue and put up my nostrils to block any future drops even though the nose bleed had slowed considerable, I could still feel it making its way down my face. Then I got my mop bucket and a cleaning cloth from under the sink, filled it with water, and getting down on my painful knees, began to wipe up the blood from the floor and the occasional drops on the wall. I cleaned up all the broken glass from the floor lamp bulb, carefully trying to miss any tiny pieces.

When I was through, I went back to the kitchen, cleaned the bucket out, and threw the cleaning rag in the trash. All the while my mind was racing, from thoughts of how I hated him, to how he turned this whole episode around to it being my fault for looking in his wallet.

Never mind his cheating on me. Never mind she was a minor. When he came out and I went to the bathroom, I looked in the mirror. My nose was not bleeding any more, but it needed cleaning, one eye was swollen and almost shut, my knees were swelling as well, and I knew I was getting a large bruise on my lower back where he had kicked me. I could feel it. I actually ached all over. I was afraid to go into our bedroom, afraid to restart his anger but I desperately wanted to lie down and put a cold washcloth on my face. I got two Tylenol and went to the kitchen to get myself a glass of water. I noticed how badly my hands were shaking.

Since at this point in our lives we did not have our own furniture, both bedrooms had double beds in them. Our youngest had a crib in the children's room and our daughter had a double bed in which she seemed almost lost.

She was such a petite little girl. All around her were her carefully placed sleeping companions; Mr. Teddy bear, her blue stuffed elephant, the small brown monkey with the cymbals, and Raggedy Ann. I carefully and quietly moved these to the floor, and as gently as possible moved her little body over to make space for me. I was afraid to go in the room where he was, even to get a gown or some pajamas.

I didn't want to take my pedal pushers off; I knew I would feel defenseless in just my t-shirt and panties in case he came after me. I knew this was a very real possibility. His way of ending an argument had always been forced sex. I felt it was his way of showing who had control over even my body, as well as my mind. I knew I would lie there, shaking and praying that he would have fallen asleep and I would be safe for the duration of the night.

It couldn't have been more than ten or fifteen minutes when I heard noises from down the hall. I held my breath and he came into the room. Not caring that our daughter was asleep, he turned on the overhead bedroom light. We locked eyes and then he said, "Get your ass in the other bedroom. Now."

He turned off the light and I slowly got up and went to the other room. I went to the dresser, pulled open a drawer and got a nightgown out. When I took my clothes off and put them on the rocker in the corner of the room. I turned back the covers on my side of the bed and climbed in. I don't believe he was even aware of it, but the entire time tears rolled silently down my face. There was no softness no gentleness to the act. It was a simple act of brutality, showing his control and contempt. Years later I would recall incidents like this and tell myself: *No wonder I felt worthless and helpless. No wonder I believed what he said about me being stupid and useless. Could anyone in the same situation not feel the same?*

My father, now living in the same town, although still out of work, surprised me with an unexpected visit the next morning. I was still pretty much estranged from my mother, plus she was still working two jobs again and her shifts varied so I rarely saw her or my brothers. Still, that morning the doorbell rang and it was him. He came inside and when he got a look at the black eye, and swollen nose and bruises he gasped and then he said angerly, "What happened? Did he do this to you?"

"It was both our fault, Daddy."

"It is NEVER a woman's fault when a man beats on her. NEVER. Your mother and I have had our fights and *she* have hit me before, but *I* have never struck a woman in my life. I'm going to wait right here and when he gets here, I'm' going to show him how it feels to be beat on by someone twice his size. Then I am going to call his first sergeant and turn him in. Let him spend some time in the guardhouse and lose a stripe or two."

I made coffee and as we sat there and talked. I calmed him down and then I lied to him. I told him my husband had cried and asked for forgiveness.

"He swears he will touch me like that again."

"Of course, he says that now. He doesn't want you to leave him. Actually, the bully has got his cake and can eat it as well. Have you looked in the mirror? You're pregnant, for God's sake. You have two other children. Someone needs to give him a lesson he won't forget. He's still a Nazi, just like he was growing up."

I finally convinced him that this was my problem, I was an adult and I had to deal with it. Before he left that morning, we agreed I would call him if and when he hurt me again and I would not just call him, but the police, and his first Sargent. I would take my children and move to his house (even the thought of moving to that filthy, mother-dominated home made me reconsider any thoughts living there again. It would be like going from the frying pan to the fire.) I could not face such a solution. The thought of my children under her roof and her treating them the way she had my siblings and I made me cringe.

After he left, I called and cancelled my scheduled doctor appointment, not wanting anyone to see me until I healed.

We never brought up the incident again except for him to apologize and swear the affair was over and he would never hit me again. I wanted so desperately to believe him. Upon retrospection, I do not know if it just that I had nowhere to go, and no solution or if I still had some little corner inside me that cared about him and believed the marriage could be salvaged. Just as usually happened, he gave a little crumb of "payback" for my forgiveness. After he beat me, he usually was on good behavior for a period of time without blowing up and he would let slide some of his petty grievances which usually made me flinch with fear and trepidation; tip-toeing around in my eggshell floored home. Sometimes it would be some sort of gift; something I had been wanting, either for my children or myself or for the home. Sometimes it was just a suspension of the tense, waiting for the other shoe to drop atmosphere.

This occasion marked a change in my inner self. Along with my girlfriend's help and guidance, I began to try to reprogram myself and my way of thinking. He wasn't going to change. It was only going to get worse. I was ready to acknowledge this, even if only to myself. Emotionally, I began to gird myself for moving forward somehow. Sometimes I would even talk to myself, saying: *Someday, someday, you are going to have a man who loves you and cares for you and the kids and is kind and gentle. In good time, it will happen. With "God's help"* I would add.

Just this small emotional promise I gave myself was enough to me a feeling of hope, however small. This time, I used the few days afterwards when he was trying to make sure he had me brainwashed into believing his apologies and promises to change were being accepted, I put a plan in motion which would change my life forever.

A simple little plan with shattering consequences which must have been planted in my heart by God.

I prepared his favorite dinner a few days later, which was a day off from his part-time job., talked to the children about being especially nice to daddy that night because he had worked hard and was so tired. I baked home-made bread and a lemon (his favorite) pie for dessert.

After he finished, he stood, and said, "That was really good. I have been wanting it. How did you know?' He smiled and turned to go watch his new program and I said,

"I'm glad you enjoyed it. Can I ask you something?"

A little warily, I thought, he said, "Of course. What?"

"Well, you know this is a small house and I keep up on everything. The kids both take a pretty long nap each afternoon, leaving me a little free time..." I paused, and then dove in, "Can we afford for me to get the paperback edition of studying for the GED and work on trying to get mine?"

He looked completely surprised. "Why?"

"Just because you finished high school and sometimes, I feel I missed a lot by quitting after only two years. I feel stupid sometimes, especially," I added, "Around some of your friends and their wives. It would be something interesting to do and I think it would be good for me to read something besides children's books to the kids and fiction books from the library. Why not do something more challenging? It would be better than sitting and watching General Hospital or Days of our Lives like a lot of housewives do."

"He smiled (a real smile for once) and said, "So you want to go back to school?"

I felt my face warm at his teasing. "I won't actually be going anywhere. I'll be at the kitchen table while the kids nap."

After a long pause, he said, "Well, I don't see any harm in it—"

He must have seen the happiness I was trying to hide and had to add his little spoiler to deflate my happiness, "You can't let anything just go to pot around here. You've got to keep up with all your chores and remember you will have the additional work and stress of a new little one."

As though I wasn't even more aware of that then he was. He had never changed a diaper or fed a baby in his life. That was women's work in his eyes.

I was so excited. His good mood carried over, probably because I made sure I acted enthused with his love-making that night.

The next morning, he even made the coffee and told me to sleep in until the children woke up. It was almost too good to be true.

A little while later he called to tell me during his lunch hour he went to the base exchange and they had the paperback cheaper than a civilian book store would have.

I wondered why he couldn't learn from such interludes how life could be so much nicer and happier with just a little effort on his part? It was almost as though he had a wall there, and he worked to keep it there. He never admitted to having any weaknesses, but in my mind, it was at great cost to our marriage and our children. Just to clarify here; it does not always take two to argue or fight. Very often, it only takes one, the abuser.

I was aware that may of his co-workers seemed hesitant to disagree with him because he could not stand to lose at anything or admit he may have been wrong and it was often "No holds barred" when he argued with anyone. I don't think he was afraid of anything or anyone.

Neither do I think size or training and fitness had anything to do with his belief in his own invincibility. If he perceived an obstacle, he conquered it and went on. End of story.

That pert of his personality did not make allowances for imperfections; in himself or others, even in his children. When this happens in a parent, it often has serious repercussions with their self-worth and acceptance of the path their lives take. Sometime resulting in a sense of hopelessness which limits their productivity.

Just the acquisition of the study guide itself made a difference in my days. I rose early, cleaned house, fed children, and got the laundry and ironing (the heavier and time-consuming tasks) done in record time looking forward to my study time. I was trying to balance my excitement over what I was learning and in not being so enthusiastic to raise any kind of regret from my husband on being allowed to do this project.

There was a slight feeling of having been cheated by my early departure from high school to marry, but I did take responsibility for my own choice. I had been so eager to leave my childhood (and mother) behind I had failed to get to honestly know the man I was marrying and to thoroughly examine what I might be getting into.

Now, I told myself *it was much too late for those kinds of recriminations, best to focus on the goals I was beginning to set, however tentatively, for my own future. I resisted putting* the children down earlier for their naps and I strove daily to finish studying so that I had enough time to truly be glad to greet them from naptime with my full, undivided attention.

Sometime my husband would query me on how it was going. I often thought he felt it might pass, this enthusiasm for the project, but he didn't say this. I would mention my struggling with the math section at times and unbelievably, a couple of times I grew frustrated with the written instructions and even wasted unnecessary tears.

My girlfriend helped immeasurably with this; she had graduated high-school and even had a year of community college under her belt. She was patient and encouraging, better than any teacher I could remember.

I did not try to rush it. I wanted to conquer this. The thought of failing the examination after all this effort was too scary to even consider. After several months, I felt like I was ready to try. I don't know how it is currently, but back when this was happening with me, an individual could make an appointment to take the exam at one of the local universities for a nominal fee and results would be mailed to the student. The exams were given often and regularly and you could take it again after a certain time period if you failed on your first (or even further) tries.

At first, my husband thought I was asking him to take me there, drop me off and then babysit out children until I called him and told him I was done. Then he would come pick me up. I rushed to explain he wouldn't have to do anything. My girlfriend was going to drive me down there, drop me off, and then take all the children (hers and mine) to her house to watch a Walt Disney movie until I was done. Then I would call her and she and the children would come retrieve me. This made my husband's acquisition to my request even easier because he didn't have to put himself out. I fully realized at some level he (like my mother with the bridal shower) not only wanted but believed I wouldn't pass the exam.

I called, found out the date and time for the examination, filled out the application form, enclosed it with a check, and even heavy in my ninth month of pregnancy, took the test. I had been told it might be as long as six weeks before I got the results so now all I did was wait.

My friend and I took the kids to free story time at the local library one day and I checked out a big stack of books to read for the wait time and for after the baby was born.

It was two of these library books which would forever have a strong influence on, my life. When I was very young, I had read "A Tree Grows in Brooklyn" (Betty Smith, 1943) more than once and now I had chosen two more of novels by Betty Smith. One (Maggie Now, 1958) immediately made me feel that *this was a story about me.* In it a young couple gets married and the man is totally focused in getting his education, including a law degree. His wife has very little education and feels inadequate around her husband's friends and teachers at the university he attends. I identified with this story-book heroine; I have never felt at ease with people who are highly educated. Even though my husband was only a high-school graduate, he was three years older in age and therefore, in life knowledge. Even later years in my life, I still got (and do now) almost tongue-tied around people who have a lot of education. I also feel a restrained but recognizable anger and jealously at many who take for granted their right and their accessibility to go further than high-school. They did not seem to feel how lucky they were for this marvelous opportunity. Very much Because of my own mother's working two jobs and my father being a largely absent alcoholic, I credited myself with raising my younger brothers as the young Maggie does in Betty's book when her mother dies in childbirth. The other book, "Tomorrow will be Better" which Betty Smith published in 1948, echoed my feeling that this writer was living my life through her books. Oh, if only I could write like that!

Each day I could hardly wait for the mailman to appear to see if the test results had arrived. Then it became a test between which would arrive first-the test results or the new baby. This was settled when I woke with labor pains right on schedule; the Friday he was due, I called my friend and then my husband hurried to take the children to her house. This, of all four of my children, was the easiest delivery I ever went through. I had barely arrived and been prepped, and into a labor suite when my water broke and I was rushed on to delivery. Ironically, I had a three-day hospital stay and on the second day when my husband came to visit the baby and I, he brought the mail…with the test results. I wished he would go home and allow me to open and read the results on my own, but he insisted on staying and sharing the results with me. The baby was beautiful, a healthy and unexpected nine lbs., three ounces and beautiful skin tones, not at all that newborn red often seen in newborns.

I tore the envelope open while he held the baby and as I rapidly scanned the first page, I found what I was looking for- the results. Not only had I passed all sections, but I had one of the highest possible scores in the English and History sections. Math (expected by me) was not as high, but it passed minimum requirements. My certificate would be mailed within the new ten days. He congratulated me, but it seemed a rather tongue-in cheek sort of congratulations, and he couldn't resist saying, "I wish I had known about how easy a person could skip all those hours at those hard desks and seats and do it this way. Well, good for you. I knew you could do it."

By his making it sound secondary to getting it the normal way, and implying that it had been easy, some of the wind was taken from my high flying sails that evening but as I held my new son when my husband was gone, I whispered to him, "Hey, big guy, aren't you proud of mommy? I can claim to be a high-school grad now. Isn't mommy smart? Aren't you proud of me?" Then I chuckled aloud in the empty room with my brand-new baby.

Of course, the workload *did* increase for me, with the new baby and the other two preschoolers. I did not complain and tried not to show the fatigue I felt so often. I continued taking my pre-natal vitamins, hoping for some extra energy. It was a blessing I did not have the studying to do although I missed it tremendously, I recognized my need for sleep was more important right now. When I got everyone down for naps, including the new baby, I laid down covered by a warm quilt and slept until one or more of the three woke up and needed attention.

My husband did not offer to help with my housework or the children, however he did start sharing rides with my girl friends' husband. This opened a brand new, rather risky adventure for me. The idea came to me one day when I was changing the bedding and vacuuming our bedroom. Remembering the ordeal of finding my husband's wallet and end ensuing warfare waged over his affair with the high-school girl, I glanced at the top of the dresser. I knew that it was very unlikely he would ever forget it again, if he did, I knew I would still examine its' contents; however, I doubted I would confront him with anything I fund in there. The wallet wasn't there, but suddenly my hands quit filling the pillow-case with the pillow and I laid it down and went to the living room where the landline phone was on the little stand by the couch. I dialed my girlfriend's number and knowing if she were busy with the kids it might take a few extra rings for her to get to answer, I sat down and waited. She picked up and without even a greeting I asked, "Hey, guess what?"

She paused, perhaps cautious about what I sounded so excited about. "What?" she asked.

"Guess what I found on the bedroom chest?"

"Oh, my God, surely not the wallet again and if it is, it's a trap-don't even touch it!"

I laughed at her and then I said, "No, and you don't need to warn me about that-no, it's the car keys."

'Well, so what? It was Dan's turn to drive so naturally the keys to your car would be there."

"You are not getting this. Think about it, Joyce. Keys. Car outside. If we plan this right, you can teach me how to drive. He will never know anything about it."

She was quiet for a few seconds and then she said, "We might. Just might be able to do it. But what if he gets sick and comes home early? Or what if it's one of those days when he goes to his part-time job and doesn't ride with Dan?"

"Didn't you tell me that Dan is trying to get on with some part-time work as well; especially with Christmas not too far away?"

"Yes, but he hasn't got a call from them yet."

"We would have to allow time for you to still do your chores, and somehow keep the little monkeys from mentioning anything to him…"

"My two oldest are so scared of him they never bring up a subject to him unless he asks them a question and then the conversation us usually his question and then 'yessir', 'no sir' or 'I don't know sir.'"

"Alright then." Joyce said, as though musing it over.

"So, it's a go?" I asked her.

"Oh, very definitely but we are not going to just leap right in. We are going to make some careful plans and have a few test runs"

"What do you mean test runs?"

"Well, we will have the munchkins with us except my three oldest. We will do this when they are in school and before they get home. And I have a baby seat for your baby if you need it."

"I have one," I said.

"Yes, but my youngest needs one too. Especially if you are going to be the one at the wheel." This was followed by a laugh from her.

Thus, began the great adventure. Our car was a 1955 Chevrolet. He kept it in prime condition so we would have to make sure it was pristine when he came home for the day. It was standard shift which made me extra nervous, but Joyce kept telling me I would have that *down pat* in no time.

It helped also, that she had a copy of the Motor Vehicle Department's little pamphlet with rules and regulations as well as testing procedures. I began to secretly study this, and kept it hidden in my underwear drawer except when he was at work. I paid closer attention to his driving as well, noting things I thought he was good at, and things he (in my opinion) was sloppy.

I thought about how great it would have been to take Driver's Education classes in school or even later, out of school and in a private driving school.

At first it was very scary. My thoughts ran the gamut from me wrecking the car and the kids being hurt and the car totaled to me successfully taking (and passing the driving test to get my license.

Joyce and I both tried to act as nonchalant as possible in front of the kids hoping their "reporting" the day's events in front of their father's would come across as pretending and playtime imagination.

First, she explained about the four gears, the turn signals, how to ease on the gas pedal, treating it to a little gas at a time to allow the transaction would be smooth and easy. She also told me if the car bucked and stalled a few times until I learned how to do this initial first step not to panic, no harm to the car or us.

"Think of it as feeding the gas to the car," she said. "You want to give it enough to tantalize it and make it want to move forward. Too much, and it will choke up on you and die out. Like too big a bite will choke you, but a little one goes down smoothly and waits for more."

I laughed at her, but I had been right all along, she was exactly the teacher anyone would want: patient, kind, and through in her explanations.

She was also right about the tricky way the driver had to balance the coordination between the gas pedal, the slow first gear and the rakes. I jerked that 1955 Chevrolet all over the road in the nearby park continually until I tried to feel the car when I gave it just enough gas and no more. She was right about another thing, as well, weekdays the park roads had almost no traffic and were the perfect place for learning to drive. Gig, wide, very open parking lots and roads with a few stop signs strategically placed to help me learn to stop and start successfully.

I was elated after that first lesson. I could hardly wait until we could do it again. When we returned home, we were careful to park exactly where my husband had left it, pristine in its cleanliness. We fed the kids all a snack and she took hers home to nap while I put my down as well.

After the first few times, I felt safe in several things: one, that my deception was not going to be discovered (not to suggest I wasn't anxious each time we had a lesson), two, my fear that the kids would spill the beans, although having snack and nap *after* the lesson put some distance between the two events, which with children at such an age was pretty normal. The third thing was the rise in my self-confidence. I begin to believe that I *could* do this, and if I could do it, I might, just might, be able to do other things as well.

Joyce laughed at me and said, "Yeah, the next thing I know, you will be running for office."

"Very funny," I answered her.

I felt pretty safe we wouldn't get pulled over in the park by any park police, thought at first both Joyce and I tried to think of what story we could tell about being over there with a carful of children, bouncing all over the road learning to drive. At first this worried me because I envisioned the policeman very irate when he saw I didn't even have a learner's permit. I could just see him taking me to the station or at the very least, giving me a ticket, a copy of which would probably be sent to the house.

Since the men in both households took turns driving in their daily car-pool, I didn't have a lesson every day and I missed it when I didn't.

"That's not how they do it," she told me. "Worst case scenario, they give you a ticket and you pay it, either by mail or I will take you down there to do it. As long as you pay it on time, it's not a big deal."

She added, "Besides, how many park police have seen in all this time?"

"None,".

"There, I rest my case."

When she began to teach me how to park, I lot all the new found confidence I had been enjoying.

"I'm never going to be able to do this!!" I told her, holding back as much of my frustration and tears as I could.

We argued about this because I had firmly placed "impossible" on parallel parking which seemed even though she pronounced me ready on all other parts of the test.

One morning shortly after the men in our families had left for work, she called. I could hear the excitement in her voice.

"Hey, guess what?"

"What?" I asked, laughing at her excitement.

"I have it figured out! I don't know why I didn't think of it before."

"What? Come on, spit it out!"

"The parking! The parallel parking! We'll got the next county over. Remember that mousey little girl we met who works in the base exchange?"

I hesitated and then remembered the timid little thing who had helped us with our Christmas lay-a-ways.

"Yeah, I always felt kind of sorry for her. Wrong personality to be working around all those G.I.'s."

"Yes, that's the one. Anyway, remember how nervous she was that day?"

"Nervous, yeah, and-"

There was a triumphant sound from Joyce. "Yes! And do you remember what she told us?" Suddenly I *did* remember.

"Her driver's license test! She had just taken and passed her test that morning and she had been really nervous when her husband allowed her to drop him off at work and keep the car herself."

"Exactly! And do you remember *where* she said she took it?"

"No. Where?"

"Bernalillo county. And do you know why she drove over there to take it?"

"Yes!" I said enthusiastically. "Because they don't make you parallel park."

"Exactly! And that's where you're going to take yours."

We drove over that very day, Joyce took the kids to play on the courthouse lawn which circled the imposing courthouse square while I took first, the written test, (and passed it easily). Then, I walked out to the car with one of the state troopers, and I saw Joyce and the kids playing. She held up her crossed fingers and grinned at me.

It was scary. I did everything he asked me to do: "turn here. Take the next left." Finally, when it seemed like forever, he told me to drive back to the parking lot at the courthouse. When we arrived and I had put the car in park and turned the ignition off, he smiled at me.

"You passed just fine, but drove a tad slow. Remember, you have to go with the flow out there with other traffic. Driving safely doesn't mean too slowly."

I nodded and I said, "Passed? I passed?"

He nodded and smiled as he signed the test paper.

"Take this on inside and give the lady four dollars and you'll be legal."

I thanked him and hurried over to tell Joyce. She grabbed me in a big hug and the kids started jumping around, wanting to be in on the excitement even if they didn't know what was going on.

"Okay, let's go inside and get that precious piece of paper."

"I'll have to come back to do that."

She stopped short and looked at me. "Why in the world would you want to make another trip when we can get it now?'

I almost stammered, I was flushed with embarrassment.

"I wasn't thinking about the cot. I don't have any money with me. I wasn't thinking. I could have taken it out of my grocery jar change, but I- "I stopped, again, with embarrassment.

"Silly girl," she said, "Come on, my treat. My contribution to the cause."

So, we went inside, she paid the fee, had my photo taken. I received my temporary permit and was told I would get the permanent license within two weeks. Joyce insisted I make the drive home so I did; clammy hands, heart beating rapidly, white knuckles, and silent prayers. A big sigh of relief when we pulled in the driveway. I refused to think about how I would somehow, someday, tell my husband.

What a day that was. Angels among us, indeed.

Chapter

FOUR

---------- ⚓ ----------

I had often wondered the age-old question of fate versus free will. Later, as times changed and *I* changed I would come to question the environment versus genetics question. I stopped asking 'Why me?' and began asking 'Why not?' I wondered how any other women shared my situation, and wished I could talk with some of them.

There was no such thing as support groups, women's shelters. Even City or state Child Protective Services were in the future.

Be it fate, or God (which I much preferred, longing for reasons and protection about my circumstances and that of my children, the unknown reasons pushing me to get that license became suddenly very clear when my husband came home a few weeks later, excited with what he considered good news.

He had gotten new orders. It seems we were going to Germany! He explained that he would be sent first, and the Air Force would send movers to pack up two different shipments. One would be the bare minimum we would need for our overseas household for the three-year stay. The other would be stored for that length of time and we would retrieve it at our next stateside assignment. I had never seen him so happy. I certainly had my reservations about being overseas in a foreign country where I didn't even speak the language. This would not make a difference to my husband. He was as fluent in German as in English. He had plans to look up a cousin who lived with his family in Stuttgart. He explained that we would be living on the economy (not on the official base, but with the "natives" as I called them to myself.)

"Now we have to get you a driver's license. Otherwise, after I leave you won't have any way to get groceries, take the kids to doctors that reminds me, you and the kids have to get some immunizations too. Then, you will have to drive the car down to the coast and ship it because we will need a car for the three years, we are there, living on the economy.

This was my chance, while he was in such a good mood.

"I have a surprise for you," I said.

"What surprise?"

"I wanted to make things easier for you (definitely not true, never occurred to me. It was to make it easier for me on my journey for an eventual escape and some independence for me and my children), so wait here while I get it."

I had just received the permanent new license, replacing the temporary one.

When I came back, license in hand, he asked, "What's this?"

"My new driver's license."

"But how did…how did you get it?"

"Joyce taught me on the days the car was here, and she took me to take the test. It was to make it easier. You won't have to take me to the commissary or the doctor's or the library. You said once how much you hated asking time off just because I didn't know how to drive."

I took a deep breath and then he said,

"This is wonderful! This is great! How did you know to do this? It's perfect. One less step for getting ready for our move."

He held the license in one hand and gave me a big hug.

"Good for you!"

The kids sensed the happy excitement and they jumped around, saying, "Good for mommy, good for mommy!"

Thereafter he began allowing me to drive our car to appointments, the grocery store, even to the park with the kids and Joyce and her children.

The day I took all the children (three now, girl, boy and boy) I didn't tell them until we arrived and checked in that this was going to entail getting some shots.

"I don't want a shot," one said.

The four-year-old said, "Will it hurt?"

"Just for a second or two. I have to get some, too"

"Does the baby?"

"Yes, all of us or we don't get to go on the big plane ride to Germany."

"Where the castles are?"

I had been getting them all hyped up about the trip and told them this place had a lot of castles we would be able to visit. Also, that we could ride a huge jet plane to get there.

"Will you go first?" asked the four-year-old of me.

"Sure," I said, trying to make it seem easy.

I put the baby in his stroller, and stood up, with the children all following me when they called our names.

I stood first, leaving the stroller in the care of my six-year-old daughter.

"Who wants to be first?" the medic asked.

"I do. I want to go first," I said cheerfully.

"Which arm?" he asked.

I rolled up the sleeve on my left arm.

I don't know if I accidently jerked or the medic was inexperienced or why, but for a brief moment the needle still in my arm, a small trickle of blood began to run down my arm.

The chaos which followed was humorous later, but right when it happened it was anything but funny. The medic pulled the needle, starting apologizing, and wiped my arm with some gauze pads. It wasn't anything at all serious, but the reaction of the children was immediate.

My six-year-old starting backing off and said, "I don't want to go on a big plane"

My fur-year-old turned and took off flat out running full speed down the corridor, screaming, "No! No! No!".

When I managed to corral him and bring him back, the medic said, "I think we should do that one first, while we have him."

While I assisted holding him, he took a sheet, folded it in half, and wrapped him like a mummy with only one arm outside the wrapping. I held the little mummy with his arm steady, who kept crying and resisting but the medic was successful in giving him his immunizations. If memory serves me right, he got three.

"There, that wasn't too bad, was it? You're all done. Now Mommy will get hers."

This time mine went off without a hitch and the six-year-old, looking at me said for her brother's benefit, "Watch me. I'm gonna be like Mommy. I'm not even goanna cry."

While it is true, she didn't really cry, her eyes did fill with tears which she fought to hold back. We did the baby and except for a brief outraged cry, he did fine.

I listened with amazement that evening when the four-year-old told his father, "Oh, there was nothing to it. I just stood up there and took it like a man, Daddy"

My six-year-old just looked at me and raised her eyebrows but was silent.

It was like we were united in a team, the children and I versus my husband. We tried hard to protect each other.

When he got there, the base had a division which would assist him in finding appropriate housing. He kept talking about the advantage we would have because of his fluency in the language and even knowledge of how things were done there.

We were given pamphlets to read with lots of instructions. Which, for the most part, my husband ignored. We were told to buy (supposedly because human excrement was used for fertilizer) our groceries (especially perishables) in the base commissary and not to eat the vegetables on the economy. I was astonished when we arrived there and he pointed out these cone-shaped wooden wagons, (called "honey-dew wagons) drawn by horses that came by on a regular and collected sewage. One could purchase miniature ones to take home to the states as souvenirs. It was not unusual to go to the small German grocers, purchase a loaf of bread (round or long ovals) with crusty golden outside, and soft, delicious insides which made the read a treat without anything except butter. Yes, we did eat it. When you purchased it, the store keeper would wrap it in a piece of newspaper and hand it to you.

Every time I would voice a tentative "Should we eat this?" my husband said, "Look at all these healthy people running around. Do they look sick? I was raised on German food, I turned out okay. We were told to boil the water, but we never did. Not for drinking or cooking or bathing. I hand-washed a lot of our clothes, but there was a German family who, for four marks (money which looked like quarters, but at that time probably was valued at four equal to an American dollar; came around and picked up my husband's work fatigues, returned them two or three days later, stiffly starched, ironed, hung neatly on hangers.)

One of my first observations of my German neighbors was that they didn't buy anything in bulk. You would see people come in and buy two or four eggs at a time, maybe two potatoes. We would go to the base commissary every two weeks (our pay period) and try to stock up on things so we wouldn't have to try and make ourselves (me, not my husband) understood. Out landlady was generous to a fault about sharing turnips, potatoes, cucumbers, and others.

Another unusual factor was that no one had a front yard with just grass or flowers. Oh, some did have flower beds in the back yard or up close to the wall in the front, but it was as though each family supplemented their food by having a vegetable garden. Once I was talking to my landlady and I had just gotten some photos sent to us by my husband's mother. There was a nice showing her nice Florida home.

"She must be rich," my landlady said.

"No, not really," I answered.

"Well, is she lazy?" she asked.

I laughed at this and asked, "What make you ask?"

"Well," she said, quite seriously, "Why does she waste all that ground with nothing but grass when she could be growing so many vegetables?"

When I repeated the conversation to my husband, he laughed along with me, but said, "Most Germans are thrifty in nature. Remember, Germany is a small country, only the rich waste their yards on useless grass to play on."

I did begin to learn a little of the language and the children learned even more. They liked learning new words in German. Places to rent were scarce, but there was an office on base where the German people could list their rentals, and there was sort of an underground airman to airman (and wives too) about places becoming available as new orders were issued and families came and went for their three-year terms. If an American family wanted to extend their stay for one more year they could apply and, depending on the job the airman had and its importance or need, extensions were sometimes granted. Of course, most were anxious to get "home" and see families and friends. One of the good things about being overseas, living as we did on the economy, was that you could save money. There was a movie theatre on base but it seemed too much trouble to get the kids ready (and arrange for a sitter), drive to the base and home just for a movie. Church services were held on base, and an individual could attend the Catholic or the generic protestant service.

Several things happened during our stay in Germany which were to have a large impact on our lives. When we first settled in, my husband would allow me to volunteer as a Sunday school teacher for some of the preschool children. This was beneficial for everyone. I enjoyed the interaction with the small children, I taught about Jesus, my own got to enjoy meeting and participating with others their age. They especially enjoyed the bible stories which they talked about all the following week. On Sunday, the lesson was about George Washington Carver. The lesson had a picture of a poorly dressed, barefoot sharecropper and I asked the children to look at the picture and tell me why they thought he was having such a hard life? How could they tell he was poor? I expected to say something about his being a slave, or being black because we had discussed these things but instead one of them said, "Well, I know the answer, Teacher."

"Okay, share it with the class.' I expected to hear her say something about his being a slave or working in the cotton fields. Instead she said, "Well, he had no shoes. Everybody knows you have to have shoes You can hardly get where you're going without any shoes."

Blessed are the children. Not a one paid any attention to his color. Maybe that's why I have come to love their company, and choose it rather than their parents or other adults. One of them even asked me once, "Teacher, isn't it wonderful that Jesus and God made different colored grown up people to match their children?"

How many years does it take to teach them bigotry and racial prejudices?

I made friends with some of the other wives who were volunteer teachers. One of these other teachers' husband worked on the flight line (where maintenance on the planes was performed. on the panes) and when my husband invited them over, we began meeting at least once a week to pay cards. They have two children so they all played together as their parents played cards.

I thoroughly enjoyed those evenings, and often one or the other of we wives would keep the car for the day and go shopping on base or like *real* tourists, go visit some of the local shops or places of interest.

I believe my husband felt some of his control might be slipping away from him and he refused to allow me to continue with the Sunday School classes. I really missed it and so did the children. He had a multitude of reasons: we were spending too much on gas, he didn't want to attend so because he used Sundays to work in the car, or planned outings where we went with our friends or by ourselves. He failed to see this invalidated his excuse of needing to save on the budget for car gas.

Although I really enjoyed having those social card-paying evenings and occasionally inviting the other couple for dinner and vice-versa, it was a combination of enjoyment and fear. Fear that he would have some kind of left over resentment of an earlier disagreement he and I had or something I said or did when they were there, I worried he would be harsh in his attitude or behavior in front of them It was very obvious they had a good marriage and cared very much for each other. I often found myself envying her.

Every now and then my husband would have a sarcastic or snide remark either to me or about me which he thought was funny, or which indicated he was king of our castle. This did not impress them, in fact, it embarrassed or humiliated them to hear or see it as well as myself.

Finally, one afternoon when we were home, my husband asked me, "Have you ever complained to Rob's wife about how I treat you?"

I was so surprised at the question I paused to gather my thoughts before answering.

"Well, have you?"

I shook my head and tried to answer strongly, looking straight into his eyes. I was afraid of where this might be going. If he thought I was talking negatively about him behind his back, we might lose their friendship, and he also, might punish me. I knew I had to speak convincingly.

"Of course not. Why would you think that? We don't discuss our husbands."

"What do you two talk about when you are together, without your husbands?"

"Well, I can't just recite it verbatim, but we exchange recipes and cooking tips, how to stop one of the kids from sucking their thumb, who has a birthday coming up, normal ordinary things like that. Why would I want to say bad things about you? You're my husband."

"Well, the other day Rob suggested I should treat you better. That sometimes I talk to you like you are one of my crew at work. He said I don't give you enough respect. I wanted to tell him how I treat you is none of his business and he can go on treating his own wife like she's fragile and up on a pedestal, but not to tell me how to treat mine."

"Did he give you any examples?" I almost was holding my breath as I asked, and I went on folding the laundry I had just brought in from the outdoor clothesline.

"Well, I don't know what he was talking about and I told him so. You can tell he's just a pussy when it comes to his family. I would never let you wear the pants in our family like he does his. Just remember, I hate gossiping women.

Once, on one of those rare occasions (it was our eleventh anniversary) he invited Rob and his wife to go to the base N.C.O. club to celebrate. There would be a band and dancing. He allowed me a new dress and I was very excited. I had always loved dancing and one of the things I missed most about my life is that we never went dancing. Before marriage, occasionally, afterwards, no.

Some of the other men at the table asked some of the other wives to dance and several asked the different partners; but I would have asked his permission, no one asked me to dance. When my husband got up and excused himself to go to the men's room, one of other airmen said to me, "I would love to ask you to dance, but I am pretty sure it would make your husband mad. I've seen this side of him at work sometimes and I sure don't want to give him any cause to put me on his black list. I just wanted you to know, it's nothing to do with you. I can see you're a good dancer."

I know I just gave him a rather weak smile. It did tell me something, though. His temper wasn't always reserved for just his family, but his co-workers were aware of sometimes needing to walk on egg-shells to avoid the flare of his temper.

Every time a promotions cycle came around, he would get his hopes up (and I would, too) but he never got past the Staff-Sargent rank he held very early in his career and in fact, retired in that rank I share a feeling of guilt in this because during this time overseas is the very first time I sought outside help for my situation. It's strange that I don't even remember what the argument was about; what he said, what I said, what really provoked him. But even with my children there, and the landlady and her family downstairs (where they could easily hear the commotion) he gave me one of the worse beatings he ever had. I honestly believe it was because I (for the first time) did not simply lie down and let him beat or drag me around, I fought back. I called me a son-of-a-bitch, a woman beater, a monster. When he finally stopped, I hurt all over my body, I ended up with black eyes, bloody nose, split lip, bruised and battered but determined it wasn't over yet. This time *I would do something.* Of course, the obligatory sex followed and all I could think of was how much I hated him. The next morning, he went to work and I went downstairs and asked the landlady to use her phone, avoiding any questions she might have wanted to ask. I called the base and told the operator my name and his name, rank and serial number. I told her I needed to talk to the first sergeant of his specific squadron. When he later returned my call, I was very honest about what had happened, I did cry, but the important thing is that he did listen. He told me not to tell him I had talked to him, but to give him the address where we lived on the economy and he would come there to see us. I wasn't sure he really would, but he did. The next afternoon, after he got home from work, a knock on the door came and my husband was totally unprepared for the first sergeant's visit. The sergeant asked me to take the children in the living room and close the door and he took my husband in the kitchen I have to doubt he had taken notice of my face and the injuries which were evident about having been beat. I never did know what the conversation was; I only know that whatever it was wen in his personal record, because he told me I had caused him to be passed over for promotion the next round. However, I *NEVER* regretted my actions. While he still gave me plenty of verbal and emotional abuse, never again while we were overseas, did he physically beat me. I am sure the story got around because there was no more card playing with our former friends and she came once to see me and I told her the honest truth. She comforted me, but it ended that friendship.

Living on the economy as we did, often made the days long and I was bored. I still went to the base library when I could and checked out all they would allow at one time and when the children napped each afternoon, I read voraciously.

During this time, there were several magazines which you could purchase at the base exchange and they were the "true romance" gender. Supposedly they were true stories, written by the women who bought and read them though at first, I thought it was a bunch of editors or writers, putting fake names on the stories and making them all up. One month I picked up an issue and took it home. I noticed that they were advertising a writing contest. Anyone could enter and send in a story. If you won, the first prize was one hundred dollars. In today's age, that's hardly any money at all, but back in the fifties, it was a lot.

I decided I was going to get some typing paper, borrow a typewriter from the landlady or the base, if possible, and write my story. I had to limit it to 300 words or under.

I don't know what possessed him to allow this freedom project but he even checked out a typewriter from special services and brought it home. I could keep it for two weeks. Each day after that, I would get up, fix his breakfast and lunch, send him off and after taking care of the most noticeable chores (making the bed cleaning up the kitchen) I would write.

I would write until the children were up and then I would feed them, dress them, do laundry or whatever else needed doing and then, when they lay down for their afternoon nap, I would sit at the kitchen table and write some more. It was a simply written story, but it came from my heart and told about trying to find a way out of an abusive life with the meager resources I had.

The next time I went to the base, I went to the post office there and mailed it in a big brown envelope, following all the instructions in the magazine.

At first, I would look through the mail my husband always brought home from our box on the base, but when days and then weeks passed, I gave up.

Oh, well, I told myself, *At least I tried. Besides, I had enjoyed the writing. I remembered being in the eighth grade and telling Mrs. Mirek I wanted to be an author someday.*

I tried to console myself in many ways but mostly I reassured myself that it was a nationally distributed magazine and who knew how many entries they had received?

When I finally received an answer from them, I had accepted failure and it was almost a surprise. It came in a white, business envelope with their magazine logo in the return address corner. Before I opened it, I thought: *I wonder if they sent every entrant a "Thanks, but no thanks" letter?*

As I opened the envelope, a paper fell out. *Ah, they went me to subscribe to the magazine now.*

When I picked it up, I opened the folded paper and inside was a brief letter of congratulations and a check for one hundred dollars,

I had to sit down and read It again. Yes, it was real! I had won, I had won, I had really won.

I knew, I just knew I could not keep this to myself. Regardless of any consequences, I had to share my good fortune., When my husband came home, I excitedly held out the letter and check.

"What's this?" he asked.

"I won"

"Won what?"

Remember when I borrowed the typewriter and I told you I was going to enter a contest?"

"Not really, I mean I remember you using the typewriter but I forgot about any contest. That's fantastic!"

He really did act proud of me. Several times that evening I would catch him silently looking at me, as though assessing me and my accomplishment.

I offered the check to him. I truly wasn't interested in the money. It was winning first place that filled me with joy. Perhaps someday, someday, I really could become a *real* writer.

I tried to insist he take it and use it but he said, "No. It's your money. You earned it. Spend it on yourself or the kids."

So, I did. The check had come right before Easter that year and I bought me a new blue dress. It buttoned down the front and was the first new clothing I had purchased for myself in a long time. I cannot remember now, but I believe it cost me something in the fifteen to twenty-dollar range. Then I took the rest and spent it on the kids for Easter baskets, and a stuffed animal for each of them. I can't remember another time when I so enjoyed spending money for something completely unnecessary, but so much fun.

The rest of the time we spent in Germany seemed time spent in avoiding confrontations. It was almost like a truce. I avoided doing anything to provoke his wrath and he seemed very aware of the possibility of adding more to his personnel records, should he resort to taking out any anger he had on me or the children.

As the baby grew, we did take some Sundays to tour the castles which picturesquely lined Rhine river. We would tour the specific castle, wondering at the grandeur it must have held in the past. Then we would find one of the small German restaurants and have the wonderful sauerkraut and knockwurst and the wonderful crusty bread.

I realize in my heart that it was my husband's influence which made our children such well-behaved and polite youngsters. Many times, people would comment to us on their behavior. They, too, seemed to be on a probationary period of peace. They played together with only a minimum of disagreements. There was a sense of walking a tightrope as we began to count off the days until we would be going back to the states.

We took one Sunday to drive to Heidelberg so my husband could meet this cousin of his. They had not seen each other since very young children. He was a professor at the prestigious University of Heidelberg. I don't believe my husband felt inferior or intimidated by this cousin (no one could make him feel that way) but I certainly was. A Professor! At a world-famous university! I was so nervous. My husband had called his cousin and they were expecting us. As soon as we drove up in the driveway, my anxiety level grew. I wore my new Easter dress, and had dressed all the children up and warned them to be on their best behavior.

Right at the very last minute, when we had been trying to get the baby's things together and leave, my eldest daughter had been playing with her brothers and she fell down. When she fell, her foot caught on the hem on her dress. I could have sewn it, had my husband allowed me the time. I could even have sewn it in the car, but "it was rush, rush, we're going to be late. Hurry up." From him and I desperately wanted to alleviate the building tension.

So, I pinned it with two safety pins; something I never would have done ordinarily.

As we drove up the driveway, I remembered my husband telling me that only very well-to-do Germans had grassy, *useless* front yards. This house was large, red brick and had a beautifully landscaped front *and* back yard. The back yard had a fish pond with koi Carp and Golden Orfeo fish which delighted my children.

They had set the table for lunch and my children again were fascinated with the setting. Each person (even the children, excluding the baby, who cooperated by sleeping through lunch) had an individually sized cutting board, napkin, small knife, and drinks. My husband and his cousin drank German beer, the children were given some sort of juice and I requested tea. Starting with the cousin, trays of cheeses (different kinds), lunch meats, lettuce, tomatoes, olives, small little bowls with spicy or plain mustard, mayonnaise and pickles were passed around. I, of course, went around to each of my children, asking them to make their choices and then assisted them. I allowed them to make it into a sandwich or eat each offering separately if it was easier for them. My husband did not offer to help with this; but then, neither did the cousin. The two men fixed their own plates, drank their beer, and carried on a lively conversation. Sometimes I could understand bits and pieces, but the wife was kin to me and the children, trying her best to bridge the gap of languages.

Frankly, I was surprised that there wasn't a maid unobtrusively coming and going to wait on us.

After lunch, the children went out in the back yard with the cousin's children and the woman and I cleared the table. I tried to offer assistance with the dishes but she wouldn't accept it, just rinsing them and stacking them in one side of the large double sink.

Their children were several years older than ours, and had a pretty good grasp of English. They were polite and tried to entertain our children who joined in with the games the older ones suggested.

Everything was going well until I noticed that the wife had seen the hem pinned with the safety pins on my daughter's dress. A tiny little frown of disapproval appeared between her eyebrows.

I think my face flushed with embarrassment, I know I *was* embarrassed, and I hoped my husband did not see that she had noticed. What kind of mother would use safety pins instead of repairing it with needle and thread? I could just *hear* her thoughts.

She must be thinking what a bad mother and homemaker I was, to not sew that hem, but to safety pin it She's probably wondering why I would bring her to this visit dressed with a safety pinned dress. Why, she's probably wondering why I didn't just change her dress entirely? Once again, the old feeling of being unworthy and useless crept over me and I wished I could just disappear. I was absolutely sure my husband never, ever, felt this way. Often, when he was on one of his tirades about my stupidity or inadequacy, I wished I had the courage to just ask him what it said about his choice of a wife if I was so worthless?

I was relieved that no one else seemed to notice, but I did. And I remembered it. Here I wanted to make a good impression for my husband's sake, and for my status as an American mother and wife. I never forgot my shame. Many years later I wondered what she said about me to her husband after we left. They had been courteous, hospitable and welcoming but I felt like the country mouse coming to the big city to meet the city mouse in Aesop's Fable for children.

I thought about the visit and my gaffe with the safety pins in the hem and finally said to myself, *'Okay, so you messed up…So what? No one noticed but you. It's not the first mistake you ever made and it won't be the last.'*

It was just another link in my life-long feeling that I was inferior, and of no value. If I had learned how to be easier on myself and not *judge* myself by anyone else's standards, I could function so much better. I should have given myself some credit. I knew (with thought) that I was articulate and well spoken. Reading and reading for all those years, years ahead of my chronical and educational age should have convinced me I wasn't stupid (as my husband insisted). I had so wanted to present a good impression for his German relatives, now I must convince myself to let it go. It was done and part of my past now.

My husband simply took it for granted that he was a superior human being and that I was inferior. How I envied that self-confidence! Because of the way my husband treated me in front of his mother and stepfather, without admonishment from them, it was easy to see they agreed with his assessment of me. His mother never felt he was ever wrong—about anything.

My husband's new orders would take us from Germany to North Little Rock, Arkansas. Here, too, there was base housing but because there was always more on the waiting list than was available our name went on the list. Meanwhile we purchased one of the little cookie-cutter houses in a close suburban neighborhood. It was a cheap little house and would be a terribly run-down community in a few years, but we planned to put it up for sale as soon as we got called one of the bade units had come up with our name. When we got the nod and could move on base housing, we did so and had no problem selling the cheap little house to another military family.

The base housing wasn't fancy, but it was roomy, with three bedrooms, dining and living area, kitchen, and just one (but large and roomy) bathroom. Best of all, the back of the unit faced a huge grassy field where all the kids in the neighborhood could gather to run and play with a generous amount of freedom and little supervision. Several times during the time of this assignment my husband would be called on for TDY duties. These temporary duty assignments would be for a month at a time. We remained right where we were, he would travel off to Tripoli, some other location for thirty days, and then home again. Personally, I thought these rotations were good for most families and for their military missions. It seemed reminiscent of the grandparent-grandchild relationships. It was fun when they came to visit, but equally welcome when it was time for them to return to their own homes.

The children enjoyed the stress-free atmosphere during these thirty-day interludes, and I must admit I enjoyed them too. We could fix Mac and Cheese whenever we wanted and I didn't have to cook to my husband's taste, but to a majority vote of the children and myself. The remote for the television was "ours" and not tuned in to his choice of news or documentaries. There was a feeling of exhilaration when he left on these assignments, and a feeling of almost "doom" two or three days before he was due home.

I always put on a good act when he arrived back, both in the bedroom and in the kitchen. He always thought my unusual enthusiasm for sex was due to his thirty-day absence, but the truth I acknowledged to myself was it was me acting the part of a love-starved woman who had missed his attention in this area.

Later, I was to admit I felt the eighteen years I spent as his wife as some kind of nightmare and that I didn't start with my *real* life until I was free of him.

Meanwhile, Arkansas I was to have the final child in our family. It was a total surprise because I continued to have menstrual periods for several months and during this time modern medicine didn't have advances such as ultra-sounds. Because at one point I had developed a large cyst which I had to have removed, at first the doctor thought this was a return of a cyst but after running a more sophisticated pregnancy test, we discovered it wasn't a cyst but a new baby.

Thus, I didn't have a true "due date", but was prepared to go somewhere between mid-December and maybe sometime in February. Size of the baby was no real help in the guesswork. I always had big, heavy babies. My first had weighed eight pounds, thirteen and one-half ounces and was twenty-three inches long. My second child weighed eight pounds and one ounce, and my third weighted nine pounds and six ounces.

When this baby was born, she balanced our family our; two boys and two girls. The girls were the "book-ends" and the two boys were in the middle.

When several months after her birth, I developed several cysts on my ovaries, and a joint decision between my husband, my doctor, and myself the decision was made to have a total hysterectomy.

I used to call my last child my little "Tag-along". Although my eldest child, the other girl enjoyed helping care for the new baby, they were never close. I didn't expect they would be, with eleven years between them. It was almost like raising two different families. There was six years between the eldest pair, and the final pair and though fate didn't match birth order with gender, it worked.

There was a wonderful family directly across the street from us, and especially during the time of each TDY absences of our husbands, the woman and I became very close. The family had seven children; very strong in their Catholic faith and with a generosity of spirit I respected and admired.

Whenever I felt depressed or overwhelmed with my own life or situation, I could think of her courage and faith and immediately start counting my own blessings and be able to erase what I had thought were my own big problems to something petty and foolish.

Her seven children were split with two sons and five daughters. The cross they were given to bear, though, was that the boys had been born Hemophiliacs. I don't believe I had even heard of this disease before I met their family.

It was during one of those TDY periods when both our husbands were gone. It was just an average Saturday and the street outside was filled with children playing. There was hollering with unabashed delight of the sunshine and abnormally warmth of a February day which felt like spring. At first, I thought all the screams were of the happy kind, joyous and excited with play. Then, something changed and I saw some children stop and just stared agog at Linda as she crouched down over her eldest son and his crashed bicycle.

I was running over towards the two of them and she said, "Can you watch all the others while I take him to the emergency room?

"Of course," I said. "What else can I do?"

"Go in my house and get my car keys from the hook on the wall, and grab my purse from the dining room table while I get Jason in the car.

I was trembling myself, and yet, she was calm and in control. I had grabbed a towel from her bathroom too, and I helped her open the back of her station-wagon to lay her son down. His eyes were closed, but I could see his chest moving and I knew he was breathing.

I didn't think anything was broken but he was bleeding a lot.

She backed out of her driveway and I corralled the other children into my house with a promised pan of popcorn and the cartoon channel on the television.

My children appeared to be the most upset by the accident; the youngster's siblings, while disturbed, seemed to review this as a simple accident and one which appeared almost customary. I didn't understand this until later when the mother called me from the hospital.

"How is he?" I asked her.

"Well, they have admitted him and given him something for the pain, but he's relatively calm. I appreciate you staying with the others Thank you so much. He's been through this before; it's not something he hasn't dealt with before."

"What do you mean?"

"It's kind of a long story, but I'll tell you all about it when I come home. If you're okay with it, I am going to stay a bit longer. Wouldn't you know, things like this seem to pick the times when George is gone to happen."

"Don't worry about anything here. Everything is fine. Take all the time you need. If you want to spend the night at the hospital, I can bed them all down here. "We've got extra sleeping space with my husband gone and even sleeping bags. I'm sure they would enjoy the novelty of getting to bunk together."

I was right about that reaction, they viewed it all as a big adventure. When I tried to gently tell the kids their brother was staying in the hospital for now, they didn't seem alarmed at all or have many questions. In fact, one of the older girls said, "Don't worry, this happens a lot to him. He will be alright." She gave me a hug and then went back to joining the other children.

Linda (their mother) got home about an hour later and as I made some fresh coffee and after she brought the others up to date, explaining he was doing okay though she couldn't tell us how long the doctor estimated his hospital stay would be. Most of the bleeding was in his knee, and they had elevated it to assist in slowing the bleeding down.

"Were any bones broken?" I asked.

"No, thank God. They just have to get the bleeding stopped."

I was to say the least, confused and puzzled at the lack of information on his condition and prognosis.

Until she was sitting at the kitchen table with a steaming cup of fresh coffee and she took a big breath and began to explain.

"I never get used to worrying about them…"

She paused and I said, "Of course you don't. I don't care how old they get, we will always worry about our children." Even as I said this, I wondered at her use of *them* instead of *him*…In my mind it was a pronoun, but plural, indicating more than one of her children.

Sure enough, when she picked up her story she said, "Both of the boys have a condition called Hemophilia. Do you know what that is?"

"No," I told her honestly.

"Well, first of all, it is passed down through the mother's genes. Females do not get it.

"People who have this suffer uncontrollable bleeding, and even lower the expected life terms to approximately one half of normal life expectancy. With someone who has Hemophilia the most common site of injuries (which are affected by various accidents) are the joint spaces, muscles, and gastrointestinal tract. Knees and ankles are the most often affected and are extremely vulnerable. And, of course these are the areas most injured by an average, active young adventurous growing boy."

I listened, horrified and she continued, "A Hemophiliac can have many different symptoms after an injury; nausea, vomiting, lethargy, blood in the stool, urine, even in children who have new teeth coming in. Even a nosebleed can have severe consequences that a normal person wouldn't understand. Presently life expectantly is around eleven years. Lots of research is being done I pray for them to find a cure. I am always lighting candles at the church and try to think positively about the boys and their future."

I didn't know what to say. I was having such a difficult time absorbing all she was telling me.

"Oh, my God. How awful. How can you stand this? I mean, obviously, you have no choice-- you have to deal with it, but…Oh, I am so sorry, Linda."

"You want to know the hardest part?"

"When I have to refuse either one of the boys a certain activity because it is one which is so accident-prone. For instance, lots of their friends have skateboards and we have forbidden them to our boys."

I nodded and said, "Well, I can see that."

I paused and then I said, "I saw Robert (her eldest) on roller skates, though. Did you allow him that activity?"

"With great trepidation. My husband tries to keep us in balance. He said what kind of life would they have if we forbade them every single thing? Think about it. Before they go outside, I want to hold them and say 'Don't climb trees, don't get into any fights with your friends, even 'play fights', no football games, even flag football. I might as well say, 'Just sit on the porch and watch life go by'."

My mind was racing through with other things her boys must deny themselves.

"So, what do they do when they are injured, like now?"

"Well, the main treatment is replacement of the blood clotting factors. This life-saving clotting factor can be made in the labs or from purified human donor blood. The doctors infuse the patient with this clotting factor, like giving a blood transfusion.

Pain relievers can be given for symptom relief but these must be anti-inflammatory because anything which inhibits the blood from clotting must be strictly avoided."

"Can it be prevented?"

"No. Since it is an inherited, genetic disease, it cannot be prevented. Special research in ongoing, especially in gene therapy."

The silence in the kitchen was deafening. I, who usually couldn't shut up, found myself speechless.

This same neighbor taught me so many things about raising children, facing life in a positive, energizing way, and what being a real friend was all about. Once, I was at her house (again, during one of the times our husbands were gone for temporary duty) when another of the wives who lived on our street drove up out front and honked. Linda's oldest children jumped up, grabbed sweaters or jackets and Linda stopped them.

"Okay, everyone got their free pass?"

They checked and showed her a coupon type paper. "How about your 'Walk-Around-Money'?" she asked. Again, everyone checked their pockets or coin purses (the girls).

She added, holding out her arms, "And last, but certainly not least, my kiss."

There was some good-humored moaning and groaning as they lined up and gave her a kiss on the cheek.

When they had tumbled out and got situated in the car, Linda waved goodbye and grinning she said to me, "She got her own and my kiddies some free passes to a movie special here at the base theater. I wonder if it's too much to hope that it be a double-feature?"

My curiosity got the better of me and I asked, "What is 'Walk-Around Money'?"

"With such a large family we never have much money to spare," she said, then continued, "So each payday or grocery shopping day, I try to stick a little aside. Sometimes it just some change, every now and then George gives me some for what he calls 'The Walk-around-fund'. You see, at school, or when the kids go somewhere with other kids, I don't want them to ever be tempted to shoplift or just take anything I want them to have at least a little "pocket money" they can spend or not spend (save for another time, allowing it to accumulate). If someone in the crowd asks, 'Or you getting one? (be it a coke or ice-cream or something) they can say truthfully say, 'I have money. (he can even show it if he wants to) I just don't want one."

"All my children know what 'Walk-Around-Money is'."

I mulled this over later, thinking what a great idea it was. All the times growing up when I had no lunch or lunch money and hid out in the restroom or lied and pretended, I had already eaten…What I wouldn't have given for a little "Walk-Around-Money".

She taught her children to have pride in themselves and their family and never, ever, let them sink into self-pity. She had lots and lots of examples to tell them which illustrated there were always people in worst situations than their own. The old tune, "Look for the Silver Lining" described her philosophy of life perfectly.

That night I laid in bed, unable to sleep thinking of what Linda and George must go through each day with worry about their boys. How did she keep from holding anger at God for giving this terrible burden to carry? How could she let them out of her sight for even a few minutes without worrying they might be hurt at any time and maybe hemorrhage and bleed to death in the hospital? I added my own prayer for their family and finally fell into a restless sleep, promising I would not let the boys know their mother had confided in me. I resolved to act the same around them as I was before Linda had shared this terrible news.

Linda and George seemed a perfect pairing. They showed respect for each other, but also a kind of playful teasing which I had never had in my marriage. I was envious. They also took their faith very seriously.

Once, she invited me to attend her church service instead of the Protestant service which was not a specific "brand" but rather a generic non-Catholic service. Obviously, the small base chapel could not accommodate a separate service for Methodists, Baptists, Jehovah Witness, and others. There was always a choice between Protestant and Catholic and that was it.

Anyway, as we walked in and found seats in the pews, she whispered to me, "Remember, you can't take communion when they offer it."

"Why not? I take it in my church."

"Well, Catholics go to confession to get forgiveness and they are supposed to do this before being cleansed and ready to begin anew. You are in a state of mortal sin right now."

I took this information in silently but must admit I felt a little offended. It was as though I had been labeled a "bad" person and I didn't like the feeling.

I believe Linda knew what I was feeling and later we did what people are warned against doing—discussed religions.

"I believe," she said, "That everyone has a right to their own beliefs, as long as they don't try to force them on others. I certainly wouldn't want to go to a church where the congregants' faith was judged by how many snakes, they could handle without being bit." When I grinned, she added, "Well, would you?"

Several months later my husband was sent to Tripoli but this time it was for a full year. Disappointedly, we had to give up our base housing but could move back to a unit after he returned. You (military families were extended the courtesy of the housing as a family, but if the soldier were going to be gone if a year or more, they no longer qualified for the housing. I thought it very unfair, be we found a little older house for rent, not too far from the base and still in the same school district. I missed seeing Linda every day, but my kids and I were invited to their house at least once a week. These were for "catching up" and were often backyard bar-b-ques which were enjoyed by the children as well as the adults.

One Saturday evening when the children and I had driven in to have dinner with Linda and her family, we were sitting the back yard watching the kids bat a volley ball back and forth across the net, Linda asked me, "How are you getting along?"

"What do you mean?"

"Well, with your husband gone, I know you probably have a full plate, getting the kids back and forth from school keeping up with taking care of the car, and the house and the shopping and school functions plus being so isolated from all your friends you've made out here at the base."

I laughed at her and then I said, "Actually, I'm not having any problems with keeping up on all that. The kids have been taking care of the yard; mowing the grass, raking leaves, all that kind of thing; what I miss most is having some grownup company. I am afraid I'll soon be raising my hand to speak, like the kids, or using one syllable words because I have so little adult conversation."

She laughed along with me. Then she studiously avoided looking at me and she said, quite seriously, "You know, we've become so close these last three years, closer than sisters even."

"Yes, I agree. You are truly my best friend."

"I know the two sides of you—the one when your husband is here and the one when he is gone, and I have to say I prefer the one when he is gone. You are more cheerful, optimistic, and a lot more fun."

I laughed again. "So, what are you saying? I should take out a contract on him?"

"That's not even funny. Don't make a joke out of this. Have you ever considered leaving him?"

I was surprised at the turn this conversation was heading.

"You're such a good Catholic," I said to her, "I thought Catholics didn't believe in divorce?"

"Well, we don't as a rule, but there are circumstances in which that might not be such a bad idea. Besides, you are not a Catholic, what's preventing you from getting away from what you live with?"

"What do you mean, with what I live with?"

"Don't play the innocent with me. Do you think our children don't talk among themselves about the raving, ranting monster you live with? You know how close me, and my girls are with yours, don't you think they share a lot of it with me?"

I know I flushed at her words.

She paused and then she continued, "I am not sticking my nose in your business, but I know the abuse must be escalating. Someday he may kill you. He already takes his punishment of your children way overboard. I've had to warn George to stay out of it when he had threatened to step in. I've seen the bruises and even a couple of times the black eye you've tried to hide with makeup."

"And then what would I do? I have no job skills except for taking care of children or housekeeping. I did finally get my G.E.D and a driver's license before we went overseas. I have very little money. By the time we buy groceries, gas for the car and pay our bills for the car insurance, my one charge card for Sears which he goes over with a fine tooth comb each month, there is very little left. He is quick to remind me how stupid I am, how useless, how no one else but him would take on someone like me with four children."

"That's just his brainwashing. You are a good-looking woman, you're articulate, you can be funny sometimes, you're very well read, and you are very good with people. I know outers like you."

"He's told me many times if I ever tried to leave him, he would blow my brains out."

"So, you contact his superiors on base and get their backing, get them to help you. Go to the Chaplin and get his help."

"You know, too, I have no family support system. When I married him, it was to escape the abusive, awful life I had there. I hardly knew him. It was like, what is it they say? Oh, yeah, going from the frying pan straight into the fire."

We sat companionably for a few minutes and then she said, "Meanwhile, maybe you could find someone. Someone who would protect you and the children, who could stand up for you and help restore your self-confidence. It would do you a world of good."

At first, I didn't understand what she was suggesting but as she returned my questioning look, she gently smiled and said, "Well, why not? Don't you think you deserve a little happiness?"

"I can't believe what you're suggesting."

"You're even afraid to say it, aren't you?"

"I'm afraid to believe you, of all people, are suggesting such a thing."

"An affair? Go ahead and call it what it is. It would be good for you."

"Boy, he would really kill me then."

"Why would he find out. You can be discreet, can't you?"

"I don't know if you realize it or not, but in my bible as well as yours there is a commandment against committing adultery or is it just that you believe it wouldn't matter so much if I broke this commandment or not since I'm not Catholic and I'm not governed by the same moral laws you are. I don't know if I should be offended by this insinuation that because I'm not Catholic, anything goes.'"

This time we both laughed together.

"Just think about this: you're got a year to yourself now. You've got a built-in babysitter, me, who would cover for you anytime. Wouldn't it be nice to dress up and be taken out to dinner in a nice restaurant, or to a movie without all the kids? To go dancing. How long has it been since you have done any of these things?"

"I would be so guilty I wouldn't have any fun at all. I'd have nightmares about what he would do to me. I don't know if you're aware of it at all, but I have had only one man my entire life. From age sixteen until now."

"And you've been faithful the whole of your marriage, right?"

"Right. All eighteen years of it.'

"Much better than he deserved. I remember the story of his little affair with the high school cheerleader when you were pregnant."

"Yes, and as the old warning goes, 'Two wrongs don't make a right'."

"Stop being so smug in your righteousness, girl. I'm not suggesting you commit murder."

"You've read Dante's works, in school or whatever, right?"

"Yeah, and it bored me to death."

"Not me, I found it fascinating, but anyway, according to his interpretation, sins of the flesh are the lightest of she sins."

"Why do you suppose he chose that one?"

"Because he made all of us to be attractive to one another and we would mate and populate the earth."

"In other words, he made us human."

"But wouldn't it stand to reason then, that since he gave us a reasoning mind, we would be able to withstand all temptation, not look for excuses to break the commandments."

"I'll bet you were a virgin when you married, too, weren't you?" Linda asked.

"Well, of course I was. Eighteen years ago, a girl could very quickly lose her reputation and never get it back if she slept around. I was the perfect picture of a "good girl".

"Well, I was, too. But— "she paused, "I also had the added incentive of never wanting to sit in that confessional booth and let the priest know what I had done."

"Well, he couldn't see you, could he? I've always wondered if it is really dark in there and if you and the priest could see one another."

"Are you kidding me? I'd known our family priest since I was born. He would know my voice. No, he kept me on the straight and narrow without even knowing he did."

I hit her playfully on the shoulder with the magazine from my lap and finished our conversation saying, "Well, will you have to confess you tried to lure your friend into the devil's work? How many 'Hail Mary's" or whatever it is will you have to do for this conversation?"

"Hey, God is all forgiving, remember?"

Just then one of the children served the volleyball straight at us and we had to scramble to avoid being hit in the head.

"Hey! Watch it out there, guys," Linda yelled at them and our entire conversation was dropped.

Chapter

FIVE

W hen a military family moved out of base housing, an inspection
was held on the unit to assess any damages and the cleanliness
before they could sign the release for responsibility of the unit.
When Linda and I found out that some of the enlisted men's wives could
sign up to be on the approved cleaner's lists and once the unit was cleaned
and passed inspection the family leaving paid the cleaners a cash payment
for their work. George volunteered to oversee the babysitting duties, she
and I could go as a team and finish one house a night. Of course, there
were other cleaners, too, but the office which handled this would rotate
down the list and call when they had a unit which needed cleaning. We
did have the option to turn down one, though, so we would go, meet the
residents, and either agree to clean it and have it done by such and such
time and date or refuse it with some excuse or another. If we did turn it
down it was usually because the residents had never cleaned the stove and
no number of "Easy-off" oven cleaner would ever get it clean, or there was
what was called "dead wax" on the floors which would take a buffer to strip
it off because the people had waxed the floors over and over and there was
a terrible build up. It would take more hours than was worth it. We got to
know the different inspectors and they were helpful to ns, as newcomers,
and gave us lots of clues as to what they looked for before passing a house.

This was a godsend for Linda and me. For various reasons (mine was
my husband's wishes) Linda (hers was the illness her boys had) we were

not working (outside the home) mothers. My eldest two children needed braces for their teeth (something I had needed when I was growing up, but never had because my parents never thought that would be money well spent or any kind of a necessity). I was determined they would have these. Obviously, we were on a limited budget which had no resources for braces. When I suggested to my husband that this would give us a way to get the children's braces and that Linda and I would work as a team and always be there together and not alone, he gave his permission and we began. We got thirty-five dollars per house which is nothing now days but way back in the sixties, it was wonderful; and no taxes on it either.

Linda said to me one evening as we cleaned the stove, refrigerator and the rest of the kitchen of a second lieutenant being transferred overseas, "You know, that Howard inspector is really good-looking, isn't he?"

"Who?" I asked although I knew very well who she was referring to. He had certainly not escaped my notice although we were nothing but courteous and business-like during out interactions about the inspections.

"Don't tell me you haven't noticed. He's noticed you, too."

"Oh, you're so crazy."

"Yeah, right."

"You are, and you are going to make me so self-conscious around him he will be hard on us and flunk us a couple of houses."

"Most likely he will pass us without even doing his job, just because he thinks you have a cute figure."

I turned around and threw my damp sponge at her and she ducked, laughing.

"On a more serious note, my friend. Be careful. Gossip travels fast on a military base and wouldn't it be a catastrophe one of your husband's friends…or his enemies wrote him about some juicy rumor about his wife and some baby-faced airman."

I stood from the floor where I had been sitting to clean the oven and looked at her.

"You're serious, aren't you?"

"Very."

"Okay I will watch out and make sure I don't encourage any personal conversations, although I don't believe I have been sending any signals like that."

"I don't think you have, either. *He's* the one who wears that dopey look around you. How old are you?"

"Thirty this year."

"Yeah and you sure don't look it. And he must be all of twenty. To him, you're the perfect older woman he wants to learn from. I bet he was first in line to see that movie last year."

"What movie?"

"The Graduate. You're his "Mrs. Robinson"

"You've lost your mind."

"Nope, you just refused to see it. Sometimes I forget you married at sixteen and have so little knowledge of the real world out there. You're one of the real innocents."

"I am not," I said and when she kept that fisheye stare on me, I finally laughed and said, "Well, maybe I am, but maybe that's a good thing which keeps me out of trouble."

We didn't discuss it again, but she did keep saying little things during out next house inspection like, "Umhum. Yes, and we remembered your hint on the dead wax, too, Howard. We are always glad when you're assigned to our houses. You're so easy to work with. You're fair, but not mean."

"I always try to be. I know both of you have children and are working for them. It can't be easy to watch them during the day and then come spend one or two nights cleaning up other people's houses," he answered.

Later Linda said, "I never noticed his dimple when he smiles before, did you?"

"Oh, Shut up."

Each spring some of the different squadrons held family picnics in which military personnel and their families would bring their spouses and children. There were games for both the children and adults and prizes. It was a fun activity and when my husband was not off on a mission, we would all go. Of course, I had to have his approval on what I wore, and which activities I could participate in. This year he was gone when it was held, but I made sure I told him in a letter that the children were looking forward to it, and I asked him if he thought it would still be alright for us to go, if we went with Linda and George and their children. There was a serious step, because if I didn't and the kids wrote something about it in their letters to him, I would never hear the end of it. When he wrote back *Sure take the kids and go. Linda and George will look out for you. The kids will have fun and it will be something for you to do I wish I was there to go with you' all.*

If he only knew how glad I was that he wasn't...

It turned out to be a beautiful day, filled with a light breeze and plenty of sunshine.

As our two families walked up to the playground and park area, the kids got all excited about the different booths which had been planned and manned by the NCO wives' club, the Officers' wives club and the Service Club.

Of course, they wanted to eat everything, play everything and see everything. We were provided with a schedule telling when each event would take place and how to sign up and enter as well as the prize.

Linda said to all our children, "First we are going to check everything out and pick who of our team will enter what."

They agreed and we secured our own place under a big tree with a picnic table. We had brought blankets to spread and sit on, a cooler with ice water and disposable cups. We had stuck a plastic container with potato salad inside the cooler as well and brought paper plates and plastic silverware. I had brought boiled eggs and the salt and pepper for them.

When we added the packaged cookies and chips and a melon and cutting knife, we felt we were well prepared.

I had even remembered to give each of my children a little "walk-Around-Money" after checking with Linda on how much she was giving hers.

When we had unloaded everything, we sat down and looked over the events: Throwing Horseshoes, Washer throwing (I'd never heard of it before), Sack races, Three legged race, Egg and spoon balancing race, Archery, Rope pulling (must have signed with a specific team) Ring toss, Baseball throw, Jump rope challenge, Dart throw, Dunking booth, Pie in the face, Topple the cans pyramid, Pennies in the dish, and Water-gun duck hunting. Of course, children could get their faces painted, too.

The smells were mouth-watering and many a child would end up with a stomachache if they tried all they wanted. There was cotton candy, lollipops, hamburgers, hot dogs, whole pies to take home or just a slice, popcorn, french-fries, candy apples, funnel cakes. and roasted ears of corn on a stick. Even homemade pickles, jams, and jellies could be bought.

The smells blended and filled the air. Gleeful shouts from children rang out and people were greeting each other without the usual consciousness of rank. Everyone wore civilian clothing and for this day, there was no formal observance of differences of enlisted men or officers. There was an unusual sense of camaraderie and friendship which was both refreshing and unusual.

As they were looking over the event schedule, Linda looked up and then, poking me in the ribs said quietly, "Well, well, well, look at who's here."

When I looked up, I saw Howard and one of the other housing inspectors walking towards up. They smiled as they came up.

Howard said, "Who's got the cleaning detail today with you both out here?"

We laughed and Linda said, "Even cleaning ladies have time off now and then. Looks funny to see you two out of your uniforms or fatigues. The big shots let you have a day off?"

We introduced them both to George and to the children. My eldest daughter was complaining because none of us wanted to go partner her in the egg toss event.

"Hey, Stanley will be your partner, won't you, Stanley?"

His friend looked surprised, but then good naturedly nodded his head and he said, "Okay but we better win."

Howard turned to Linda, "Hey, will you handle all the kids so she and I can enter?"

He pointed towards me. I don't think Linda thought she had a choice. She said, "Sure, but come back as soon as it'd done so George and I can go do something and you guys can baby sit."

Howard leaned over and giving me his hand, pulled me to my feet. "I know where the egg toss is, come over this way."

When signed up for the egg toss, there were two to a team and you were each given a spoon and lined up on opposite sides. The partners would try to be the first ones to meet in the middle, after tossing the raw egg carefully back and forth to their partners on the spoon. Hands were not allowed, and it was important to be gentle and slow so the egg wouldn't break each time it changed spoons.

We didn't win, but we were one of the three last partners to break our egg. It was a lot of fun. I carefully avoided looking straight at Linda when we got back to the big tree. She and George went off to try their luck at horseshoes and Howard and I played with and entertained the kids too small to go around on their own.

The rest of the day was spent in taking many turns on different events. I hadn't ever realized how much fun it was to be free to enjoy myself without my husband there, always frowning, nit-picking every single thing the kids did, being afraid to say the wrong thing or be embarrassed by what he said or did to us in front of other people. I thoughtfully admitted to myself I had never had this kind of happiness and freedom since my marriage. Eighteen years of being held under some else's control, living on the edge of fear I would be facing some kind or reprisal for some misdemeanor infraction I didn't even recognize.

Being completely honest with myself, it had been so long since any one had flirted with me or paid me any attention, I thoroughly enjoyed Howard's approval and without acknowledging that (at least on his part) his attention was anything except friendship I felt pretty, flattered, and it had been such a long time since anyone had so obviously offered me even kindness and acceptance for who I was I wanted the day to never end. I could barely remember the years before I had married, I was so young and inexperienced. Later that evening, I admitted to myself that there had been some physical attraction there, as well although Howard had not said one solitary inappropriate thing nor had he suggested any other meeting or meaning to our behavior that entire day.

As I saw the interplay between others (husbands and wives, children and parents, friends) I temporarily lost the joy and enthusiasm for this wonderful day. After all, it was almost like Cinderella. A wonderful day, but as always, even wonderful days come to an end. The clock hits midnight and the spell are broken. When he came home, we would go back to our "normal" lives. I drew very quiet and even morose as the day began to dwindle down and families packed up and went home. Trying to forestall the ending, I stayed behind with Howard, his friend Stanley and some other volunteers to put things away, pick up trash, pack up leftover supplies and collect lost and found items which would be held at the Service club for later seekers.

Linda had taken all the children to her house, and George had stayed to help with the cleanup.

As we stood around, checking everything over, Howard turned to me and said, "Stanley and I can give you a ride home. It's no problem."

Before I could say anything, George said affably, "Oh, her kids are at my house and we live across the street from one another. We've got it covered. Thanks Anyway."

"Yes, but thanks anyway," I added. "It was really fun today. I'm glad you could come and hang out with us."

Then I remembered Stanley and I turned to him, And you, too, Stanley. Thanks for being such a good sport with all the munchkins. I know they drove you crazy."

"No mam, not at all. I come from a big family. I enjoyed it."

On the way home George aid, "Boy, I'm give out, how about you?"

I laughed with him. "Sure am. But it was so much fun."

Each hoe children all still seemed to have a fully charged battery and were equally divided through Linda's house, some watching television, some playing board games, some in the backyard, catching fireflies in jars.

I accepted Linda's offer of a glass of wine and we sat on her back patio, relaxed and quiet for a few minutes.

"None of them are going to go peacefully to bed, you know," she said.

"I know, but I sure will. I'm suddenly exhausted, aren't you?"

"Yes, quite frankly, I am, but I am so glad you went with us. I knew you would enjoy yourself."

"I did."

"You certainly spent your day occupied with our inspector friend. You two must have had a lot to say to each other."

Even though it was dark, I felt my face warm and was glad Linda couldn't see it.

"He is very nice, Linda."

"Oh, I certainly agree. In fact, he may be one of the few men I would describe as *sweet.*"

105

"I suppose you think I was leading him on today, don't you?"

"Not deliberately, I don't. What I think was that you felt his admiration and approval and you basked in it. I can't blame you for that. Why wouldn't you? You sure don't get that anywhere else. However, I feel I have to remind you that..." She paused here and reaching down for the wine bottle next to her chair, she refilled out glasses and then continued, "You better be careful. He's just a kid. He told me he wants to make the military his career. He probably has a spotless record currently. Surely you wouldn't want to do anything that would get him into trouble. Never mind the chances you are taking that some busy-body or other will let the cat out of the bag; deservedly or not, and your husband will accuse you of all kind of things, though you are certainly quite innocent. You wouldn't want to be responsible for that, would you?"

Even though she couldn't see me in the dim light on the porch, I shook my head negatively and said softly, "No, I wouldn't."

"So, therefore, my dear friend. You have my full support in whatever you decide to do in handling this and you can come talk to me—or not—anytime you feel the need. Meanwhile, enjoy what had to have been a wonderful boost to your self-confidence today. It would appear your young admirer doesn't agree with your husband's summation that no one else would ever be attracted to you except him.

I found myself thinking and rethinking about that day far too many times over the next few weeks and though I had expected there to be a little awkwardness when we cleaned houses and Howard turned out to be one of the inspectors, it failed to materialize. He was glad to see me and it showed. I was glad to see and banter with him and made no excuses to avoid the inspections or push them all on Linda.

Finally, one afternoon when Linda had to leave early for a meeting with her priest to discuss one of her girl's First Communion, the inspectors were late to arrive for the inspection. Sometimes this happened, but they would have called if they had to reschedule.

I wasn't expecting any certain inspector, I knew it might be Howard or Stanley or some of the others. I had gotten a sitter for my own children because the inspection had been arranged to suit the clients who were being transferred. I was not in a particularly good mood because the money for the babysitter would be coming out of my share of the fees we charged.

I was surprised at how happy I was to see him. He had a big smile on his face, too. He and Stanley went through the house with their clipboards, checking everything out. When they were done, they signed the inspection report, I signed off my responsibility and we stood, talking a few minutes outside the now locked up unit. His responsibility included turning in a copy of the report so Linda and I would get paid, but we were done.

"You know," Howard said, "It must be very hard for you to take care of everything with your children when your husband is gone for an entire year at a time sometimes. If there is ever anything, I can do for you, let me know. You can leave word for me at my housing office and I would be glad to help you out. I think it's wrong for the military to displace families when the man of the house is off on a year-long TDY. Then when he gets back you will have to move again and wait for when housing becomes available again.

I was a little embarrassed when I replied, "Oh, we're doing fine," I said.

"Does the house you're renting have a yard?"

"Yes, a big one," I said. Then I asked, "Why?"

"Well, I could come cut the grass and edge it up when it needs it. That might be one thing off your list."

I was impressed by his offer and knew he was genuinely making the offer out of a desire to help. I can only imagine what Linda would say if she knew he offered (or even worse, I allowed him to come over to my current house) to help me with anything. I could imagine the scenario of him coming over, even for the most innocent of reasons, and after my husband came home one of the children mentioning that *Howard* had helped with the yard while he was gone.

"No, no, we're doing fine. I appreciate your offer and your concern, Howard."

After thinking it over, I decided to keep his offer to myself. There's no telling what Linda would make of Howard offering to come work on my yard. I giggled a little, imagining her take on the subject.

Because of my background and the utter, complete control first my parents, then my husband had always had on me, I was never one to take the initiative on anything. Over the next few weeks, I must admit I sometimes had some very erotic thoughts about Howard. I did acknowledge and realize that he had (as Linda called it) a "thing" for me. However, it takes two to tango, or so they say, and I would never have had the courage to make the first move to encourage anything closer than a friendship and he was too shy, too young, too morally bound by his military code to know how to proceed towards an illicit affair with some sergeant's wife while he was overseas. Mentally, I lay awake in bed some nights and tried to visualize how it would feel to have someone so young, handsome and virile make love to me. Someone like Howard would probably be gentle and caring and thoughtful; totally unlike what I was used to with the only man I had ever been with (my husband). The thoughts and dreams made me restless and guilty, but they also filled me with a longing for something I would probably never have again. Make no mistake, while fleeting and almost illusionary when we first married there *was* some kindness, some gentleness, some sweetness to our relationship. What had caused the man who was tender and gentle the first few months of our marriage to make him almost unrecognizable? For, honestly, at first, I had seen that side of him, too. I considered that he had never really loved me but because I had been so determined to stay a virgin (be a good girl, that was the standard) until I was married, he confused sex and love, too. He thought he loved me and truth was he just wanted sex. If that were the case with him, then he had a right to feel cheated, too.

I always felt bad afterwards, after lying there, thinking of Howard but often (later) when my husband was sent for more than one tour of duty to Vietnam, I would wonder if he were killed, would I find someone else? Someone totally different who would treat me special, who would respect and protect me? Or would I stay free for the first time in my life?

Immediately I would feel ashamed that I could even have such thoughts. After all, he was the father of my children and even if I had no love for him as my husband, didn't I owe him something for these eighteen years? Truthfully, I was dreading the day he would be returning home again and the thought of resuming our sexual relationship made me almost physically ill. I admitted it. I did not have any remaining love for him. Not at all. The thought of being free of him finally, totally, filled my very being. How would I ever pretend otherwise convincingly? When he came back this time, how could he *not* see through me completely? How could he be fooled?

It reminded me of something my mother had said to me when we were still on speaking terms and I confided about my husband's infidelity and asked about my father's own past in that area.

She had said, "The secret to a successful marriage in so far as the male species is concerned is that a man wants and expects a chef in the kitchen, an educated and disciplined nanny for his children, and a whore in bed."

My husband had never been one to accept me just lying unresponsive and placid during the sexual intimacy of our marriage, no, he fully wanted me to be very involved and seeming to enjoying every minute of it. I found this charade very hard to perform and I believe that's where women are so very different from their male counterparts "Women," said Linda to me once, "make love, and men make sex. Women expect and deservedly so, a neat and tidy little package tied with a romantic and meaningful little pink bow. Women can't separate the two; they wear their hearts on their sleeves for men to see and break."

Once when we were having such a conversation, I asked her, "How do you account for the famous romantic male poets who wrote such convincing sonnets?"

"She chuckled and said with her expressive twinkling eyes, "Well, that's easy. They were inspired by the women in their lives. Show me a romantic male and somewhere their past is a wildly romantic woman who taught him how to love and appreciate women; be it his wife, lover, girlfriend, or even his mother."

Many, many years later one of my friends presented me with a birthday present which I still treasure. It was a small easel and sitting on it is this verse:

"Behind every successful woman is herself."

I had to agree with this friend and that's one of the things that worried me. I, (like most women I knew or read about) couldn't dissociate love and sex. Men might (and most often do) easily separate the two (without feeling dishonest about their feelings and actions), but most women felt disloyal in trying to pretend emotions which simply were not there. How could I be such a good actress when my husband returned from this year? How could I pretend the same eagerness and hunger for him that he would be expressing for me after sch a long separation?

I remembered a former friend I had long since lost track of (easy to do when military families lacked the roots, but moved so often). Her name was Janie and we were friends during a three-year tour of duty in Montana. We were "couple" friends, and would often meet on the week end for an adventure visiting some of the local sights or perhaps meet for dinner and card playing. I liked her husband equally as well as I did her, though he was extremely quiet. I found out later they had divorced and when I heard the reason, I had difficulty in believing it. She had been the one wanting the divorce, even though they had a child by the time they divorced but even this shared child could not keep them together. Janie told every common friend that she left him because she couldn't face a lifetime of boredom with him. She said he was unimaginative, *too* predictable and just plain *too* good, *too* kind, *too* boring. He lacked any excitement about life. Whenever I thought about her later, I wondered if she had found what she was looking for and if so, what kind of man was he?

I needn't have spent all that time worrying about my husband's return so much because he took a thirty day leave and it was almost like a brief honeymoon type of reunion. He had saved some of the extra pay he got from the military for his overseas assignment, and we took the children to Disney Land. He was unusually patient with them. The only real exception to this was he had imagined our eldest daughter as the young preteen she was when he left. She was a freshman in high-school now and he did not approve of her desire to be given more freedom than she had been allowed before. He refused to even consider allowing her to date, and vehemently argued about having any boys over to the house. He made the concession of allowing her a few girlfriends over for a sleepover but even then, it was not the joyful, fun time it should have been and just fell sort of flat. I believe her friends were uncomfortable with my husband. He was too rigid in his expectations. I also feel they could feel the tension in the air at our house which wasn't there at their own homes.

My daughter would come to me, trying to have me align alongside her so she could experience more of the freedom her friends enjoyed, but I was much too afraid to attempt such a partnering.

The saddest day of my life during this time was when we prepared to move to our new assignment. I knew I was going to miss Linda and George and their children. She had been absolutely the best friend I had ever had.

There was even a bitter-sweetness about seeing Howard for the final house Linda and I had cleaned for inspection. I knew at times in the future I might even regret that I did not take things further with him, but I also knew my deeply ingrained old fashioned morality (like the feelings which kept me a virgin until marriage even having friends who teased me about being a "Little Miss Goody-Two shoes") which, had I succumbed to the attraction I felt for Howard, would have haunted me with guilt and regret. I may not have been able to completely hide it. I think I read some meaning in the last conversation I had with him but then, who knows? I may have been misinterpreting what I saw in his eyes. I wondered in our military crisscrossing of lives and assignments if I would ever run across him again? If so, would he be older (and thus, wiser and more worldly) and would I be more adventurous? Would the attraction be there for either of us if we did meet again somewhere, sometime?

I knew that the entire "thing" with Howard was not merely my imagination for several reasons. One, he wanted to make a career of the military and wouldn't do anything to jeopardize his performance or personnel record. Two, the inspectors were responsible for making sure what was initially in the unit when it was leased to a military family remained in the unit unless the new family coming into it specifically wanted it taken out and not sent on to the new assignment with the military family leaving. A few times I had said I was going to miss the pretty china cabinet which was in the unit, left from the exiting family. I did not have one, although I had a set of nice china and silver. While Howard was "checking" us out, and when Linda was in the other room with Stanley, checking other parts of the house, Howard said to me, "Would you like to have the cabinet?"

"Sure, I would. Who wouldn't?"

"I can change the inventory on this paperwork and have it shipped with your own furnishings to your new assignment. No one pays any attention to this. Once they are signed, and inspection passed, it's done. The movers will take everything listed to go."

I was shocked. "We (notice how quickly I linked us in the wrong-doing of his proposal) can't do that. If you got caught, you could be court martialed or something." (This was the worst possible infraction I could think of and that Howard would even consider doing something which

111

would put his military goals at risk was unbelievable and made me feel almost faint).

"No, I could always pretend it was a mistake."

Emphatically I said, "No! Indeed not! Every time I looked at the thing, even if we (there was that inclusionary "we" again) got away with it I would feel guilty and I probably would hate the thing. Besides, what would I tell my husband?"

"That it was probably a mistake. Or blame me."

"You are a little crazy, know that?"

Just then Linda and Stanly walked in the room. "Who's crazy?" Stanley asked. (Was that a knowing smirk on his face or my imagination?

"All of us," Linda said, "who live military lives."

So, I didn't get me a free china cabinet but I *could* have and at great risk for someone else. I saw the depth Howard was willing to go to please me. I realized it was not bargaining on his part because after this final inspection, I would never see him again (in theory, anyway). In other words, there was no way he could manage any kind of repayment from me.

And so, we moved to our new assignment in Fort Worth, Texas. One of the more pleasant surprises about this new assignment was that the couple we had been close with for a while in Germany were assigned to this base as well. We picked up our family friendships almost as though we had never been separated by the assignment in the middle.

Chapter

SIX

---⟡---

It did not take long for the "old" husband and father to reappear. I suppose a good part of it was that during the previous year when he was gone, due to a variety of reasons (such as the children being older and our total acceptance of the free life we led while he was gone) the family seemed aligned in two different, opposing camps. The children and I versus my husband.

One of the biggest mistakes I ever made involved our oldest son. His birthday was on September first and in Texas September first was the deadline for entering school. Even a day later and the child had to wait an entire year which of course made him a year older than his classmates except for any others in the same predicament. He was disappointed, he wanted very much to be sent off to school with his older sister (her birthday fell exactly a month later.) So, after much discussion, it was decided that if we could send him to New Mexico to live with my two brothers (My third brother was off on a three-year stint in the Navy). and mother, he could come home at the end of his first-grade year and move straight into second grade in Texas. We checked with the Texas Board of Education to make sure this was true (it was).

Knowing how my childhood had been, I can't imagine what possessed me. Perhaps I thought things would be totally different now. My parents were divorced, my brothers were in high-school (practically grown young men and more responsible; and one was off in the Navy), my mother had finished her nursing schooling and supposedly was just working one job now.

So, we shipped him off. He was excited about getting to go and stay with his uncles. Looking back, with the false validity of hindsight I now realize he was only about to turn six and, in his mind, it was like the gift of a glorious "one-on-one" special vacation his siblings would not have.

I gave him lots of pre-addressed and stamped envelopes for him to have his uncles and grandmother to help him write letters. I saw him off at the airport with his little pinned-on tag for a child unaccompanied by an adult, holding back tears. Perhaps I was already having second thoughts about this. I told myself if he finished the first half of the year at least, they would accept him as a transfer student. Each week I sent what money I could spare to help with the groceries and school supplies. I never received any acknowledgment of the money or my letters but when I called and talked to one of my brothers, I would talk to my son and one of my brothers would then take the phone and update me on his progress and activities. Now and then they would use the envelopes I had given him to send me school work or pictures he had done at school. Of course, I always shared any communications I received with the entire family especially his siblings.

Thank God this particular child of ours was extremely bright. He would have done just great in school; had he been allowed to start while in Texas living with his family. He had almost (with just a little assist from his two-year older sister was already recognizing sight words and beginning to read. wasn't until he was returned home after only two months (not the complete semester we had planned on) that I found out what he had been put through. My son did not share everything in front of his father but over the next few months, innocently and without intention to blame his uncles or his grandmother, he let little things be revealed. For example, right before Christmas, I asked him, "What did you and your uncles do for Halloween? We missed you so much and you never sent a picture of what you were or anything."

He grinned and said happily, "Uncle Sam took me to pick out a costume and I was Casper, the friendly ghost."

I chuckled. "I bet that was fun. Did they take you trick-or-treating, too?"

"Sure. And I got to wear my costume the day after Halloween, too."

"Oh, you did, did you?"

"Yeah. And the day after that, too."

He must be confused, I thought. "Did everyone get to wear their costumes to school more than one day, too?"

He shook his head no and said, "Nope, just me."

"How any days did you get to wear it to school?"

"Till my teacher sent me to the office and the assistant principal, Mrs. Woods, called my uncles and told me I couldn't wear it to school anymore."

I was silent, horrified. Surely this was a six-year old's confused mind. Surely my brothers did not allow this first grader to wear his Halloween costume day after day until the school put a stop to it.

"What did the other kids in the class think when you got to wear it so many days and they didn't?"

"Well, at first they were they told me I was stupid because I didn't know Halloween was over. Then…"

He paused and thoughtfully, he said, "But I think they were just jealous because they asked the teacher why they couldn't wear theirs every day."

In my mind I pictured this poor little bedraggled looking orphan child dressed in a red flimsy acetate jumpsuit with a white Casper the ghost mask hung around his neck and a thin rubber band to school every day for a week or more. I hoped with all my heart his teacher had been kind and patient and allowed him to retain his pride as best he could. Did he feel embarrassed and ashamed to be different from his classmates? The next time I spoke on the phone with my brothers, I asked them to be honest. Was this an actual event? Did it really happen?

Sheepishly, I thought, my brother admitted that sometimes they got up late and allowed my son to decide what he wanted to wear. They had allowed him to get on the school bus after they left sometimes and yes, the school called and said he couldn't continue wearing his Halloween costume to school day after day. My brother admitted he felt guilty they didn't even know he was wearing it day after day until the school called. He said he allowed the school to think this six-year old boy (on his own choice) to change his regular clothes and wear the costume just because he loved it.

After I hear that this incident *did* occur as my son reported it, I began to listen more carefully to his stories of his life with his uncles and grandmother.

There were evenings when he either missed the bus ride home to his stop, or was supposed to be picked up by one of my brothers and they "forgot".

For instance, one day when we heard a siren he turned to his siblings and with a voice full of braggadocio, he said, "I got to ride in a police car once."

Rather than draw more attention to what he was saying, I decided to listen and judge the truth of it for myself.

First there was the expected disbelief by his siblings, "You did not!"

"Did so," he said emphatically. "And the policeman let me turn the lights and siren on."

"Liar, liar, pants on fire!" said one of his siblings.

"Yeah, one night when Uncle Sam was supposed to pick me up after school, and he told me not to get on the school bus after school. He told me to wait right out front of the school and he would come in his car to get me."

"So," said his brother, fully curious about the story now, "So then what happened?"

I listened intently from my position as driver on this trip to get Saturday morning haircuts.

"Well, I waited and waited," he said, almost enjoying drawing out the suspense of the story ow that he had the interest and belief of his siblings, "Somebody the house across the street from the school called the police and told them there was a little boy sitting on the curb with his lunchbox and jacket all by himself and it was almost dark."

He paused in his story, and then he continued, "The policeman came and asked me my name and how I got left behind. He thought I missed my bus."

He looked at them, paused and then he said, "Here comes the best part. The policeman took me to get an ice cream cone and—"

My other son said, "No, you're making that up. Policemen don't just go get kids ice cream cones. They have to ask their mommies or daddies first."

"Well, this one didn't and I can tell you I even got to choose the flavor I wanted. I got chocolate fudge."

"Humph, Well, what happened then?"

"We drove to the police station and—"

He was interrupted by his brother once again, "Well, when did you get to turn the siren and lights on?"

"Right before we got to the police station."

"Then what happened? Did they lock you up in a jail cell?" My daughter, who had been quiet during this entire tale finally spoke up, not so much with disbelief because I could see she believed the basis his story to be true but she spoke with the trace of a giggling tease in her voice.

My son looked at her and said, "No, of course not. I was just a kid. They don't lock kids up."

Then, as though tiring of his tale-telling he said, "Nothing much. The policeman called Uncle Roy and told him where I was and he came and got me."

"How did he know how to call Uncle Roy?" my daughter asked.

"Because I learned how to write my name and address and phone number down in first grade, that's how. I told him it was 505-642-1876."

Now my daughter said, "Well, that was pretty darned smart of you."

"Were you scared, sitting on the curb with it starting to get dark and all?"

Now the story was destined to take a turn to end it with him being the hero and *my* thoughts thinking of the many things which could have happened to my son.

He said, successfully ending the hero, "Nope. Not a bit. I knew Uncle Roy would come for me because he said he would."

I mentally thanked God, after all these months since the incident for being with my son and giving him an angel's blanket of protection.

I wondered, as well, after he had returned to our family, about other signs of his life away from us. Before he had made his journey there and back, he had had a strong distaste for being told it was bath time. Now this, in itself, wasn't too unusual. It isn't uncommon for small boys to want to postpone bath (or bed) time. But when he came home, he suddenly had developed a love for bath time. He would take his little fleet of boats and spend so much time I would have to go in the bathroom and let some of the now cold water out, and add hotter until his water wrinkled hands and feet made him look like an aged old man. Other family members would complain at his lengthy time in the bathroom.

When I finally asked about this change, he quite seriously answered me. "When I lived with my uncles, I never took a bath."

I laughed at him. "I am sure you are exaggerating. You mean you *never* took a bath?"

"Well, hardly ever. 'Member how you used to have to make me take a bath?" He paused and I nodded my head and agreed, "Yes. Now you have practically turned into a fish. It's hard to get you out of the tub."

"Well, the uncles never made me take a bath."

"Oh, and did you like that?"

"At first."

"Then not so much after a while?"

"You know what my favorite thing to do was?"

"No, what?" I asked, giving up on the bath info for a while.

"Well, they had this neat old storage shed in the back yard. It had a tin roof. You know the kind I mean?"

I nodded.

"Well, I learned how to climb up this big ole' tree and from there I could climb over to the roof of the shed. I could take all my little cars and trucks and play up there. It was like having my own tree house."

"Wasn't it just a little bit dangerous?"

"Not much, once I learned how to get there from the tree. Besides, I liked it up there. Sometimes I would play there clear until it got dark and I had to go inside."

"Since the uncles didn't *make* me take a bath, pretty soon I decided to take some on my own."

"Did they wash all your clothes for you or did your grandma do that?"

"The uncles."

"Do you know what I didn't like the most?"

"What?"

"When it was time for the grandmother nurse to come home from work."

"Why?"

"She was scary."

"Scary? What was so scary about her?"

"Well, she had red hair."

Well, lots of people have red hair."

"Yeah, but she wore these big white nurse shoes that went clump, clump, clump when she came home from work and started up the stairs."

I tried hard not to grin as he recited these facts about my mother. I could visualize her in her white uniform, nurses cap, stockings and shoes and her bright dyed red hair.

"Yeah, and she wore this red, red, *really* red lipstick."

"So, what did you do when she came home from work and… (I almost lost it when I got to the sound of her shoes) she came clumping up the stairs?"

"Ran."

"You ran?"

"Yes, fast."

"Where did you run to? The uncles?"

"Sometimes they weren't home yet."

"So, if they weren't home, where did you run to?"

"To a good hiding place."

"Then what?"

"I would hide until the uncles got home and the grandma went to bed."

"Did the uncles know this?"

"Sure. They told me it was a great idea. The hiding."

Yes, I thought, *I bet they did. The grown-up uncles probably thought it was a funny, and wonderful idea. How many times had I seen them "run" when it was time to hide from the people who ruled them with fear?*

Meanwhile, my husband had to redirect his strict and sometimes unreasonable demands to the weakest of my children, my second son, Joseph. Whereas before the oldest son got the full brunt of my husband's insistence for our boys to "act like a man", "quit being such a sissy" "Don't be such a mama's boy". It almost seemed like crying (for the boys) was forbidden. Boys were simply not allowed to cry.

This was always my quiet one, my timid and so eager-to-please child. Although we all were very aware of time as the afternoon hours drew closer to time for the man of the house to come home from work. As the hands on the clock moved closer everyone could feel the tension begin to rise. Unlike some other husbands and fathers, he was *never* one to go "hang out with the guys" for a few beers after work. I reasoned it was because they never invited him. He held the position as crew chief on the flight line and was considered unreasonably difficult to please for those under his supervision. They certainly didn't want to spend their own free time with him.

Anyway, we would feel the tension increase as his homecoming drew closer. I was busy making sure the evening meal would be ready to serve immediately after his special news program with Walter Cronkite, and the kids would scatter as far away from his path as they could without being so obvious, he would notice and get mad at the lack of acknowledgement of his arrival.

The dinner itself was fraught with traps and mis-steps which might cause anyone to be targeted. The irony of the family always bowing their heads in prayer before eating was not lost on me. It never ceased to amaze me that this was one of his "never" break rules and yet he never attended church (whether the rest of us did or not), we did no family bible study or reading. To illustrate to the extreme steps he took this rule, there was a never to be forgotten example of how far he would go to exert total control over all of us One evening, we all sat down to a meal of home fried-chicken, and forgetting all but his love for getting one of the two drumsticks, my youngest, (This was prior to our having our final child and daughter) reached out to secure a chicken leg to place on his plate so he would have one when we began eating. Instant mayhem took place, my husband reached out with his fork to stab Joseph's hand still clutching the chicken leg. The rest of us looked on in shocked and stunned silence but of course, Joseph broke out in a blood-curdling scream and instantly dropped the chicken leg.

Being honest, it was not *that* hard of a stab - the imprint of the fork was there, and it was red and I knew it hurt. However, the blood did not rise to the surface.

The other children looked from their father to the screaming Joseph. I stood without speaking and took Joseph to the bathroom where I ran cold water over his hand over and over until the redness began to go away. I tried to soothe him emotionally, but it was hard because I viewed the entire incident as an example of his father's barbarian nature. *What an animal,* I told myself but I told Joseph, "You know the rule about grace at the table, honey."

"I just wanted a chicken leg," he whimpered, "and I forgot."

We went back to the table even though Joseph was reluctant and by this time didn't have any appetite. They had waited until our return to have grace. I believe my husband knew he had gone a step too far, at least in my eyes because when he noticed Joseph did not even eat any chicken during the meal, choosing just the mashed potatoes and gravy, the salad and green beans, he did not comment. Studiously, neither did the other children. Thereafter, even though the other children always left at least one chicken leg on the platter for Joseph, his taste for the drumstick never returned.

This was when he began his severe fear of the dinner hour (as I termed it). Before my husband caught on to my ploy, I began trying to allow Joseph to eat early, when he still had an appetite, and so he could just eat a taste or two of whatever we were having. When he began to notice Joseph's lack of appetite at the dinner table, he began to search for the reason.

"What's the matter, Joseph? How come you're not hungry?"

Joseph shrugged his little shoulders, and with his glassy look of fear in being caught in trouble, he replied, "I'm really just not that hungry, Daddy."

Looking directly at me, he said, "Did they have a late snack today?"

"No, not really. I always give them an after-school snack since they eat lunch so early at school. But school lets out at 2:45 p.m. so it shouldn't interfere with dinner."

He dropped the conversation then, but Joseph started have strong bouts of nausea when it got time to come to the table for dinner. Sometimes it would end in him throwing up-even with very little in his stomach. When this started, I brought the little play table and chairs into a corner of the kitchen and would fill his plate and let him sit at his own little table and chair. Two things resulted from this: One, Joseph's nausea lessoned, and his appetite got considerably better. It would appear that it wasn't his digestive track which was causing the problem. Two, this rankled on my husband who viewed this as his capsulation to a child's (Joseph) whim.

After several heated arguments about allowing him to continue eating at his own table, both Joseph and I tired of the constant wrangling with him, and Joseph caved in. On his own one evening, he forced himself to the table with the rest of us.

Suddenly, on *his* own, unexpectantly and thankfully my husband "let it go", and resisted what I knew was an almost irresistible urge to comment on Joseph's return to the table.

This was no real or lasting solution for the issue with Joseph's eating and it eventually had an unexpected and life-long consequence on his overall physical, gastronomical, and emotional health. Long into adulthood he was forced to deal and live with hyperglycemia. When I visited, he and his wife (after they have been married several years) I would watch as she packed his lunch, then added a snack for mid-morning and mid-afternoon and then he still ate dinner with his family and sometimes *still* felt the need of a bedtime snack.

Yet, he had no difficulty in maintaining a perfect weight for his body type and lifestyle. The rest of us envied what seemed an effortless weight control and fought the usual up and down battles to keep our weight under the best guidelines.

I am not so sure the episode was forgotten as Joseph moved from childhood to manhood because although he *got along* with his father as adults, they were not really close (actually I would not describe his relationship with *any* of his children as close).

Without me being aware of it, things were taking a gradual change in our lives. Slowly (almost unnoticeably), I was changing. But then, so was my husband. And, as surely as the sun rose and set on a regular basis, I began to believe I deserved better out of life. I began to believe and understand that my children deserved better. And, though it was almost imperceptible, my husband was changing; not much, but still...Old hopes somehow never completely fade and I lived, as most humans do, with optimistic and a vague hope our lives would change. I cannot deny that at times when he was at his worst, I wished him dead but argued with myself I didn't really mean it.

I wondered later if he noticed I no longer jumped as fast (to his chagrin) to respond to his orders or to answer him. Not that I refused, just that I wasn't as quick to respond.

The children noticed my willingness (regardless of the consequences) to attempt to take their side or alleviate their punishment for misbehavior in his eyes. They began to come to me and try to enlist my aid in their battles especially our eldest daughter. She was not allowed to wear even the mildest makeup, unlike all her friends and could not go on a date, even to school functions. It took everything we had to argue for her to at least be able to attend the events in a group of her girlfriends, and we knew it was hopeless to win an argument for dating. His stand was that when she was old enough to drive a car, and get a license, he would allow her to date of course, with loads of special restrictions attached. Her Cinderella bewitching hour was age sixteen and by age fourteen she was "champing at the bit" to have the freedoms her friends all had.

There was a big swimming competition at the pool on the base, and because all of our children had taken free lessons for years and could swim like fish, I allowed them to enter their age and style categories. The competition was held on a Saturday and we were all excited about it. I had promised my daughter a new swimsuit, and we went shopping that week to find her one. This was long before the bikini was "the" thing, and most women still wore either regular-cut two-piece bathing suits or one piece with perhaps a little risqué high cut leg. I knew her father would have a fit if she did got even the very modest (to me) two piece swimsuit of the time, and did not get the one piece old-fashioned suit al the older women wore. I allowed myself to be persuaded to the purchase of a two piece (which I considered the more modest of our choices) and she was thrilled but I was very apprehensive about our choice.

The morning of the swim met dawned bright and sunny and there was a heightened sense of excitement as we gathered our towels, swimsuits and our camera, loaded with a new roll of film, high hopes and expectations. There was already quite a crowd assembled and all my children were entered in various categories even the youngest who was in the Tadpole category.

They had put bleachers up and my husband and I chose some good seats with a good view if the finish line. The oldest went off to locate friends and coaches with my stern admonishments to pay attention to the announcements over the speaker so they would not miss their specific contests and the time to line up. Many of my daughter's friends had their suits on, but wore coverups of one sort or another or had large-sized towels wrapped and knotted around themselves. We spoke to several acquaintances and were settled down to enjoying what promised to be a fun day when I felt my husband stiffen slightly beside me where he was sitting when they called for my daughter's age and category. To this day, so far in the future from that one, I cannot even remember which was her first event. I looked to tray and determine what he was looking at, and it was our daughter who was lining up (minus her towel) at her place in the swimming lanes.

With a calm, seemingly unruffled expression he said in an aside to me, "Where did she get that suit?"

"We got it this week. She had completely outgrown last years."

"And you allowed her to flaunt her body in something like that?"

Trying to keep everything looking normal, and keeping my voice down I replied, "I feel hers is appropriate and not revealing in any way. Look at the other girls. She is so proud and excited. Look, she is waving at us and smiling. Don't ruin it for her, please."

I prayed he would embarrass her and cause a scene. There was some relief when he said, waving back at her like any proud parent and said in a moderate voice to me, "I will take care of this later, when we are home. I cannot believe you allowed this. Have you no shame? That is your daughter out there. First it was the nagging about makeup and dating and now this. It is so getting out of hand."

I felt a small (very small) measure of relief that the consequences would be temporarily postponed and any confrontations not be allowed to ruin the children's day. Perhaps he would have softened some by the evening. I knew this was unlikely, but once in a while he took his gripes out on me, with a milder version of his displeasure for the children.

The starting signal was given and I watched my daughter's lithe figure hit the water. My husband surprised me by showing his unexpected support for her effort by standing to urge her on as she easily pulled to a quick pace in the lead. The results would be given at the awards ceremony after all the events finished but it was very clear she had won. She lifted herself from the water, grabbed her towel from her brother, who had been holding it at the finish line for her, and quickly wrapped and knotted it around herself before looking up to the stands and grinning at she held a "thumbs-up" sign to us.

What should it be? The good news or the bad news first about that day? When I looked at the photos we got back from the Base Exchange where we had them developed, they looked like any other family pictures of that day. Be smiles from the award platform as each of our children placed no lower than third in any of their categories. There were a couple of ties to their credit, but the rest were clear cut victories. Any parent should have been very proud for such a showing. Trying to be gracious as others congratulated us (and the children), I mentally determined that I would not let him spoil their accomplishments. I set out to brag about and to them, something they were unused to.

While the children and I basked in their successes, my husband was giving what I always saw from him: his back-handed manner of giving praise. When he accepted the invitation to join some of the other family for dinner at the popular restaurant just outside the base, I was surprised (but pleased) that the kids' glorious day would be extended for this almost unheard-of experience of eating with their friends.

One of the other wives looked at me and said, "Wow, that daughter of yours did so well, didn't she? You must be very proud of her! Maybe she will end up at the Olympics one day."

I smiled to show I was not taking this compliment seriously, but I appreciated her words. My husband smiled at her too and replied, "Yes, she did good. Although she needs to apply herself as diligently to her academic endeavors."

The woman looked a little surprised and she said, "My daughter told me your daughter is on the Student Council, and the Honor Roll as well. It doesn't sound as if she is lacking in that department, either."

"Children should not be praised too lavishly," my husband told her and continued, "It is my personal belief that it makes them lazy. Yes, she gets good grades but there is always room for improvement and it doesn't come easy for her. She has to use the midnight oil often and study for those grades."

I never once saw him assist (or even offer) with any of the children's homework assignments. The only time he had anything to do with the school was to go speak with her home room teacher when we got a note that she had missed turning one assignment on time, which explained her lower than usual or expected grade. I was awed by her bravery as she handed him the note for his signature. Further, I was amazed that contrary to his usual ranting and raving when faced with either disobedience or poor performance by any of the children, he made an appointment with her home room teacher and gave instructions that as punishment for this transgression on her part, she was to bring every single book from every single class she had home every day for the next two weeks whether she had homework from any of the subjects or not. I wondered how forcing her to carry the weight of all her books each day was teaching her anything except how heavy her textbooks. Later in life when she had a son of her own and computers and the internet came into existence, she mentioned to me that children had things so much easier than when she was growing up.

She asked me "Remember when Dad made me carry all my books home every day for two weeks? How much easier for me if I could have just gone online and done extra assignments."

Now, as the children chattered, I noticed while the other children (for the most part) looked at the children's menu and made their own decisions about what they would eat, mine looked at the menu and then deferred to their father for what their choices were. It would seem their exuberance for the day could not be dimmed. This day would be long remembered and I was happy for them.

One tiny little word of praise, I thought. *Would it hurt for him, their own father to give each of them their due and hand out one tiny little personal bit of praise?*

I had no appetite, dreading the evening to come when we got home. I knew the confrontation that would come would take away the glitter and shine from this thus far happy day and I felt the unfairness of it. As I glanced at him now and then during the evening, *I couldn't help but under (as I had so many times before) what had changed him? Was it me? I was so in love with him when we first married. I had tried all our married life to please him. I felt there was no sin I had ever committed which deserved the Jekyll-Hyde transformation from the happy, handsome, and optimistic person he used to be. Surely there was something basically wrong in his personality and upbringing with his stern and miserable mother which had set the stage for this brutal, uncompromising, unhappy man?*

Finally (all too soon in my eyes) goodnights we said, children bid goodbye to their friends and we were on our way home.

My youngest had fell asleep on the ride home and I picked him up to carry him to his bed. Usually my husband would do this chore, but I knew he was (should I classify it as relishing?) preparing for the confrontation with our daughter about the swimsuit.

I sighed as I lay down my son, took his tennis shoes off, and lightly covered him. The yelling had already begun. The other two boys had taken this opportunity to escape to their rooms. I am sure that they did not know what has raised their father's ire, but whatever it was, they were just glad they were not the target. It wasn't that they felt no sympathy for their sister; far from it. There was pity for her, but mixed with it was relief that they had escaped his wrath this time.

"Why are you mad at me, Dad? What did I do? Whatever it was, I am so sorry. Why are you angry with me?"

"Because you embarrassed me in front of everyone there."

Puzzled, she looked at him, then to me, then back to him as she asked, "What did I do to embarrass you?"

"Dressed like some kind of slut, that's what! Where is that obscene swimsuit you wore, flaunting your body for all to see. That's what. Where is it?"

It took a minute for her to understand what he was saying, and then she looked down at the swimsuit, wrapped in her towel she was carrying in her arms.

"My swimsuit? It's here, Dad. What's wrong with it?" She looked to me and I stepped closer to her and said, "I was with her and I approved of it. She didn't sneak off and buy it with her friends. I'm her mother and I felt she looked decent and I was not ashamed of her. I think you are looking at this wrong. All the suits we saw in the stores were like this. She had completely outgrown last year's suit."

"So, you let her dress like a whore, you, her own mother. You say you have no shame. What kind of mother are you? That you would let her wear such a thing?"

Then he turned to her and said, "Take that piece trash and throw it in the garbage right now. I never want to see you in anything that obscene again. And you," he said, turning to me, "If you cannot judge what you provide for our children, I will take her shopping for what she needs. I'll wager that if I went tomorrow to find her another suit, I would be able to find a one piece which would be appropriate for a decent young lady to wear."

It ended with my daughter cowering before him with tears and then him watching as she threw the suit in the trash bin. As she did that he said, "You both disgusted me today. You, "he said, pointing at her, "Get upstairs and go to bed. Keep this is mind the next time you let those harlot friends of your influence you against your upbringing."

He turned to me and said, "And you…see if you can guide our children to make better choices. What's next? Sitting down and serving them alcohol with you as equals?"

He stormed off and I slowly exhaled the breath it seemed like I had been holding forever. As soon as he was settled in his recliner with his beer and the day's newspaper, I went to my daughter's bedroom and holding her in my arms, tried to comfort her.

"How could he call me those names? I'm not a bad girl, Mom."

"I know you're not. This is really my fault. I shouldn't have let you pick that one. There was nothing indecent about it. You need never be ashamed of your body. God gave it to you and as long as you act appropriately, with your innocence and Christian faith, you can hold your head up high."

I wiped her tears and held her close.

"I hate him, Mom."

I pulled back from her and looked into her eyes.

"No, you don't hate him. You hate the way he behaves. He's your father."

"I hate the way he behaves. I hate the way he humiliates me and the boys. I hate his unfair rules. I hate not being able to do what other girls my age are allowed to do. I wish he would go away on a longer mission. I pray all the time for him to be deployed again. We are so happy when he is gone."

While I continued to hold her in my arms she said, "You know it's true, too. You just want to pretend otherwise. I wasn't surprised he didn't have a single congratulations to the boys or about how we did in today's competition. I do hate him, and I can't wait until I am old enough to leave this family and have a normal life. I just hope I don't marry the first man who asks me, just to escape him."

I was horrified at what she was saying. "Don't even say such a thing. You will graduate high school and escape by going away to college. I will not stand by and watch you make the same mistakes I have with my life. You're too smart, too strong for that."

Finally, she quit sniffling, and assured me she was okay, and I left her to go say goodnight to the boys. They asked about her and I reassured them she was fine.

Going back, I viewed that day and it's resulting confidences my daughter had shared with me, I began to see what staying with this monster was doing; not just to me, but to my children.

What memories would they have about their childhood if I did not gather myself and provide them with role models of good, loving, patient and understanding families.

I asked myself if this is what I had envisioned as my life when I left my horrible childhood behind me, expecting him to be my knight in shining armor?

Chapter

SEVEN

--- --- ⚜ --- ---

I do not believe nor did I then, at sixteen that I am a brave person. Often later in life when I watched the bravery exhibited by some women, I am awed by their determination to set and reach goals for themselves. I am not ignoring the effect being abused during my childhood, then additionally eighteen years of marriage by the monster of a man certainly succeeded in tearing down any self-confidence or ability to believe in myself. And yet somehow through faith, friends, angels along the way, creeping into my life began to grow a determination for escape. For a better life for me and my children.

Once I admitted to myself that I must be realistic; no more pipe-dreams of some hazy or magical happening which would change everything. I *knew* if I waited until I got enough courage to face my husband in a real confrontation and tried to leave him, he might kill me. It sounds far-fetched and like something from a fiction book, but this was no cursory imaginative feeling on my part. The physical abuse had been steadily increasing in violence, both towards me and my children. I had no real resources and support system therefore no one would come to my aide and face up to him for me. I reasoned, and rightly so, that I would be "on my own". Only someone who had seen it or lived through similar situations could understand the overwhelming fear I had for this man.

There would be no calvary coming to my rescue, no brave bodyguards. I did realize however, I couldn't face him down in person. I would have to attempt the escape when he was on one of his lengthy TDY missions. And I would have to have a real plan…the money to get away, a place where we could go and have the most safety. I would, of course, have to take the car. And most important of all, I would have to have a job. Mentally, before he left for a year in Tripoli, I began my list. Just the very thought of his enraged face if I were to face him in person and announce I was leaving.

I later wondered if he was surprised when we saw him off at the airport (for what was to be the last time) and for the first time in any of these "goodbyes", I did not cry as usual.

Mentally, when he got on that plane that time, he was gone from me and our life together. Now I just had to make it true.

The one true friend I had at the time was another angel in my life. My husband and I had about two thousand dollars in our savings. Not much to start a new life with four children, no job skills, and living in a small three bedroom rented house. It was worth considerably more in the early seventies. It was a joint account and she advised to take all but maybe five dollars, because he would try to cut off all my meager resources. She told me that in Texas, all funds or acquisitions we had accumulated since marriage would be fifty-fifty split, so not to put it in an account in my name. While others might think it naive of me to trust my friend with all I had in the world and nothing but her word she would return it when I got divorced, I had her deposit the total amount in her own account.

Next, I began taking typing and shorthand at the local community school. I took these classes in the evenings from 7:00 p.m. until nine. It was perfect for me. I had time to make sure they had supper and were well into their homework when I left, and I was home in time to supervise baths and bedtime. Then I would study my own assignments. My eldest daughter freely gave of her own time to dictate to me so I could work on getting my shorthand speed up. When I think back to that period of time, what a difference a recorder would have made! Or, an electric typewriter or computer. Instead I had a Smith-Corona manual I had purchased from a pawn shop.

These classes were held at the close school where my children attended during the day. It was a rather large complex of an elementary school from Kinder through second, a large third through fifth grade, a middle school of sixth through eighth and a high school. Most of the students were from the nearby Air Force base, and local farmers' children.

Meanwhile during the day while my three oldest children were at school, I kept a little four-year-old along with my own youngest daughter. This gave me some extra money in my escape fund I didn't have to explain to my husband. The fund grew slowly, but I found other ways to supplement it with just the children and I, we did not have the unnecessary prime meals we were used to having when he was there. We ate a lot of macaroni and cheese, biscuits and gravy, hot dogs, hamburgers, meat loaf, sandwiches, tuna, peanut butter and jelly and other filling, and what is called "comfort food" in today's menus. The kids didn't purchase school lunches anymore, except for Fridays—Pizza days—which I felt they deserved as a reward for less fried chicken, pork chops and *never* steaks.

The base movie theatre didn't usually get "first run" movies, but they were still movies my children had not seen before and the tickets were cheap. This was long before the VCR and DVD were to come.

We did have a television, but shows were rather limited and cable special channels were a long way off.

Still, we were happy. There was more laughter in our home, and the boys played Little League on baseball teams and the rest of us tried to go to each game and cheer them on to victory.

I loved my classes and wondered why I did not feel this type of enthusiasm for school years ago when I hated it? Even I could see the results. The day I successfully finished a timed typing test at fifty words per minute (generally the required number when applying for an office job) I was thrilled beyond words. The shorthand was a little more difficult, but the improvement was showing, weekly, even daily at times.

When I could successfully take dictation and then transcribe it with a very minor word or two (usually unimportant because using the before and after text of the word I could figure it out in transcribing) I began to prepare for finding a job.

I applied at the school district where the children were attending, and was surprised when I got a call for an interview. I was beyond nervous when I went for the interview but all the people, I met that day were equally friendly and helpful. The superintendent's secretary interviewed me, and later was to become a cherished friend.

I was hired as the school's attendance clerk. It didn't pay a lot, but it was my first real job and I was both proud and excited to be earning a real paycheck. It helped a great deal that since my work would be done at the middle school where my eldest son went to school, it would be was convenient for me to drop my youngest at the preschool program (held at the elementary school, along with my second son, second grade), then my eldest daughter at the high school and finally my eldest son and myself at the middle school. Even though I would be using very little of my new secretarial skills, I still kept practicing on them. The superintendent's secretary told me that there would be a chance for me to move up to a better paying slot somewhere in the district so I put forth every effort to do move that just what was required, but helped whenever and wherever I could with other duties. I manned the front desk in the middle school, organized my little office clerk students in their collection of attendance slips clipped to the outside of each teacher's door and filled out an attendance report for the middle school each day with copies for the file, the middle school principal, superintendent's secretary. I monitored the calls from parents about their children kept at home due to illness. As time went on more duties were added to my responsibility especially when I mastered some initially assigned to me, and I demonstrated I had other skills to offer as well.

I was sent to check out the girl's bathroom sometime to look for loiterers or those trying to skip a class. Since my office was in the middle school, there wasn't as much of this as the high school had thus, it became my job to monitor their bathrooms' as well. Many times, I caught student smokers. These students were usually defiant, and unfazed about being required to go to the office where parents were contacted for a meeting before punishments were assigned.

The district did have a truancy officer and it was also my job to notify him in writing when any student's attendance showed unexcused or too frequent absences. One afternoon, the assistant principal at the high school, his secretary, and myself walked around the grounds of the high school because his office had received an anonymous tip that several students were skipping class and hanging out in the back of the school. The back of the high school was fenced off to keep students from going along the small creek bed which bordered the back of the school property

133

and acted as a barrier to the land that belonged to a farmer and bordered the school property. The three of us were quietly walking along this order when we reached a part of the chain link fence which had been cut and left with enough of a space for people to get through to the creek. A we noted the fence, we heard several voices coming from nearer to the creek itself.

The vice-principal was in the lead, and the other secretary and I brought up the rear. As we made our way forward, I know we were not prepared by what we saw when we emerged from the tall weeds, small saplings and grasses.

There were several students sitting under one of the bigger trees, laughing amongst themselves; smoking and watching something beyond our view. When the vice-principal yelled, "Hey! All of you! Come on up here where I am. Right now!"

Immediately they scattered and ran, cutting through the brush like it wasn't even there.

We could plainly see what they had been looking at with such interest and ribald humor. There was a boy and a girl engaged in sexual intercourse on a spread-out coat. The boy's jeans were down around his knees, and the girl's skirt and sweater up over her breasts and who knows where her panties were?

Both the other secretary and I gasped in surprise, and when the vice-principal yelled again, "Come on, get on up here, and get your clothes together the boy said the most surprising thing of all, "Wait a minute. Just wait a minute, can't you? I'm almost done here."

Then the vice-principal started down the slope to the two students and the girl screamed and attempted to push the boy off her.

The vice principal said loudly, "You're finished right now. This minute. Get yourself up and pull your pants up."

The vice principal turned to we two women and said, "You two go back to my office and write a report up and look up parent notification numbers on these two. I'll escort these back and we will keep them in the office until we reach the parents and they come to meet with me in my office"

We turned to head back to the school and then I looked back at him. He was standing next to the girl and I saw where the panties were. She had them wadded in one hand and she had started to cry. The boy was defiant and angry but certainly didn't seem afraid.

"Should we tell the parents what they were doing?" I asked hesitantly.

Wryly I thought he said, "I don't think either of you would be comfortable explaining that, do you?"

I shook my head negatively and he said, "No, just say they have violated major school policies and they won't be released from school today until the parents come to pick them up from my office."

The other secretary and I went back for the school and the vice-principal added, "And have the maintenance men come see what they are going to need to repair this fence as soon as possible. Might help to have some "No Trespassing" signs put up on our side of the fence as well."

And we walked back to the school the other secretary chuckled a little and said, "I'd say they violated school policies alright; fornicating on school grounds."

"Wait a minute," I said, grinning, now that no one else was around, "technically it wasn't on school grounds because doesn't the fence divide the two properties?"

"You're probably right, but I'll let the boss determine that."

"I'm glad I don't have to talk to the parents, aren't you?"

"Yeah. What will be their punishment, do you think?"

"Either suspension for a certain period of time or maybe even expulsion for the rest of the semester r even the year. I bet they wish they glad only been smoking, don't you?"

She laughed along with me. "You know, I took a Human Sexuality class at the university last year," she said and continued, "and I remember discussing how different the hormone levels, in fact, the entire make up of sexual behavior is totally different for the sexes. The profession said that males reach their so-called sexual peak in their late teens and earlier twenties and women not reach theirs until their late thirties. No wonder there are so many older women lusting after the young studs."

"I don't know if I believe that," I said. But when I remembered the attraction between Howard and myself although it had not amounted to anything, really, there was something definitely there.

"I can't get over him being so brazen as to asking the Vice Principal to allow him to "finish".

"Well, he was definitely in the mood, wasn't he?"

"How do you think this episode would look on his college resume and application? He is a senior this year, after all."

That afternoon she invited me to go with her for the faculty meeting for the high school teachers. She confided in me that she would not be at the school district next year. She was expecting and planned to stay home after the birth of her first baby.

"There will be an opening for my position and you should apply. It would mean more money, more responsibility and more status."

"But I have no real experience for something like that."

"So what? I didn't either when I started here. Your title would be secretary to the high school principal, but you would be working for both he and the vice-principal and both of them are wonderful to work for. You would still be off during the summer months, except two weeks prior to school opening to get everything ready and help the registrar with getting the new students in the right classes for next year. You'd get to use the skills you have been learning and the days go fast, it's not a boring job. You'd like it."

The more I thought about it the more excited I became. The next real challenge I had was to find another place to live. I did not want to still living in the little rental house when my husband arrived home. I wanted more security than that. I even envisioned buying a home for the kids and I. Did I have enough money for down payment and closing? Could I get one with low down payments? The children and I began looking at houses for sale on the weekends and they were as excited as I was.

Meanwhile I became must ore devious in the letters I wrote to my husband. I filled hi in on everything the kids were doing and what I did to take the car in for inspection, the grades the kids were getting. But surely, he had to notice there was no longing from me in his absence and I seemed to be managing alone better than I ever had in the past.

Two things happened during that year that I would never have forecasted in my life. In the fall as I moved towards my first full time position in the high school office, I began a relationship with Don, the Vice-principal in our office. I don't know how it happened, really, except

I was ripe for some warmth and approval in my life. Married at sixteen, eighteen years of bitter, abusive life with someone who beat me and my children, humiliated us stripped me of any self-confidence I was extremely vulnerable to anyone who showed me any kindness or understanding.

My husband had already cheated on me twice; once with the little high school girl and once with a nurse he met while working his part-time job. Both times I had forgiven him, and trying to patch our marriage up. Howard had showed me that I could be attracted to other people, and though I felt it morally wrong to commit adultery, I loved for some connection to another human being who could see me as I really was and withhold judgement.

It began simply enough. Innocent teasing and joking in the office, seeking each other to sit by in faculty meetings and at lunchtime. He was a big bear of a man; friendly and happy, and generous with his praise for a job well done. He was married, his wife Ann, taught school in the high school. Probably the main guilt I felt was because I liked her. However, there didn't seem to be a closeness in their marriage and I sensed their biggest tie was the two young boys they shared.

I don't even really remember how it started…My heart began to flutter when he came in the room unannounced, he asked my opinion often (which made me feel he respected and trusted it).

Finally, one evening when my eldest daughter was home early and watching the others, he invited me to go for a drink with him after we got off.

"Will Jane be there?"

"No, she's on the planning committee for the Junior/Senior prom and both boys have scout meetings. I'm at loose ends and thought I could persuade you to come have a drink. How about it?"

I have to admit it, I immediately thought, *here it goes, my husband is gone, after several of the bachelor teachers trying to "hit" on me since I started my new job. He's just wanting to try his luck to get in my pants. Then I was ashamed for thinking this. He had never been inappropriate with me about anything.*

I hesitated the barest minimum seconds and then agreed. There was a small out-of-the-way little cocktail longue not too far from the outlying part of the school district and we went there. I called my daughter and told her I was in a meeting and would be home in a little while and she seemed pleased I was going to do something fun for myself.

We each drove our own car, and he waited to open my door and escort me inside. His hand was warm across my lower back, and we chose a small table in the far corner.

Nervously I looked around. I realized I had been just a baby when I married. Not old enough to drink or drive and I had never been to a cocktail longue or bar before, even with my husband. The closest had been to the NCO club on base.

When the waitress came to take our order, Don asked me what I would like, I didn't know what to say. I didn't drink. Not even wine.

"What are you having?" I asked him.

"Jack Daniels on the rocks."

"I don't know what to order because I don't drink."

He laughed and said, "Better order one of those frothy women's drinks then. Maybe something with pineapple and juice and coconut and whipped cream."

"Oh," I said, delightedly, "I love pineapple and coconut. That sounds good."

I did love the drink and learned it was called a Pina Colada. At first, I drank part of it a little fast; it was delicious and so cold but Don said, "Take it a little slow, it tastes like fruit juice, but it could hit you all of a sudden since you're not used to it. You're driving, you know." There was no music, except for a piano player. He had a big glass mug on the piano with money in it and when I asked, Don told me he played for tips. You could go up and ask for a special song and he would play it for you.

Right off the bat I leveled with him about my nervousness. "Are you going to tell Jane you took me for a drink?"

He looked a little surprised at my directness and he raised his eyebrows and asked me, "Why not? Do you feel it was wrong of me to ask you? Is there something illicit about this?"

"Isn't there?"

"I guess it all depends on the interpretation. Do you feel guilty?"

"A little," I said.

He laughed. "Well, don't. A drink is just a drink after all."

He changed the subject then and we began to talk about our children (he was crazy about those boys), our pets, our jobs, some of the students. We laughed a lot and I had such a good time. Within that conversation I learned about his birth family and I began to share some things about my life.

At one point he said, "Why didn't you ever go to college?"

I felt myself blush and I said, embarrassedly, "Who, me? You've got to be kidding. I only went through tenth grade and have just a G.E.D."

He looked genuinely surprised at this. "That's hard to believe. You catch on to things so fast. You know, it's not too late. Weren't you taking some courses at the community college that meets at our school evenings and weekends?"

"Just secretarial courses to help me get this job. I don't think I'm smart enough to dream of college classes."

"You should never say something like that. It is so defeatist. It's as though you are programing yourself for failure before you give yourself a fair chance."

"What kind of a guy is your husband?" he continued.

I hesitated for a few seconds. When I paused, he asked, "Does he drink?"

"Not excessively," I answered.

His eyebrows raised a little. "No? I'm a little surprised."

"Why is that?"

"Well, for one thing, a lot of military men drink; exceptions to the rule, but a lot do. For another, you deem very reluctant to voice an opinion sometimes, even when it turns out you are right about something. That's usually a sign of a controlling partner in there somewhere."

"So, you think I am too timid, too passive to be independent or have my own opinions?"

He laughed softly. "Not exactly. I minored in psychology for my graduate work and I am really fascinated at what makes people tick."

That struck a chord in me as he said it. I had often thought if I ever had had the chance to go to college, I'd like to take some psychology classes.

"So, does that mean you have wondered about what makes *me* tick?"

"Not just you—everyone, from students to other teachers and the staff at the high school. For example, what do you think of our principal, the illustrious Mr. Stevens?"

"Well, he's good to work for…He's patient, even with the problem students. He seems to have a strong faith, talks about his church all the time."

"Those things seem true to me, as well; but have you noticed that he is very, very, what I would call *strait-laced* and rigid?"

"Example, please."

"hum…Well, the other day he called me into his office to show me something. Can you guess what it was?"

"Not a clue," I said, wondering.

"I'll give you two examples, related to the same beliefs. Th first one was when he took me to the big window in his office and pointed out a certain car. He asked me, "See that car, Don?"

When I acknowledged it by asking, "What about it?" he enlightened me by saying several times a week an attractive red-haired woman drives up in that car, parks it and waits for a big 'old cowboy in a red pickup truck. She gets in his truck with him and they leave for a couple of hours or so. Before school lets out though, he brings her back, they both drive on in their respective vehicles."

"Not getting the point," Don continued, "I asked him 'So what?' and he told me he was thinking of getting the license plates and using a friend in the sheriff's office to find out who the vehicles belonged to."

"What in the world for?" I asked Don.

"He told me he believed he had caught those two red-handed having an affair and that he believed one or both were probably married and cheating on their partners."

"You're kidding me."

Don grinned, wryly I thought and continued. "Yes, and he wanted them to get caught."

"What made him think it was any of his business?"

"His church is very strict about the ten commandments and about consequences for sins.

Especially, I might add, about sins involving morality; human sins to do with sex. Makes me wonder how his and Margorie's personal life is."

I did not comment on his remark except to ask, "So what do you think he intended or was even thinking of doing about his theory about these sinners?"

"I think he wanted them caught and some kind of severe consequences to fall on both of them. But," he mused thoughtfully, "I also sense he was at least just a little bit envious."

"But why would he be envious? He's been married all those years to the same woman and I always though he seemed happy."

"He's the kind of man who preaches righteousness but all the wall he longs for something exciting in his life, something bold and risky. He's afraid his life will come and got as it is now; mildly successful, boring, and certainly predictable."

I thought about this and then I asked "You said two examples, what was the second one?"

"To demonstrate the extent of his disapproval of anything so sinful it exhibits the weakness of human frailty, like God having made humans attractive to the opposite gender, like..." He paused here and queried, "Have you read Dante's works?"

I think no, I know he was very surprised when I nodded in the affirmative and said, "Yes, and I know where you're heading with this—where Dante put the people with sins of the flesh—in the very outer limit as he considered it the least series offense against God because God had made us attractive to each other."

"Yes, exactly! Well to get back to our hypocritical principal and his war against sinners, remember when those boys and girls broke into the school and partied in the gym that time?"

"Yes, what about it?"

"What was their punishment?"

"Hum...I believe it was two days suspension, and volunteer service, cleanup the gym and athletes had to miss two games."

"Right, sounds pretty fair, wouldn't you say?"

"Yes, I think so. There wasn't any expensive or extensive lasting damage."

"What did he fight so hard to punish the young couple having sex; not even on the school grounds technically, I might add? What was his recommendation for them?"

"He wanted to expel them and make sure the senior's records confirmed notices to be added to his college applications."

"Right. I rest my case."

"Didn't the school board overrule his recommendations and give suspensions and a research paper done in several afterschool sessions on the topic of morality?"

"Yes, again proving my point. He's obsessed with pepe being puritans. He would have been perfect living in the age where people like Hester Prynne in Hawthorne's "Scarlet Letter". No sign of forgiveness in the story for Hester and none from our principal either."

When I later tried to be fair about my descriptions of Don, I no longer failed to notice his fine mind and intelligent conversations as well as his wonderful sense of humor and his physical attractiveness.

"I guess you've read that classic as well, haven't you?" Don asked me that evening.

When I nodded, embarrassed, he said shaking his head "And this woman calls herself stupid."

He called the barmaid over and asked for our tab and said, "Well, this has really been enjoyable. We'll have to try and do it again sometimes. The committee meeting is over by now and Jane's probably gone to pick up the boys from scouts unless the leader dropped them off."

Curious, I asked, "Will she ask where you've been?'

"Nope. She doesn't really play check up on me and if she did, I'd tell her. After all, there's nothing wrongful about having a drink with a friend, is there?"

Again, I was embarrassed and I mentally cursed my propensity to blush at the slightest provocation.

"Often, I go play a game of pool with a friend or if there is another high school football game close by, I go to it. Jane is a good person and she trusts me. I am assuming by your reaction and questions that it isn't like that in your marriage?"

I shook my head no and thought to myself *How wonderful to live in a trusting and caring relationship like that with another person.*

I wondered what the atmosphere would be like at work the next day. As I laid in bed that evening, I still had a pleasant glow, I assumed was from the drink and I drifted off wishing my husband could be more like Don.

This relationship I eventually found myself in was not something immediately jumped into—not by either Don or myself. It began as a special friendship and an appreciation for the things we had in common. Each of us had a need which was not being met; mine was for acceptance and security for a feeling of safety worthiness. I think his was a feeling he was being taken for granted, and the "middle age crazy sort of reassessment of his life and a feeling humans often get when they no longer feel young and they have already achieved most of the goals they had set up for their lives.

Because we shared a bond in our love of reading, we began to share books. When either of us finished a particularly interesting or entertaining book, we brought it to school and traded it to the other with our critique.

I no longer remember exactly how long it was until we began to meet more regularly and more often. I *do* remember (most vividly) when our relationship changed and oved into the physical stage. We had met at our favorite place, a slightly out of the city heavily wooded roadside picnic park for drivers. There were no other vehicles there, it was quiet and had an "out of the world" sort of atmosphere I don't know how we got on the subject, but somehow I was telling about the doctor in his Don about going to the base doctor for an appointment and how my husband had beat me up the night before, and make-up or not, nothing could hide the black eye or the bruise on my cheek.. The doctor had tried to be sympathetic without putting blame and he told me that sometimes our knights in shining armor don't turn out to be such knights. Then he asked me if he could do anything to help my situation. He offered to make a phone call and said there were procedures in place which would allow him to intervene for my children or myself. He also cautioned me often these situations escalate but they never go away on their own without any attention. Somewhere in the conversation when the doctor got back to going over the tests we had done, he reviewed my request for having an Intrauterine Copper Contraceptive put in place and taking me off the birth control pills and I had told him "My husband thinks I am too skinny and that it's the birth control bills." The doctor had replied to me, "Well, *I* don't think you are too skinny and *I* am your physician, but I also don't feel there's a problem with us changing from the pills to the IUD.

When I was relating this meeting with the doctor to Don, I started crying, and he reached out and pulled me to his chest. He allowed me to get my tears under control and then, keeping his arms around me he said, "What a sorry bastard."

He was one of the few men who still carried a handkerchief and he pulled it out and wiped my face. Then, it seemed like the most natural thing in the world for him to tilt my face up and kiss me.

It was easy to pretend we were totally alone. He held me and then he kissed me again and he whispered, "I agree with your doctor. You are definitely not too skinny. In fact, you're perfect. I have heard some of the teachers ask you how you have such a figure after giving birth to four children."

"Really?"

Now he laughed. "Really."

"I hate to bother you with all my problems."

"You're not bothering me," he said."

"Well, that surprises me," I told him. "I could swear you were getting very bothered."

Now he really laughed.

"Well, I am, in that way. You're certainly right."

Softly I said, "Let's get in the back where the gear shift and steering wheel and drink holder are not all in the way."

"Are you sure about this?"

"Very."

We climbed in back and stretched out, and it was all very in just a few minutes. I have to admit I did not get much relief or satisfaction except that I enjoyed the arms and the kissed and cuddling part. Immediately he began apologizing about being so quick. He kept saying, "I know it wasn't good for you, and I'm sorry, but I just couldn't control myself. I have been wanting to make love to you since I first met you."

I kept reassuring him I was fine and to lighten up the situation I added, "So, all along I thought you were attracted to my fine mind and our conversations about literature."

When he took me to my car, opened the door and ushered me inside, he leaned over and kissed me again. "Drive safe, please drive safe. I don't want to lose you now that I have found you."

Now I look back and even alone, I blush, thinking about the battle going on between my sincere (abet my old-fashioned and outdated feelings that adultery was still wrong, wrong, wrong) belief I was "giving in" because I felt sorry for Don or because I felt I "owed" this physicality in our relationship to him, the first male to ever show me kindness and understanding. Unbeknown to Don, I shamefully equated this relationship to two kinds of food: gourmet (which most definitely involved true love, understanding and forever planning; and comfort food which was good for the moment and was a temporary fix for the *"real"* thing. So, I mentally questioned my own motives (out of shame and guilt) was I just settling for the hamburger when all along I was looking for the steak? That I spent mental time trying to excuse or justify it, truth was I was ashamed of myself, both during the affair and even I must admit for the rest of my life.

How weak a person I was to try to excuse *my own* behavior by labeling my part in the entire affair as a kind of "thank you" for his goodness towards me. When I admitted this, it was almost ludicrous I could believe it. I was very disappointed in myself. *It's as though I said to him (of course I didn't and wouldn't) 'You've been so terribly kind and good to me; I'm offering my body to you in payment. The only real truth I finally admitted to myself was that I didn't love him in the same way he thought he loved me and yet…I didn't want to give up our relationship and him. What a coward I had found myself to be. And what a dishonest and selfish friend to Don. When, once in a while I tried to be completely honest with myself, I thought, 'What is the difference between me and a common prostitute? Am I being honest with him when I let him believe I felt the same towards him as he confessed he felt about me?, Admitting that I know I don't love him, yet I accept his kindnesses and support and allow the physical side of our intimacy in exchange?*

When I once told him in the early stages of our physical relationship, "I don't like being like a teen-ager, in the back seat of an automobile with you on a dark road somewhere", we began to meet in motel rooms.

Once when he had a coach conference in another city, I got someone to take care of my children although my eldest was capable and competent enough to be put in charge and I joined him there. Of course, I did not go anywhere near the conference instead he insisted I take some money and go get my hair done and a manicure while he was in meetings. Then we met in a very nice restaurant for dinner and even went to a country-western dancehall and had a wonderful time. He was a good dancer and we laughed a lot and I could almost believe in what he was saying about a future. The next morning, we went out to breakfast with me still guiltily looking around everywhere, waiting for someone to recognize one or both of us and call out a cheerful greeting, then we went bowling. I had never been and he had great fun in helping me pick out a good weight ball and in gently laughing when at first, I got those "gutter" balls. It was a wonderful week end and I cried silently all the way as I drove home.

I don't know if I was surprised or had a vague expectation that it would come, but Don began to speak of leaving his family. His intentions gained in strength after I filed for divorce.

I had found a lawyer downtown, close to the county courthouse where my petition for divorce would be eventually heard. Feeling guilty and somewhat shameful, I asked him if there was any chance my husband could try and get custody of my children.

"No," he answered bluntly, "For one thing, the assignment he has in the military keeps him in constant uncertainty as to how long or where he will be stationed and any judge wants to see children have at least a semblance of stability."

Gathering my courage, I blurted out, "What if he tries to say I'm not a good parent because...because I haven't always been faithful to him while he's gone?"

"Just curiosity of course, but have you?"

"No."

"Has he?"

"No."

"Well, there you go. Not that it matters. He could have photos of you and a man coming out of different motel rooms all the time and that in the judge's eyes does not prove you are an unfit mother. In fact, one might say it's contrary to that because you didn't bring this man into the children's home or life. No, I'll take care of all that."

When he asked me for the real reason, I wanted a divorce, I told him truthfully about the eighteen years of verbal, emotional, and physical abuse the children and I had gone through.

He listened intently and then he said in what would become his familiar, brisk and "to the point" way, "I can smell a lie and I don't smell one here. I believe you. I have had my share of clients most of whom I have turned down as clients who have lied about being abused but I can hear it in your voice and see it in your eyes and quite frankly, in your tentative and uncertainty about what you are doing. Don't worry anymore. Let me do the worrying.

He did not charge me for that initial meeting and the low amount he set for his services I found out later, indicated he had sympathy for me and my plight and was really very sincere about his desire to help me get through this.

After that, he was fully, completely and always on my side. He thought of all his female clients as his "Girls "The only thing he asked me when I got ready to leave his office was, "What took you so long?"

"Fear."

"And how did you overcome that fear?"

"Friends."

He said he would get the paperwork ready for my signature and get a court date on the calendar and call me as things progressed.

"I don't want to live the rest of my life in a lie," Don said once. "I want to marry you and stop hiding my feelings. I want to show you what life can be with two people who share the same hopes and who have a deep understanding of what is important and what is not."

If I did not show the same enthusiasm for his intentions, I did not deny them, either. I felt as though I was on some kind of merry-go-round, spinning furiously faster and faster with no hope of getting off.

Meanwhile, I continued adding regularly to my "escape stash". One day when I arrived home from work, the kitchen floor was awash with water where the refrigerator had stopped working and all the ice had melted. I called a repairman out but the news was not god. He informed me it would cost more to try and get it repaired (partly because of its' age) than it would be to replace it. After he left, I mopped the mess up, then sat down on the floor and began to cry. I knew it was foolish and it didn't help anything. Tears were never a solution and I, of all people should accept and remember that. The children were trying hard to comfort me.

The youngest said, "Well, let's go get a new one, Mommy."

I had to smile at her simplistic and innocent solution.

"We don't have the money for that," I said.

"Well, you could write a check."

I thanked God again for blessing me with the resilience and humor which comes from a child. This comment coming from him reminded him of when I was pregnant with his little sister and I voiced my desire for another desire to "balance" our family at two and two. He had listened and then he said very seriously, "Well, don't worry Mama, if we get a boy and you save the receipt from the hospital bill, we can take the boy back and swap it for a girl."

This same child had wanted a candy bar at the store once and when I said I didn't have the money for candy, just milk he had said, "Well, you could write a check for the candy bar, couldn't you?"

I didn't even try to explain why I didn't want to write a check for a nickel, just giggled several times during the day when I thought about it again.

Now I laughed and hugged her before I said, "When you write a check you are promising that you have enough money in the bank to pay for the check, sweet pea, and we don't."

"Well, since it already late, and we haven't eaten, let's go spend some of the money we do have and get burgers and fries at the place down the road."

My eldest said, "Shouldn't we save that to help get a new refrigerator?"

"Well, it's not enough to really help. I think we deserve this and we'll worry about this tomorrow."

My eldest (an avid reader like me) said, "That's what Lillian Roth said in her autobiography remember, Mom? She tried so hard not to cry over her life by saying she would cry later, you remember the book you gave me?"

How could this child, coming from me, her uneducated, unsophisticated and emotionally hopeless mother, be so intelligent and so knowledgeable? It wasn't the first time I had asked myself this and I realized it was a strong force in the effort I was making to provide them with a better life.

I went to work the next day and shared my story of refrigerator woe and as we began to discuss it in the office (with teachers coming to check mailboxes and any memorandums before it was time to report to their classrooms), Jane and Don came in and I saw Don in conversation with his wife just inside his office. The door was open but I could tell they were in agreement about something.

Then Jane turned and said to me, "Hey, problem solved! Don and I just recently got one of those fancy new refrigerators, makes its own ice and defrosts itself you know, the thing they are advertising all the time?"

As we listened, she continued, "Well the company wouldn't give us much of a trade in for our old one, even wanted to charge us to haul it off so, we kept it. It works fine, not much to look at, has to use ice trays and be defrosted now and then when the frost builds up, but like the Little Red Engine That Could keeps right on chugging along. Keeps everything cold. Freezer is small, but we just keep it in the garage now with extra soft drinks for the boys."

"Yeah, and you have it. I can get the boss to meet me here, and if nothing is scheduled right before or after lunch, we can take it over and plug it in."

"Oh, I couldn't accept such a gift. And you said you're using it."

"Not really using it. No, Jane and I insist. Even the delivery is no charge. We won't accept 'no' for an answer."

Jane nodded her head as well and insisted.

Later I would add this generous gift to my backpack of guilt in my betrayal of Jane.

I did not live very far for the school in my little rented house and Don went to his home with Mr. Stevens (how strange I always called the principal by his titled name, Mr. Stevens but always thought of Don by his first name. It was not a break-down of respect or lack of courtesy. It just always seemed natural. Even the teachers would ask for him by first name when they came in the office to see him). They picked up the refrigerator and came back to the office, got me and we took it to my house. I was a little self-conscious about my little rental, but I kept it spotless even the carport where they backed up the truck and unloaded the refrigerator. It was a medium sized refrigerator, but very, very clean and the minute we plugged it in, it hummed into activity. Don and I filled the six ice trays and put them in the small freezer, and then we all went back to work.

An interesting sideline to this is that almost a year later when the children and I had found our home to purchase, we moved the same refrigerator with us and it kept on running, efficiently and faithfully even long after I no longer worked at the school.

Realizing that I had only so much time before my husband would be sent home to the states, I moved to put the next step of the plan in motion. My friend had been trying to help me find a job that paid more and offered a path in which I could have opportunities to move up. She advised me that I needed to think of not just surviving now, but the future. I agreed.

One morning she came to my office and when we took our coffee break that morning, she told me about a job posted on the jobs available with the county.

"It's a county position with lots of perks. Free parking each day, paid holidays, work throughout the summer, something you won't have here at the school and supplemental financial assistance if you sign up and take courses which further enhance your job skills."

"But wouldn't that mean working and living downtown? I love my job here, I like living in the area..."

"Yes, and I would hate for you to leave here, but we would still talk on the phone every day, we'd see each other on the weekends and the holidays and this would get you away from the base area, if they send him back here. "What are the qualifications?"

"Typing test, forty-five words per minute, hopefully with no errors and shorthand of seventy words per minute, good transcribing skills. Hours are eight to five, hour for lunch and two fifteen-minute breaks."

"Wouldn't I have to have some college hours?

"No, it's not for a probation officer or assistant, but for secretary to the Volunteer director."

"I've never heard of a volunteer director for probation officers."

"Actually, I think it would be right down your alley. No offense, girl, but you are practically a bleeding heart when it comes to helping the down and out. You're a great one for people deserving second chances. Look how many you gave hour husband before you finally wised up. You'd have to set an interview and go in for that and you could find out more about it."

"Well, I guess it wouldn't hurt to look into it."

"Yeah, and the offices are in the annex, right next to the county court house. There all kinds of lawyers there, you could find one to file your divorce and be right there for your court appearances when it's time for the case to be presented before the judge."

I thought about it and y pulse increased with the anxiety I suddenly felt. *Was I really going to do this? Was I going to go through it and escape?"*

Before I said anything else, she said, "A couple of drawbacks—"

"What?"

"The county has their paydays set up on a monthly basis. You're have to plan and budget carefully. Of course, assuming the judge awards child-support and assuming you're going to be new "ex" is decent about paying it, you might have it set up where you get it mid-month and that would help."

"I am so used to every other week…"

"I know, but I also know how determined you can be. You can do this."

"How much child-support do you think the judge would award?"

"I don't know, but you have four kids and they will take that, his salary, what you get paid or can expect in salary and expenses for each of you. That's the other thing. You need to go ahead and hire a divorce lawyer so he can guide you on the steps to take and what to expect. Besides, I think it takes about two months for a divorce hearing and a divorce to become final and real."

Then she said," And your children will have to change schools because they will be in a new school district"

"Oh, no. They love their schools. They are going to hate that."

"Perhaps not when they understand all the circumstances. And didn't you tell me once your daughters wanted to take dance and there's no place out here which offers extra-curricular classes in anything like that"

For the next several days I discussed everything with my friend and then I scheduled a day off, and made an appointment at the county Probation office. I admit there was not just an element of fear about many facets of my plan; the interview and testing, what to wear, how to locate the office so I could be on time, what questions I would ask about the details of the job, but also the sound of the job presented a strong interest for me. I did think I would enjoy working with people. After all, if the judge saw fit to give these people probation instead of sentencing them to jail or prison, they must have some good qualities, deserving a chance to turn their lives around. Maybe as the volunteer director's "Girl Friday" I would get to go to court with her sometimes I was fascinated by this possibility.

I set up a stand-by plan so if I was late due to traffic and distance coming back from the interview, my eldest daughter had keys and I had explained I had an appointment with a lawyer and she might have to be in charge until I got home if I was running late."

"When she heard the word "lawyer" her eye widened and she asked, "A lawyer? What for?"

"I have planned to discuss everything with you and your brother tonight when the little two are in bed, but basically I am considering filing for a divorce from your father."

I don't know what I had expected but certainly not her response. She reached out her arms and hugged me and she said, "Oh, Mother, I am so glad. I am so very glad. Yes, yes, and yes again. "Maybe…maybe," she said a bit mischievously, "I will live at home while I go to college. Maybe I won't try to get as far away as possible,"

"That's a little mean, don't you think?" I asked but smiled just a little.

Finally, one evening prior to the big interview, I took my two oldest into my bedroom after the two youngest were in bed and sat them down.

The next day when my friend asked me how our talk had gone, I said, "I was so surprised at their support. They are happy about it. My son even said it was about time and *we* should have done this a long time ago. They included themselves in the decision just as though they had been in on it from the beginning. And I had been almost afraid to talk to them."

"Afraid? Afraid of what? Your right to be happy? There is nothing to be afraid of. Listen, children are more perceptive and understanding than we give them credit for. What famous person said, 'The Only Thing We Have to Fear is Fear itself.'?"

"Oh, I know that one! I remember being so impressed when I read about it in school.

It was Franklin Delaware Roosevelt (March 4, 1933). His quote on his March 4, 1933 inauguration address was "The only thing we have to fear is fear itself."

"Smart-alec!" she laughed when she gently punched my shoulder.

"Says someone who has never be beaten by a bully."

"Bullies stop when someone has the courage to stand up to them and convince them they are no longer afraid."

"Did I ever tell you what he told me after he beat on me one of the last few times? I think he saw in my eyes how much I hated him and how much I wanted to leave him."

"What?"

"He said if I ever left him, he would wait and find a good place to hide no matter where I was, and he would step up with a gun and blow my fucking head off."

"Sure, he's going to threaten you with that. That's what bullies do to keep their victims in line. By the way," she added, "I believe that is the very first time I have ever heard you use the "F" word."

"I apologize. I know it embarrasses you. It does me too. I hate the word."

"Don't apologize. I view it as another advancement in your journey towards independence and freedom. Let your feelings show, voice your opinions-the men do it; I believe, to belittle and humiliate us."

"Well, it works, doesn't it?"

"Only if we let it. We need to fling it right back in their faces. And...we need to start raising our sons differently so the next generation of women has it easier."

Now we both laughed together. "Aren't we the brave ones?"

"Yeah, when we are by ourselves."

I never told my friend about Don and I but I often wondered what she would have thought or said if I had. Somehow, I feel she would have supported it, if only because she felt it probably helped me begin to gather some badly needed self-esteem. She had often told me I needed to try and stop feeling I had to prove myself to any and every one.

I had begun to feel I had some value and worth and could hold my own even among those who admittedly were more educated or qualified than me.

One week, Don invited my friend (who was secretary to the superintendent), the middle school secretary and myself to lunch. When we asked where we were going, he refused to tell us, saying only that it was to be a surprise. When he told me Jane would be there, and in fact the lunch was her idea and way of thanking us for all the many tasks we did to make things easier for the teachers under our care in our schools.

Since Don had a large station wagon and we would all fit, he drove and we all rode with him. I think most of us were surprised when he took us to his home. Jane welcomed us warmly and had set a lovely table in the dining room. There was a linen tablecloth with matching napkins and the wine and water glasses were unmistakably real crystal. It wasn't just that it was a large, expensive home, but also that it was sparkling clean and decorated beautifully. I was uncomfortable from the beginning, and probably because of my guilt, and could hardly manage a word. We were served wine, shrimp cocktails, Then the rest was a good old Texas Country comfort food dinner: Chicken fried steak, mashed potatoes, jalapeño cornbread, corn on the cob and apricot cobbler for dessert. I am ashamed to admit I was jealous. I wished she had been a terrible cook and everything had turned out awful. However, it was all delicious. Her home was large and lovely, the yard was mowed, landscaped flower-beds full of colorful flowers. The children were at school, so there were no distractions from little people and Jane had taken the day off to prepare and cook.

What could Don possibly see in anyone like me? It almost made me mad at him. That he had it so perfect and was an ungrateful wretch who didn't appreciate what he had. The grass was definitely greener on his side of the fence and no matter what I could not imagine I would ever have this kind of surroundings and life. Why did some people have wonderful childhoods, then continue right on throughout their lives with whatever they wanted? Not needed, but merely wanted? It didn't help that Jane was sweet and friendly to all of us. I wanted to credit her innocence about her husband and I with her being stupid but I knew she wasn't. I knew from her personnel file that she had a Master's degree in education.

Finally, I did admit to myself (just to try and make myself feel better) I was prettier. I had a better figure, and better education or not; I was more articulate and had more personality. She knew nothing about literature; taught biology and spent her time dissecting frogs and eyeballs, or whatever.

Don seemed perfectly relaxed and while he didn't brag on his home or possessions one could tell he was proud. I tried to act courteous and remembered to compliment Jane on her lovely home and the wonderful meal (without choking on the words). I even remembered to write a little thank you note and put it in her school mailbox the next day in which I requested the recipe for the Jalapeño cornbread.

I was perceptive enough to know Don was avoiding talking about the luncheon because he realized I must have felt uncomfortable there.

I had asked for the day off, prepared for care of the children and their getting home from school. I had carefully selected a blouse, skirt, vest and neck scarf and pair of black heels to wear. I had put my hair up in a chignon because I it made me look professional and intelligent. My friend had given me some quarters in case I had to pay for a parking meter and wanted to give e money to buy lunch, which I refused

"I'd be too nervous to eat anyway," I said.

I had not told anyone but my friend where I was going or why but I could see the curiosity in Don's eyes, and I ignored it. I assumed he thought it had something to do with my filing for the divorce.

Luck seemed to hold out for that day. I remember it was warm and sunny, traffic was extremely light and there was plenty of parking spaces left in the county parking lot. I found the address easily and had plenty of time to spare. I went inside the building located the restroom, sed it, checked out my hair and makeup and went to locate the office.

I checked in with the receptionist and sat looking idly through a magazine as I waited to be seen.

The office was modern, tidy and had a friendly and open atmosphere. The people coming and going all smiled and greeted me as though they knew me.

When they called my name, the receptionist motioned me which door to take and I took a deep breath and knocked on the door before turning the knob and was told the "Come on in."

Mrs. McPherson was an older woman, probably in her late fifties with sparkling blue eyes and dark hair attractively sprinkled with silver. She wore a navy-blue suit with a white ascot and she had a warm, wide, welcoming smile.

She invited me to have a seat and then she looked at my application she had on her desk and asked me a few questions.

She then said, to my delight, "I am going to forego the usual tests on your secretarial skills, I am going to assume that you read the qualifications for the job and wouldn't be here if you didn't meet them already. We didn't contact your present employer," she looked down and said, "The school district because we went to ask your permission first. I didn't know if you had told them you were considering a new job or not. You know, the old "one bird in the bush worth two in the field" thing."

I had no idea what she was talking about except I did register (with some relief) that I wouldn't have to take the steno or typing tests. I did fully realize I could pass both without any problem, it was still a relief not to have to "prove" it.

She then the field open to me, telling me to ask all the questions I might. After she said, "I will be your direct supervisor if you take the job, then we have an assistant director and a director of the department. We are a county agency, of course, and work closely with many judges and with lots of lawyers. Our appearance is certainly important, as is the way we present ourselves in the courts.

We train volunteers to work one on one with probationers to try and help them keep all the rules which guide them through their terms of probation. We want them to be successful. There is a lot of confidentiality in our work which we guard very carefully. The pre-sentence department gets details of charges against each prospective probationer, and prepare a pre-sentence report for the judge and the client's lawyers as well as the district attorney's office. We keep a copy of that file with us and of course, it gets shared with any volunteer we pair the probationer with. None of this information should be discussed by our employees to family, friends or anyone not directly involved with our mission and function."

"What do the volunteers do?

"They are important and we are one of the few probation departments in the state which have a very successful rate of probation terms reached. Even the judges, who were reserved and tentative about the program when we first began it are very supportive now. The give rides to the probationers for job interviews, doctor visits, mandatory appointments with our office, home visits where the probationer lives, visits at the probationer's employment, they assist in the probationer finding work, applying for assistance from the local food banks, unemployment office, welfare assistance, educational opportunities. Hopefully they bond with the probationer and the probation officer to form a triangle for successful probation. However, it is very important the volunteer is well trained and understand completely what they can or cannot do. They must check with the probation officer when confronted with anything they do not understand or know about the rules so they can advise the probationer correctly if he or she needs some direction. It is not their duty to act as spies, and yet, they are responsible to report back to the officer any missteps the probationer may have made or is making which would interfere with their probation rules.

This job involves two evenings a month when we meet with the volunteers for training purposes. At this meeting we thoroughly go over the conditions the probationers have to follow, what the volunteer's relationship should be with the probationer and problems which may arise in the successful completion of their responsibilities. They are reminded they serve a purpose; not of warden, or the fence which keeps them from being sent to jail if they don't follow the rules and their probation is revoked, but a guide to successful release when their probation is finished.

She continued with a stern look, "And absolutely no personal relationship other than guide, assistant probation supervisor between the client (probationer) and the volunteer or the probation officer. I prefer to think of a relationship of friends, just not *best* friends.

Before I left, she had taken me into the director's office and she left me there with him for a few minutes and he took this time to tell me how probation began.

You could tell he relished an opportunity to talk of his long-time career in probation. "Probation first began in the United States when John Augustus, a Boston cobbler, persuaded a judge in the Boston Police Curt in 1841 to give him custody of a convicted offender, a "drunkard", for a period and then helped the man to appear before the judge, rehabilitated by the time of sentencing."

"I didn't know much about probation," I said, "but I do believe some people do deserve a second chance and that one mistake does not make a career criminal."

He smiled and agreed. By the time Mrs. McPherson returned to retrieve me, I felt I already knew this man and I really wanted this job.

Mrs. McPherson gave me a tour of the department and introduced me to a lot of people. I knew I would never remember all these names.

When we once again reached her office, we went inside and she said, "You need to go outside to Nancy and have her give you all the paperwork.

She will see it gets to personnel and finance and everywhere else they need it. Welcome!"

"You mean I have the job?"

"Oh, but of course I'm sorry I guess I didn't say that, did I? Can you start in two weeks' time? Is that enough notice for your present job?"

I felt a clutch at my heart. How could I ever tell them? But I nodded.

She went on, "Nancy will explain everything. She's been here over ten years and is the director's right hand "man". We have wonderful health insurance for you and your dependents, vacation is two weeks, paid every year and you can accumulate up to thirty days if you are so inclined. You're going to like it here. I have been here thirteen years and wouldn't think of working anywhere else. I am sure you will think of lots more questions, but things will go smoothly. Everyone works together here. We are a great team."

Chapter

EIGHT

All of a sudden, things seemed to be moving at breakneck speed. I had made it a habit to sit down each evening and write to my husband. I felt it was my duty, and I would collect whatever letters or drawings the children had prepared for him, and mail them all the following morning. If it is true that God moves in mysterious ways (and I do fully believe this), I believe sometimes humans do, as well. We often do things and later regret it, are proud of it, or wonder …*Why did I do that? What could possibly have possessed me?*

I think the set of circumstances which happened next might well have been a little nudge from God to do the right thing and that was to bring my intentions of getting a divorce out in the open. The lawyer had told me their office would put notifications in whatever newspapers legally was required and send the registered papers to my husband, but he had gently advised me to write or call him before he did that. "It was," he said, "the right thing to do, after all."

Don and I had planned to meet on the Thursday after I got hired by the probation department, and when we did, I told him I was giving my two weeks' notice the next day.

"I can't believe you're going to do this. Why? You will all on your own out there. I won't be close enough to keep an eye on you or your kids."

"Well, for one thing, it pays considerably more money, which I need."

"I have always said if you ever needed anything, I would be there."

"Pease, Don. You're a married man with a family of your own to take care of and support. Further, I'm working hard to continue to grow in my independence. I don't want to depend on *anyone* else, even you. I am an adult, a mother of three children and I can and will support them myself. You are a kind and generous person and a truly valued and trusted friend, but I have to move forward."

"I told you *I* want to get a divorce. I want to marry you. I love and want you. As soon as possible. I'll go home tonight and talk to Jane."

"No! No, please listen to me, Don."

He interrupted me, "But you are cutting me out of your life, just as sure as if you took a knife and just sliced me right out."

"No, no, I'm not. We will still see each other, and somewhere down the line, if we still feel as we do, and if it seems right and not a decision made in haste or a feeling of guilt or necessity, perhaps it will come to pass. Meanwhile you must allow me to make my own difficult choices and try to move forward. Let me try and straighten all my problems out for myself, without your help. If I run into a situation where I absolutely need something, I feel you can help with; I promise, I'll contact you. These are big life-altering decisions and we can't just leap into things. Remember, patience has its own rewards."

A little sarcastically I thought, he said, "Yeah, and haste makes waste, too but where does that leave us?"

When we said goodnight that evening, we kissed but we did not set up a new meeting date. I insisted I would call him, but he needed to allow me some time to try and handle things right now.

The next day I was in the copy room, running some copies to pass out at the afternoon faculty meeting when he came in.

"Here," he said, extending a small piece of paper out towards me.

I took it and asked, "What is this?"

"You know the little rural post office down the road to the school?"

"Yes, I've gone in there a few times, what about it?"

"I rented a postal mail box. You can write me there instead of the school and no one will know."

"Well, they won't if you make sure you either destroy them after you read them or burn them or whatever,"

"Kind of like being spies, isn't it?" He asked this with a grin he tried to make real.

"Okay. It's a good idea. Just don't expect daily reports on my life or progress in the big world of probation and criminals."

"Have you told your husband yet?"

"About what? The divorce or the job?"

"Well, either way, I'm sure it's going to be a shock and the worse news he has ever received."

"I'm calling him tonight, and very anxious about it."

"I wish I could be there for you; or at least give you a hug right now, but I will be thinking about you. Don't be frightened. He's too far away to do anything but yell or cuss. If he asked for an emergency type leave to handle this, is it likely they would give it to him?"

"I don't think so, but I don't really know. Would a divorce be considered an emergency?"

So, that night, having fortified myself with a glass of white wine and strong verbal support from my friend, I waited until all the children were either asleep or in their rooms doing homework, sat out to call him. I still regard that call as the hardest one I ever made. I went in my bedroom and using his complete military address, spoke with the long-distance operator for foreign calls. It was no quick accomplishment. It seemed to take forever. She was so helpful and explained each of what seemed a very complicated series of steps. She explained that it would be daytime where he was, night time here.

My mouth was dry, my palms sweaty, and I knew my pulse was racing. When I heard his voice at first though a little distant, I could clearly recognize it and understand him.

You could sense immediately his distress, I had never called him when he was deployed and most times if a soldier had emergency calls, their superiors would call them in to talk to them about any messages coming through. I was sorry for this and when he asked hurriedly, "What's happened? Are the kids alright? What's the matter?"

"Nothing. The kids are okay, and nothing drastic has happened I just wanted to tell you, person to person and not in a letter and before you received the papers, I have filed for divorce."

There was compete, dead silence on the phone at first, then he said, "What the hell? You are filing for divorce? Since when? Why? You can't even wait until I get back to discuss this? I knew from the cold tone of your letters that something was going on but I never anticipated this. What's going on? You found someone else, is that it?".

I refused to answer his question but I said, "I cannot go back to the life we had before. You have abused me and the kids for the last time."

"You're crazy, you know that? What a bitch you are."

"No, not crazy, but finally realizing I don't want to live the rest of my life and the kids in a constant state of fear. We are so much happier when you're gone. I am tired of being afraid. And of being knocked around for no reason. I'm done."

"Well, you better be afraid now. If you think you have been afraid before, you only thought you were, I will blow your fucking head off. If you think you will take my kids away from me, you're more stupid than I thought you were."

"The papers are on their way by registered mail from my attorney. They will explain everything. You can go to your military legal aid for assistance if you need to and that will be free for you"

"What about all my stuff? My guns and stamp collection, my books and family stuff my mother gave me?"

"I will box it all up and send it to you. Make me a list. I don't really want your stuff; your cameras, your weapons and swords, your souvenirs from your deployments and from Germany."

"Have you told the kids?"

"Yes, we discussed it together."

"And I guess you have turned them against me, right?"

"No, I have not lied to them. I have tried to be fair, but honest. Surely you must know how terrified they have become of you. Don't you think they were witnesses to all these things? They were right there. They're not blind or deaf."

"This is not over. You're going to be very sorry for this. You will regret it, I promise you. Eighteen years and you give me a 'Dear John 'call. Thanks a lot, you piece of crap. You're not going to find anyone else to tackle a woman with four children. Especially someone as stupid and worthless as you are. No one else will have you, you'll see."

"I am hanging up now," I told him. "You are angry and upset but if you remember, I told you when I called your first sergeant in to the house when you beat me so badly that time that someday I would leave you. I deserve better and so do the kids."

"Don't you dare hang up on me!" he yelled.

I did hang up and ended the conversation and I was trembling. Even thousands of miles away he could terrify me.

The only thing I told the children was that I had talked to him and told him about filing for divorce. I did not give them details. I did not feel it was fair. I was supposed to be the grownup. They knew what our life with him was like and what it was like with him gone.

I gave notice at the school and everyone seemed genuinely sorry to hear I was leaving but most understood it would be a step up for me, with a future ahead. I waited until lunchtime, I had brought a packed lunch that day to eat at my desk, precisely so I could tell Don about the call. He was, as always very supportive and again offered to help in any way possible.

"You seem remarkably calm this morning."

"I feel calm. I think the worst part is over. Facing him down, even by phone, was a big step for me. You have no idea."

"Did he try to reason with you? Did he promise to change? Did he swear he loved you and wanted another chance?"

"No, no, and no."

"I just don't understand him. You'd think after eighteen years and four children he would try to salvage it."

"He has to always win," I said softly. "It never occurred to him that things would ever change."

Before my final day at the school Don did one more thing for me which would forever change my life. I would never be able to repay him. He did it without asking me, or even pitting the idea in my head.

One morning as I came to the office he was already there, early, and with a big grin on his face.

"Wait," he said, when I sat my things down on my desk and started to take my coat off.

"What?"

"We've got an appointment and we just have time to make it without being late."

"Appointment? What kind of appointment?"

"You'll see. Don't worry about the office, I've arranged for your attendance clerk to stand in for you. The boss knows about it, in fact, he helped arrange everything. Even Jane is in on it"

I began to get a feeling of being out of control and worried about some kind of confrontation coming up. *Had he talked to Jane about his feelings? Even shared the entire sordid (on my part) story?*

He wouldn't…would he?

"Come on, come on, we have to hurry. He cracked the door to Mr. Stevens' office and said "We're leaving now. We shouldn't be too long."

"Where are we going? What's going on?"

"It's a surprise."

"I'm not very fond of surprises as you may have guessed by now."

"Oh, you'll like this one. At least I think you will. I'm not answering any more questions. You will get all your answers soon."

My mind was filled with questions, but I was quiet until we reached our destination.

He pulled into the parking lot of the beautiful red brick private university which loomed over several acres. It was such an idealized sight for a university; almost like a movie set. Several buildings had ivy-covered walls, and college students were coming and going around the campus; some as a leisurely pace and some as though late for their favorite class.

"Why are we here? What are we doing?"

Don came around to my side and assisted me out of the truck. He ushered me inside the main entrance into a beautiful marble-floored entry-way and then into the office. When the smiling receptionist came to offer assistance, he said, "Hello. We have an appointment with Mr. Radcliff. He gave our names and she had us be seated while she went inside the closed office door behind her.

When she came back out, she said, "He can see you now, go on in."

When we got inside the door, a distinguished looking man of about forty-five smiled, came around the desk to shake hands with Don and said, smiling, "Ah, it's great to see you. Your high school is having a pretty good season this year. I keep track, you know. What does it take for you to come visit? Have a seat and introduce me."

"Chuck, she is the young woman I told you about on the phone last week."

We shook hands, this Mr. Radcliff and I, and I was at a serious loss. *What were we doing here?*

After he offered us coffee, water or a soft drink, which we both declined, he looked at me and said, "Don tells me you want to go to college."

I was stunned. I looked at Don, speechless.

Don laughed and said, "Believe me, she's not always this quiet. In fact, she can talk your ear off sometimes."

"All I ever did was tell Don one time I had always wanted to go to college. I loved school."

"She even loves working in our high school but she's leaving our school for something much more exciting."

Mr. Radcliff said, "Would it surprise you to learn that Don, Jane, and I have been having dome very interesting conversations about you and college recently?

"Yes," I nodded, "Very much."

"Well, how would you like to go?"

"I can't."

"Why not?"

"I have no money for college."

"So, what if I told you that right now there is a way you could go on a grant for absolutely no money? Not even for your books."

"I would say there are other considerations besides the cost."

"What?"

"I am a single parent with four children. I have to work to support them with the necessities. I can't go traipsing off each day to class. How will I pay the mortgage, the food bill, all those things?"

"What about working a job in the daytime and going to school three or four nights a week?"

"I have heard about odder students getting a degree by being given credit for life experiences."

"And?"

"I am not interested in that. If, and I say if because I still think you're building false drams here, I wouldn't want that. I would want the same degree plan as an eighteen-year-old, just starting on the path.

"And," I said, looking pointedly at Don, "I wouldn't let some wonderful sponsor or kindhearted person with money to spend giving me charity to attend school"

Now Mr. Radcliff and Don both laughed,

"Well, you give Don and Jane t much credit here, they are not poor, after all, they are teachers but they are certainly not in a position to give away sixty thousand or so in college tuition, either."

"But you said..." I began before he interrupted me. "They told me you have taken a new job with the county probation office."

"That's right," I answered, still not understanding what was going on and what his pint was.

Mr., Radcliff said, "There is a fairly new grant being offered to qualifying and interested students to help fill a desperate need in the Criminal Justice System in our county. I won't go into the reasons for the need; more crimes, more lenient judges handing out probation terms instead just shifting all violators to jail for even misdemeanors, overcrowded prisons, what it is, it's a wonderful opportunity for students who are willing to work and work hard to get a free college degree. It does involve sacrifices on the student's part"

"Like what?"

The student has to serve an apprenticeship in the system which you would already be doing,"

"But I would be getting a salary for that, it's not a volunteer position."

"Doesn't matter, and..." he paused, "Assuming you complete the degree, you have to continue working for the criminal justice area for at least three years then you can do what you want."

Again, he paused and he said, "That means even if you hate the job in the beginning or anywhere along the way, you have to see it through or forfeit the scholarship. And you have to maintain the same GPA as other students in degree plans. And you can't get fired, either."

He chuckled at this as though it would not be an issue.

"I don't know if you are aware of it..." I swallowed, and then, looking him straight in the eyes I said, "but I don't even have a high school diploma."

"Ah, but you do. I have a copy of it, helpfully provided by Jane and Don. It came from your personnel file at the school."

"But I really don't."

"Did you or did you not earn a G.E.D.?"

"Well, yes, but I didn't know if that counted for college entrance."

"Of course, it does and the grades you got on the exams were explementary. I would expect those kinds of grades to carry over with your colleges."

Don laughed and he said, "At last, she begins to believe."

He turned to me and said, "Here it is. Your chance to really build a future for you and your children. Think it over before you let this go by. It will not be easy, children, new job, school but both Jane and I believe you can do it."

"So, do I," Mr. Radcliff said.

"Can I go home and read all this information and think it over? It's seems so impossible. I feel like I am dreaming."

Before we left his office that day, I was given an application, and a fistful of papers including information on a new student orientation and a volunteer "buddy" from the student body who was earning extra credit for his job as sponsorship of a new student.

On the way back to the school office, Don and I stopped for lunch and he also called Mr. Stevens and told him we were on our way back.

"I want to pinch myself," I said to him. "Can this really be true?" Yes," said Don, and

Believe me you are being offered a real deal. I got a partial scholarship for my first degree and I had to serve two weekends a month for a year out at the state hospital."

"Really? I would have liked to see that."

"Hey, I once got bit by a patient because when I was playing cards with him and he was losing."

"You're making that up."

"Nope," he said, raising his right hand.

I almost stuttered but I made myself get it out. "I don't know what to say or how to thank you. And Jane…I feel so damn guilty."

"You may not believe this, but she really likes you and she like to help others. This was her idea originally. Stevens and I fell along with it because we agreed we should support it."

I looked at him curiously and said, "Don, don't you feel guilty, too? Don't you have any remorse about our betrayal of her?"

He flushed and started folding and unfolding his napkin and looked down at what his hands were doing.

"Yes. I do. But I would do it again. I wouldn't trade five minutes of the time we spent together. I am honest when I say I know I am a good father. I am a great football coach," He grinned at me, "Yes, I'm a lousy husband, but if I thought you would have me, I'd move out of the house today and ask for a divorce."

We were both quiet for a few seconds and then he started, "You know, she and I don't even—"

I interrupted him, "Stop. I don't want to hear it. Please."

I began to feel like there were a few "cracks" in Don's armor. Perhaps he was not the compete "knight" I visualized him to be. I even wondered if I were the first dalliance he had been involved in? Then I felt ashamed of myself. Who was I to point any fingers of guilt? We were both guilty of betrayal and of violating our wedding vows. Neither one more culpable than the other.

Chapter

NINE

------------ ☙ ------------

Of course, I accepted the opportunity, although I had the same old doubts about my competency, but after discussing it with my three eldest children, they encouraged me and promised to do everything they could to help me succeed. My classes wouldn't begin until the following fall.

Meanwhile, the children and I spent a lot of Sunday afternoons visiting new housing developments in the area we thought would be best for all of us. It would be a difficult year, there was no doubt; with the youngest in Kinder, the next would be in sixth then we would have a middle-schooler and the eldest would be in school.

We looked at brand new homes and at older homes. Tainting all this with the fear of my husband coming home during late summer and hunting us down. I tried to move forward staunchly with my plans but more than once a strange noise in the house would wake me in fright and I would sit up, listening intently for signs of intrusion. I slept so lightly I believe I heard every creek of the house settling, the wind outside the windows and I would try to calm my breathing down. Many times, I just gave up on going back to sleep and got up to have a cup of warm milk. Contrary to popular belief, it never made me sleepy.

The day I was to go to court, I halfway expected to walk into the court to find my husband had gotten leave and come home to face me in court. With less than two months left on his deployment, it was unlikely, but I was still frightened. I met my attorney and looking hurriedly around the somber quiet court, found to my huge relief that he was not there.

I was sworn in and asked a very minimum of questions, mostly swearing that all four of the children were of my husband's *issue*. The judge called my husband's name several times, verified that he wasn't in the court and spoke briefly to my attorney up at his bench. Then he went through the conditions of the divorce decree. He ordered child support payments of a certain amount to be paid by a certain date each month and standard visitation and primary custody to me but with certain visitation rights. I don't think I heard anything until I was released from the stand and the judge hammered one time and said, "Divorce Granted."

I met the attorney at his office and we went over everything so that I could fully understand it all. All the time and on the way home I kept saying, "I'm free! I'm free!"

Mentally I kept thinking over and over, *I am free, free and. single. I am a single parent.*

I had only been at the new job about two weeks on the day I went to court for the final hearing. Because of the times my ex-husband had been gone on deployment, I was not intimidated by the many things I realized I would be newly responsible for; things he used to consider his responsibility. Filing my own income tax each year, making sure I took care of the maintenance on the car regularly. I had received a letter from the military, having to relinquish my military I.D. It was part of the divorce settlement that the children would be entitled to theirs and the use of it until they each turned eighteen and to the medical care. I was so thankful for this. If it hadn't be addressed, I would have been financially strapped to provide for their coverage. I had signed permission and applied for my eldest to take her driver's education at age fifteen instead the usual sixteen required by the state, as my attorney had advised me to do. As soon as she qualified and could get a license, she and I planned on her getting her license and a car. That would help a great deal with their transportation to school, extra-curricular activities, my school and work schedules.

As if touched by guidance by God the next weekend we found the perfect little house. Only two blocks from the school where my youngest two would be attending school; they could walk each other home each day. It was new, and in a nice little subdivision. We loved that it was a corner log and we would only have one side and one back neighbor. The house was reasonable, would have the loan to include a privacy back fenced in yard and four bedrooms. Three of the bedrooms were, to be sure, relatively small, with a larger one as a master with its own bath. The kitchen was small, with an adjoining dining room, separated by a breakfast counter and place for barstools. The living room had a fireplace, something I had always wanted and a nice patio for a porch swing and grill for outdoor summer bar-b-ques.

We got all the application paperwork and took it home to fill out, and the four of us chattered happily all the way home.

After supper that evening, I sat down and wrote my ex a letter telling him I was trying to buy a small house for the children and I. I told him my attorney was sending him some paperwork and would appreciate it if he would act as co-signer if need be, so I would be sure to qualify with just my salary and the child support. I added my own plea for his assistance, should it be necessary, and told him I knew he wouldn't let his anger and animosity for me keep him from providing a home for them. I reminded him to send me his list so I could crate up all his thing and send them to him when he arrived home. I knew he had requested reassignment to Florida his considered home state where his mother and stepfather lived.

This is where I made probably the biggest mistake of my life (other than marrying him in the first place).

I wrote him his letter then wrote a short one to Don sharing my news about the finalizing of the divorce, how the new job was going and all about the new house. I even shared the possible of an early moving-in date from the mortgage and title company to allow the children to be able to start at their new schools on the first day of the new term. Unfortunately, I also told him that I missed him, and still appreciated all he had done for me when I most needed it.

Three days later I got a call from Don.

"I don't know how to tell you this; but be prepared."

"For what?" Suddenly I felt my stomach clutch and my mouth go dry.

"You must have written me and your husband both at the same time and been very tired and careless or both because I opened your note and found your letter to your husband and he must have gotten mine."

"Oh, my God. What will he do to me?"

171

"Well, maybe nothing. Or maybe he will come after me."

"How revealing was the letter?"

"You did mention you will always love me, perhaps not in the same way I feel about you; but still…"

All I could say was, "No, no, no. How could I have been so stupid?"

Don changed the topic, trying to wipe the sounds of fear from my voice, telling me how happy he was about the house and asking questions about the job and all about the scholarship.

"Look at it this way. There's nothing you can do about it. Just put it aside for now and wait and see when he gets it."

Every day I waited for a letter from him, or a raging phone call, but nothing arrived.

Then, approval was given for early move-in promised by the mortgage company as per our request for the start of the fall term at school.

We hired a moving company, Don and two friends from school came to help, and my girlfriend and her husband. It took all one day (a Saturday) and part of the next before we got it all moved in and beds set up. Another week as we begin to enjoy the additional space and the feelings of being homeowners and no contact from my ex.

Then it came. The mortgage and title companies called. They were turning down approval on the loan unless I could provide a co-signer. They send me a copy of a letter to them from my ex in which he stated he would certainly not co-sign, that in his opinion, I would be a terrible credit risk. He listed some fake loans he claimed I had defaulted on but he had taken over (and thus were in his name now). He told me I had only been at my job for under a month and they couldn't vouch for me. He even told them when he was back in the states, he intended to take me to court and fight for full custody of our children.

I sat down and cried most of the evening not because of the obscene, hateful and threatening letter he also wrote to me and to the children about what a piss-poor mother, wife, and person I was but how I had had sex with another man while married to their father. Of course, as I might have expected, there was nothing in those letters about his many dalliances with women over the eighteen years of our marriage.

He also sent me the payment coupons for the car payments. I had already made up my mind to pay these, after all, I had possession of the car and intended to keep it. With the coupons was another hateful, angry letter in which he wrote: *I understand it all completely now. That's where the divorce and buying a house and the new job all came from. I found out, too, that you stripped our bank accounts. That's where you got the money for a down payment and closing costs. Well, get your new boyfriend to cosign for your new house. I will never do it. I feel sorry for the kids, but not sorry enough to help you pull this off. Don't fool yourself about this. I will never just accept this. You will pay for this. I promise you that.*

Two days later I got a call from the mortgage company saying they were going to turn down my loan approval without a co-signer, based on my salary not enough credit in my own, personal name; just jointly my ex-husband and mine, jointly. I would have to find another place to live and move out immediately. I knew that if I asked him, Don would cosign for me on the loan. But this was part of my journey. I wanted to buy my own house. Mine in my own name.

I called my best friend, crying so hard I couldn't barely be understood and she immediately dropped everything and came over. After a big hug she said, "Calm down and we will look at options. It's not the end of the word. The good thing is you are already are living here."

"Can you even imagine the cost of moving again? The time to search and find something I can qualify on my own, the kids are already registered in their new schools. It's just too much. I can't do this."

"It's just a little bump in the road. You can do this. First, call the mortgage company who pulled back their approval on the loan. Make an appointment with the builder, or whoever is in charge. He has a big stake in this as well. He wants this sale to go through. You cannot deal with this on the phone. You need to meet face-to-face. You need to act strong and tough and not give an inch. Be firm in your position. Repeat many times that they already have given you possession. In your opinion, they had no right to withdraw the approval. Here, sit down and make a list of the things you will say. Remember, you can hint about taking a full-page ad in the newspaper; going public with your story. Look at all the bad publicity. The word discrimination against women borrowers should be brought up when you talk to him. Threaten an attorney getting involved. Don't be ugly, just firm. You always present yourself good. Hell, you even talk like a college grad already. You'll dress for the part; a business suit, heels, hair up in a

French twist or chignon and maybe even carry a pair of gloves with your purse. Don't wear them, no one wears dress gloves anymore, not even to church. Just carry them.

She began a list and all of a sudden, I just couldn't help myself; I started laughing, really laughing. What might be called a "belly-laugh".

At first, she looked at me, puzzled, but then she burst out laughing, too. Every time we tried to stop one or the other would look over and we would both get carried away with laughing once again. It was uncontrollable. It was loud. It was wonderful and it was just what we needed.

Finally, we were both reduced to just grins.

"You're suggesting I become an actress, with a carefully formulated script and everything."

"You got it."

Later, in my life I would wonder where I got the audacity, the pure, unadulterated courage to try such a stunt. Born out of desperation, I thought.

Furthermore, it worked.

The building contractor and his boss company were courteous, great listeners, and easy to talk to as well. I turned down their offers of coffee, water, or anything to drink. I was shaking so badly I was afraid I would spill it all over myself.

The builder chuckled at one point and said, "I don't want the public to see a picture of a mother with four children sitting of the curb of one of my houses, being evicted. I have been in this business forty plus years and I know lots of mortgage people. I already have another one in mind. I will call them and get all your paperwork to them and get back to you as soon as I can.

When I seemed at a loss for words now, he said, with a reassuring smile. "Don't worry. You are not going to lose your new home. Make your payments regularly, or even early and you will begin to establish your own credit rather quickly."

"How long do you think it will take to get back to me? You understand, with school starting soon, and myself in a new job..."

I waited, as they say, on the preverbal pins and needles until about a week or so later the call came from the new mortgage, ready to set up the closing with a new title company.

I still don't think I had a clear mind about it until I went to the closing, signed all the papers, and gave them my cashier's check for the closing costs and down payment. Too, the first payment wasn't due for another two months so that gave us a little money to pay deposits on utilities, buy a few things I didn't have at the rental house; garbage cans, door mats for outside the front and back doors, some light bulbs and a few other things not provided by the landlady when I was renting. It helped because I had to pay more down on the conventional loan, since my ex sure wasn't going to use his V.A. loan and had refused any assistance on my getting this house at all.

I did make a smart move beginning with my first house payment. I added fifty extra dollars earmarked as extra payment on the principal every month. I was determined to pay the house off early, and save some of that interest money.

My parents had never owned their own home, but had always rented. I felt this was the first real step in my life towards independence and stability.

The next was jumping into my first semester of school myself. We moved into our home in the early spring, and I was eager to get started on the new adventure. Back to school at thirty-four. The very thought of tackling classes among a bunch of college kids gave me nightmares. I had quit school after finishing the ninth grade; who did I think I was to attempt this challenge?

I got another boost which reduced the stress in my life a great deal. I had been encouraging the children to write their father. I wanted them to still have a relationship with him; hopefully, a more normal and rewarding one. My daughter showed me a letter she received from him in which he said he had asked for and received permission to stay another year at his present station. He reassured her he would keep writing them and when he did return to the states, he would be living in Florida and she and the other children would get to come down and reacquaint themselves with their two cousins and with his mother. He even said they would go to Disney when they came. They were excited at this; what child wouldn't be?

The two eldest, with the most memories of him were a little suspect of this; my eldest son said, "What if we go and he keeps us and you never get us back?"

"That's not going to happen."

"How do you know that?"

"Because I will turn myself into a fire-breathing mama dragon and come charging down to Florida and bring you back."

"Real funny, Mom. I was being serious."

"Well, don't be. Our life is on a good track"

The first week of June I met with my assigned advisor at the university. It was a Catholic university and she was a nun named (or called) Sister Sophie. When we sat down and figured what we should do, I was overwhelmed with everything but by the time I went home that evening I was signed up for the first semester. I would be taking fifteen credit hours which she advised as being too much, being a new freshman on a regular track. My major would be psychology, my minor Criminal Justice; this would start me on the track for accumulating hours through my job at the probation department.

She advised me to consider taking some C.L.E.P. (College Level Examination Placement tests). She suggested I pick a subject I felt knowledgeable in, pay the small fee, and if I got a certain score, I would be given the credit towards my degree. They held these examinations once a month at the university and you must sign up in advance and pay the fee. If you didn't get the accepted minimum score, you had nothing to lose but your invested money but you could accumulate the class credits immediately.

I was hesitant at first, but what did I have to lose? No one but my advisor and myself would know if I failed and I could even wait three months and try again if I wished. I carefully examined the brochure, and selected "Classic Literature."

I got the day off from my job, and drove to the university and resented myself at the testing class. There weren't many of us there, probably less than a dozen. We were given our respective exams; I wondered how many were taking the one I was signed up for, but then, I took a deep breath and after being told to turn our exams over and began, I got lost in the exam itself.

It was like coming home in a way. I had been such an advanced reader especially of the classics, I found myself among old friends: Dante, Lord of the Flies (William Golding), Emma (Jane Austin), Kidnapped (Robert

Louis Stevenson), The Scarlet Letter (Nathanael Hawthorne), Gone with the Wind (Margaret Mitchell) and of course, my very favorite of all times; To Kill a Mockingbird (Harper Lee).

I felt I might be over-confident, but I knew I had achieved at least a minimum score. Every day I checked the mail, looking for the results but it was well into June when I received the letter. I read it several times just to make sure I was reading it correctly. Oddly, it did not give my score except to say I had passed and my school records had been posted to indicate that I now had three college credit towards my degree.

I was ecstatic. This inspired me to sign up for another exam, this time I signed up for child development ages birth through age five. This too, seemed rather easy (after all, I had four of my own and they had survived my parenting skills).

The classes I was attending on Monday and Wednesday evenings and on Tuesday and Thursdays were going well, too. I was still rather intimidated by the other students with their bright comments for the teacher and each other, their confidence and eagerness to raise their hands and add their opinion, even if it differed from the professor's. I still was lacking in the self-confidence these young students exhibited. Not that there weren't a few "older" students, some were vets, coming back from overseas assignments and taking advantage of their educational benefits.

We settled into a kind of routine or sorts. I have to give my two eldest lots of credit. Without them I doubt I would have made it through. I had a lot of support from the friends I had made at the probation department and I did my share of transporting the clients I was assigned to the local food bank, job interviews, and other necessities. Most had no private transportation and had to depend on us and their assigned volunteer. I tried very hard to be objective; helpful, but not a crutch.

There was some shifting going on in our department due to a rising influx of new probationers. I rationalized it wasn't just more people committing crimes, but the judges (knowing the over-crowding in the jails and prisons) were probating more convicted individuals instead of handing out incarceration sentences. I had lost most of my fear of my clients, even the ones who showed their bravado with trying to manipulate favors from one or the other of the probation team.

The hierarchy in the department was like a pyramid. At the very top were the judges, both in the District (felony) courts and the misdemeanor courts. Then came our department director, his assistant, and section heads. My supervisor was the director of all volunteers and their missions. There was a person who studied and wrote applications for grants which would be beneficial to the department and to the individual probationers. We had a director over the team that wrote all the pre-sentence reports for the judges to use in their decisions on sentencing guidelines. I often thought this department section (researching cases and writing pre-sentence reports for the judges to help determine an appropriate sentence) should have been my work assignment with my writing skills, I would have been good at it. We had a director for probation officers (and their assistants) training. We had a special section which dealt with al out of country probationers. These were people had broken the law in our county, but were assigned to a probation department in the county in which they lived and worked. They sent monthly reports for our own department to read and evaluate. We had a lab which tested required urine samples regularly for those probationers who were on probation for drug-related offenses. We had an employment director for probationers who diligently sought business people or employers who were willing to offer jobs for someone on probation. The probation officers were assigned two to a team, one female and one male in order to effectively monitor the assistance gender made sometimes. Obviously, we needed a female office to take a urine sample from a female probationer and a male for the male probation population. We also had a director who was familiar with and constantly looked for educational opportunities the county could provide to improve the probation's employment skills for better success in meeting his probation requirements.

I became a master at hiding my real feelings when sometimes I had to deal with someone who had committed a really horrendous criminal act, and yet (wrongly I believed) was still given a probated sentence. Hidden inside I carefully kept my prejudices and beliefs and the largest of these were the probations who had committed crimes against children. One of the courses I took at the university was entitled "Violence in the Family" and several times in the weeks of this course, I almost just quit. The case studies were hard to accept and I thought the professor spent too much time trying to explain the "why" the offender had been driven to commit the offences against the child-victim. I never spoke of my feelings on this in class. I couldn't ever admit I had been a victim of child abuse, and then eighteen years of partner abuse as well. I didn't want to hear the by now familiar "Why didn't you leave?"

I also didn't entirely believe it was a circular offense. I didn't believe every child who is abused grows up to be an abuser. I felt there could be many who became doctors, nurses, social workers, psychologists or physiatrists so they could help others heal from their pasts.

I don't know where I found the courage but one day, in this class about family violence, the professor was talking about instincts versus learned behavior. He was talking about how society would probably be better off if more people spoke up about these cases instead of pushing it down inside and hiding it from themselves as well as the outside world.

He also said we, as a society, should be more responsible to teaching others appropriate behavior instead of "minding our own businesses". He spoke of the famous case where Kitty Genovese was attacked three different times one evening in New York and though thirty-eight witnesses heard, no one called the police or gave assistance. The professor called this "The Bystander Effect".

Then he spoke of a woman in a laundromat one evening when a crazed killer with a gun came inside and when he started shooting people, she immediately placed herself between the shooter and her child, saving his life. The professor asked if the class believed it was the motherhood instinct which prompted the woman to save her child? Or was it because society would hold it against her and blame her for protecting herself, instead of her child, if she had chosen that action?

I raised my hand and when he called on me, I answered, "I believe the mother did protect her child out of instinct. Even animals will protect their young."

"What about the way society raises teaches our mothers to care for their offspring? To take care of their young? What about all the parts of our culture which emphasizes the holy bonding of mother to child? What about the way even the most horrendous serial killers may idolize their mother? The new born human is certainly unable to take care of themselves and therefore it's very life depends on the care it receives from its mother whether biological or adopted or however the bod was established. They are so much more vulnerable than many other species. We're taught that to gain approval from society at large, we must take care of our young. Also, to propagate the species, we must protect the young. If it is instinctive, how do we account for the way some mothers will abandon their newborns right after they gave birth to them? Aren't they worried about how society will perceive them and judge them?"

"I don't believe a mother protects her young to, in reality, protect herself from being isolated or ostracized from society. I believe it is an instinct to protect a part of herself from harm; out of love and sacrifice. And your argument leaves out the exceptions to the instinct rule. What about the killers which have been documented as caused by a hatred of their own mothers? Where does this fit into your theory"

"Well, then, said the professor, "What about a dog willingly giving up his life to defend his master? Or a hero on the battlefield giving his life for his buddy? What makes one individual do these things and not another? Are we back to nature versus nurture again?"

It was a very lively discussion and I was so proud of being able to give my opinion. Several students stopped me to say they had agreed with me. One even said, "Well, the professor is a man, what does he know about a mother's love?"

It was not important who was right or who was wrong in this discussion, it was the very fact I got so involved with the lesson and the class that I spoke up; I had my say; something I had never really felt free to give. Nobody laughed, no one pointed a finger at me and acted like I was stupid or had no right to speak up. It felt good. It felt exhilarating. It made me feel liberated.

By the time fall arrived and I had to choose my classes for the new semester, I had fifteen college credits accumulated on my records from five C.L.E.P exams and nine credits from the classes I had attended in person. I was well on my way. I began to feel comfortable in my student role, my probation employee role, my role as a homeowner and even my new role as a single woman who could accept that as I grew more confident and assured of my value and worth as a mother, woman, I sensed an interest from the opposite sex. I even was invited out for dinner or a movie from fellow co-workers or classmates. I readily admitted to myself that I wasn't ready for this part of my rebirth as yet, but I was beginning to accept the thought that one day I might find someone to love and who would love me enough to accept a woman with four children—maybe enough to face a life together in love and trust.

Looking back, I don't really even remember much of those two years. I didn't realize how lucky I was to have had children who were so good. I certainly could not have accomplished my goals without their enthusiastic help. Many times, when preparing for an exam, my eldest daughter and I would study together at the dining room table. I would quiz her using her notes (she was a meticulous student and took wonderful notes) and she would quiz me on mine. Often even the youngest would bring something she had brought from her class and she would carefully do what she called her "homework" with us.

The most amazing part of this whole period was this thirst I had for the classes and exchanges with instructors and other students. To be perfectly honest, my school was taking first place with me and even though my supervisor was pleased with my job performance at the probation department, she would have disappointed to know my job was definitely in second place.

Once I discovered my eagerness for the courses I was taking, and I got my first report card, with a 4.0 GPA, I was certainly "hooked". I do believe my example set a goal for my children because as my grades continued on their golden path, my children's grades went even higher than ever before. My daughter and I had begun to discuss her hope of attending the same university as I did, although her master plan was to become a teacher.

When friends or co-workers in the probation office asked me how I had kept up such a demanding schedule, school, job, children, I had no answer for them other than I was enjoying myself, being able to make my own decisions and better still, to find I was making the right ones.

My advisor asked me once what I was trying to prove? When I considered her question, I thought because every success I have, no matter how small, whether to do with school or work was one more little bit of evidence that the eighteen years of being told I was stupid, worthless, and of no value was wrong. I must admit though, there were times I thought I just had everyone fooled; if they only knew me better, they would realize my unworthiness and that I wasn't nearly as smart as they thought I was...

The more I realized I could handle both the classes and the schedule, the more committed I became.

Finally, one day I sat down with my advisor and she said, "You have almost done the impossible here. You're accumulated enough hours in both psychology and criminal justice to make your degree a double major, and you are going to graduate this coming May. I'm very proud to advise that you have been on the dean's list for the entire time, and have been nominated for the "Who's Who in American Catholic Universities for both years."

I was stunned. There must be some mistake somewhere. Me? Are you sure?"

She laughed at me. "Yes, and you did it the hard way; no credit for life experiences for you, my dear. You did it right along with the youngsters. You should be proud."

Four-year degree completed in two years; but of course, I went straight through. I never took a summer off, and during spring break and Christmas, I took independent study classes with two different professors. I reveled in her praise; I wanted to shout and scream and brag, but I didn't. I held the treasure inside tightly to myself and savored it like a treasured gift.

I thanked God nightly for the blessings and when I walked across that stage and was recognized as having earned B.A. degrees in Psychology and Criminal Justice, Suma cum Laude, I thought I might stumble and faint. I knew I wasn't smiling; I was much too nervous.

Afterwards my advisor said, "You looked mad or upset when you walked across that stage. I was worried about you"

I laughed and explained, "I was neither. I was nervous. So nervous."

Most of the clubs in our town had Tuesday night special for ladies which meant no cover charge so often my friends and I would go out together for a drink or two and listen to the music and dance a little. I enjoyed these fun times, but we always went as a group and had an agreement we would never allow any of us to go home alone (or with anyone we didn't know (Well!).

But no matter the job, the school, whatever; Saturday nights were the most fun. Several couples, including my married friend and her husband, and two other couples plus myself would go out and dance and enjoy each other's company until the clubs shut down at 2:00 a.m.

However, I had made myself a hard and fast rule which I tried never to break; I saved Sundays for family time with my children. We might plan a short trip to a museum or an upcoming movie we had been waiting for, bowling, hiking or a picnic. Once every now and thing if we could afford it, we made the trip to San Antonio to visit Sea World or to Houston when we visited the Astro-world theme park. We tried to make it at least one day at the annual state fair and also the rodeo.

Often, my eldest daughter's boyfriend might join us on these excursions. Also, I noticed that I would feel a twinge, just a twinge, mind you of envy when I saw families complete with a daddy. Too, it wasn't just that I felt my children might have enjoyed having a grownup male figure in our group but I yearned for someone of my own. Someone to tell me when I looked especially nice (or not, as the case might be). Someone who could make me smile just by holding my hand or walking towards me with a welcoming smile. *Was I destined to be done with that part of my life?*

PART TWO

Chapter

TEN

⚘

Five Years Later

I had been promoted to assistant probation officer, then two years after that, full probation officer. The department itself had grown exponentially; with four big offices as well as the main one (down in the annex to the county court house). I was assigned in the south office, close to home and except when I spent all day on Thursdays (court day) was rarely anywhere but home or the south office. Eventually, I was made unit supervisor which meant I supervised the probation officers assigned in the south office.

After receiving my first two degrees, I immediately signed up for graduate school, and two years after that was awarded a M.S. in Psychology. Still, the longing to keep finding challenges which would prove my value; to the job, to my children, and most of all, to myself, I was currently enrolled in doctoral classes.

I had made close friends with another probation officer, and we hung out together a lot. I knew when I examined it, that he felt a different kind of draw towards me than I did him, however, I treasured our friendship and he did not try to push the relationship any further. I appreciated the fact that he allowed me this closeness without the troublesome physical side rearing its unwelcome head. I was dating a little now, but no one; as they say, "Swept me off my feet". My daughter was delaying college for now (against my advice) but eventually, though I could not predict our futures at that time (she did receive a degree in education and achieved her goal. I like to think my example helped her accomplish this).

She had dated her boyfriend for two years and they were planning marriage, my eldest son had (against my wishes, but with my signed permission at eighteen) joined the navy. The third graduated high school the week I received my Master's and we had our cap and gown photos taken together. My baby was in second grade and spent a lot of her time daydreaming that I would find a prince charming and she would suddenly have what she called "a real daddy."

My ex-husband proved to be the coward my friends had always said he would be—he made one visit during the children's school years, driving from Florida. He stayed with some old joint friends of ours and since my eldest had her own car and license, she drove her siblings to meet and spend one evening with him. He had mentioned to her there would not be a scene if I would like to come, he was "past" all that, but I said "No, Thank you," to that idea.

During this time, I had two proposals of marriage (*Ha! So much for your words that no one else would ever have me!*) I mentally told my ex. I wondered if I was to live the rest of my life out without any real love or passion? My friends kept trying to match me up with their friends, coworkers and relatives and while I accepted some of these invitations, for the most part I either found them boring, unacceptable (no real careers or goals), custody of too many children (*done that, been there, through with that*, I thought.) or only interested in a fling. Here I was, almost a Ph.D. in psychology and at a loss with no relationship of shared love or trust. I found out my ex had married a woman with three girls and I wondered if he abused them as he had us?

One Saturday evening my best friend, Betty and I were having a girl's night, and over a glass of wine we were looking at our lives and evaluating if we were satisfied or what we would change if we had an opportunity to go back somewhere in the past and make different decisions.

At first I said vehemently, "I certainly wouldn't marry my first husband again."

"Yes, you would. You wouldn't have had your kids if you didn't."

"Can I tell you something?"

"Uh-Oh," she said, giggling, "Here comes the wine talking."

I laughed and said, "No, No, seriously, listen."

"Okay, okay, go ahead."

"If he had not been such a monster..."

When I paused, she said, "Go on, if he hadn't been such a monster, what?"

"Well, I'm not admitting to anything, we're just talking about hypotheticals here..." I paused again and she giggled again.

"Go on," she urged me.

"Well, of any of my physical experiences (in my mind I was primarily thinking of Don here) my ex was the best lover I ever had; up until he turned evil and I believe I just flipped the switch then and tuned him out. When we first married, he did court me, and was gentle and there was no forced sex especially after having beat me up. He didn't start our marriage being abusive. It just crept up on us. He had the capability of being a kind and good man.... maybe that's why I stayed so long. I kept looking for the earlier version."

"Good luck with that. The earlier version was the act, the performance. The latter was the real him."

"So says the woman who has been married over twenty years."

"Well, but Ronnie has his faults, too"

"Like what?"

"Well, like he has had too many jobs to count, like my little business has supported our family for years. Ever been there when he strolls in and goes over to the cash register and just helps himself to a few bucks so he can play the lottery or go to the horse races?"

I nodded my head affirmatively.

"And you may not think I ever noticed, but he always ogles the women. Think how that makes me feel? Like I'm being constantly compared and judged; sometimes not on the winning side either."

"But he always shows signs of affection, he has a wonderful sense of humor, he's fun to be around," When I paused here, she giggled once again and I said, "I think your wine is showing now, too."

"Probably, but you forgot to mention he's a great dancer, too."

"Yes, he is," I nodded.

"Now," she said, "Let's get back to this confession of yours..."

"Confession?" Already I was regretting having brought the subject up."

"You know what I mean. How many others besides your ex have you had?"

I waved my hand in the air and said carelessly, "Oh, too many to count."

"Oh, come on. Let's heard some juicy details."

I refused to elaborate, but if I had been honest, I would have had to admit there had been others. There were the two who had proposed marriage. I wouldn't marry them, but I had had brief affairs with both and while not exciting, no fireworks going off, no bells ringing or any prince charming recognition events; they were fulfilling in their human contact and pillow-talk. No, wait. Upon reflection, there was that young guy who proposed within two months of meeting me. He had invited me to speak at his university class about probation work. He had a Ph.D., but was a good ten years younger than me and taught a criminal justice class. I enjoyed speaking with his class, and I also enjoyed attending the military ball he invited me to that spring. He was one of the professors there. I made my own formal for the event, and wore my hair up, and that evening he proposed. I am talking tongue in cheek now; because truthfully, I always think it felt like I could have been his mother. Not in actual years, but certainly life experience. I finally kept saying "No, you just want to be married," When, less than two or three months later, I had stopped accepting any invitations from him, I received a wedding invitation from him and he had scrawled across the bottom, *You were right, I just want to be married, and not to some co-ed.*

And of course, there had been Don. We were still friends, and still occasionally spoke or met for a drink or lunch; sometimes with Jane included. I still was friends with some of the teachers and staff and many, including Don and Jane had come to each of my graduation ceremonies. I still found him kind, generous, with that wonderful sense of humor and optimism. I would forever remember the helping hand he had extended me as I began to rebuild my life. Sometimes I lay in bed and remembered what it was like to be enfolded with warmth from another, to have secrets from everyone else, just shared specifically and tightly with this one special person. Someone who liked walking with his arm around my waist, who opened car doors for me the old fashioned way One who would pull my chair to seat me at the table, who asked me what I would like, rather than just tell me what we were going to eat or drink, or do. Was this a forever lost part of my life from now on?

Not according to my little crowd who kept trying to "fix me up". One evening when I answered the phone, a strange voice said, "Hello, we're never met but I'm a good friend of Ronnie and his wife, in fact he works for me. He's been bugging me every day trying to get me to call you up and take you for at least a drink or a cup of coffee or something."

"His wife had been doing the same thing to me."

"Well, what do we want to do about it?"

"Well, I'm dating someone right now."

"Oh, Ronnie didn't tell me I might have some serious competition."

I laughed and said, "Well, I don't know about it being serious, but he's a nice guy and I'm not really all that excited about blind dates."

"Me, either."

"Are you from here? I wonder because I don't remember your name from their list."

"No, we both work for the same company but I just got transferred to this location from Mississippi."

"Wow, you're in for a culture shock. Have you got you some Texas tennies yet?"

"What are Texas Tennis?"

"Boots, of course. Everyone here has to have a pair of boots."

He laughed and responded, "Does that go for those giant ten-gallon cowboy hats as well?"

"Why, sure."

"Well, I won't keep you on the phone but should your current 'not so serious' guy get married, or hit by a truck or move out of state, tell Ronnie so he can tell me and I'll call you again. I've enjoyed talking with you and sooner or later I'd like to get to meet you."

We said goodbye, and at that time I got a kind of okay feeling about him. Maybe after I did a little more research on him with my friend and her husband, I might rethink my decision.

One Saturday evening, approximately a month later, I had almost decided not to go out with my friends on our regular Saturday night clubbing date; I had quite a bit of homework to do before Monday.

However, my friend could be nothing if not relentless and her repeated entrees from her had persuaded me to go. I made them promise to bring me back home early if I decided against staying very long.

We were going out to a big barn of a dance hall, and they had a very popular country-western band playing. I loved all kinds of music, country-western, pop, jazz, even classical and a little opera. My little group of friends were all die-hard Country Western fans though and it was rare I could swing them for an evening of something else.

Regardless of the fact that I did own a pair of nice boots, I rarely wore them out dancing. Simply put, they hurt my feet. Although I sometimes wore shoes with a small heel, since I wore regular high heels to work each day, I was completely comfortable, even dancing in them.

Most of the judges strictly forbade female officers of the court (including female members of the Sheriff's department, City and State Police departments, Texas Rangers, Parole and Probation officers, Constable's office and staff to wear pants inside the courthouse and various courts.) It would be years before this changed and as far as I know now, it is still "no jeans", just nice pantsuits or slacks.

Thus, when I got dressed that evening, I wore a Little Black Dress" only it was blue and it had a bit of a flare to the skirt. I had my hair pinned up, out of the way and off my neck.

My friends came to pick me up and my eldest and her boyfriend were at home making sure their siblings didn't burn the place down or get in a free for all.

It was not unusual for some of the other workers from the company (who weren't married) to show up with an extra friend or two, male and or female and when we arrived that evening. I noticed right away this had been the case on this night. My crowd had put together several tables and had quite a gathering. As I stood by my friends' side, awaiting the shifting and movement to accommodate the new additions to our group, one man sitting wedged between two others smiled at me, and raised his drink as though to toast me.

He pantomimed the words "May I get you a drink?"

I shook my head negatively but gave him a smile.

When everyone had rearranged themselves, the waitress came for our drink orders and everyone did a round robin around the table with their names. The man who had held his glass up and offered to buy me a drink leaned over and said, "I'm sorry, with all this noise, I missed your name. Mine is Roy. Roy Smith."

"Jackie," I said, noticing his beautiful smile. His eyes could not have been any bluer.

"Would you like to dance?"

"Sure," I answered and then wiggled my way out of the back where I was sitting to stand and move towards him. He reached for my hand and led me to the dance floor, and then drew me into his arms.

I am five ft. two, and I have always liked men taller than I am; hopefully by a few inches or more. For some reason It makes me feel safe and protected. It also makes me feel petite and feminine. He was a perfect fit for me. I thought he was probably about six ft. one or two and I just sort of nestled into his arms.

I think many people in our country-western culture believe the same way, but there was a time during this period when pop songs often crossed over to be hits in the country-western feed and vice-versa. The song that was playing when we met and danced our first dance was *Help Me Make It Through the Night*", made popular when sung by Sammi Smith. Of course, we weren't lucky enough to have the real Sammi Smith but the singer with this particular band was doing a good job vocalizing it. Within the songs of this era were many beautiful ballads. You could understand the words and the message behind them. Maybe it's like they say, "in the eyes of the beholder" but in this case it would be "in the ears of the listener". Songs like *Lady*" by Kenny Rogers, *He'll have to Go*" by Jim Reeves, and *I will always Love You*" by Dolly Parton." Each person dancing to these favorites (and many others) felt as though the songs were about them and to them. Many a heart has been lost (or broken) to music.

It is my own belief that many people may have taken the words of that song to heart and that why it was such a run-a-way hit with several different artists.

I was so conscious of his body against mine and his arms around me I felt might suddenly know what the phrase meant "our hearts beat as one". Then immediately, I forced myself to stop being so silly. I didn't even know this man. I did acknowledge I didn't want the song to end. I wished it would go on forever. It didn't, however and he escorted me back to the table. Right before we reached the group, he bent his head down a little and whispered in my ear, "I see you don't follow your own advice."

I looked up at him and said, "What do you mean? What advice?""

"Well, *you* aren't wearing *your* "tennies.""

I stopped walking and looked up at him and said, "You!"

He grinned and replied, "Yes, it's me. The one and only current reject in your life."

He looked all around us theatrically and added, "And where is the much discussed "serious" one you're dating right now? The one you turned down my invitation for coffee with such admirable loyalty?"

I started walking on to the table without replying to him. *My face felt warm; surely, I wasn't going to let this idiot have the last word? He would have to turn out to be a smart ass,* I thought.

As I sat down and took a sip of my drink, he reached over, patted my hand and said cheerfully, "Hey, I'm just teasing you. Don't get mad. I just think it's funny. Admit it, don't you?"

"I'm not mad," I said, trying my best not to grin at him. Of course, I *was* lying. I *was* mad. I felt embarrassed and as though he were making a fool of me or having a good laugh at my expense "What do you think is so funny?"

"Well, that Ronnie and his wife tried to get us together for so long, then I reluctantly call you and somewhat relieved, I was told to buzz off. Then we both come out with our circle of friends,"

I interrupted him, "I'm not your friend, we just met."

"Sorry. We both come out with all these strangers who are pretending to be our friends and we end up meeting at last."

I couldn't help it, I started laughing out loud.

"You know how I'm going to look at this?" he asked.

"No," I said, still laughing. "How?"

"I'm going to look at it as though it's such a shame we wasted so much time when we were so obviously meant to meet."

"That's nice. Are you a romantic?"

"No. Not really."

"You're not married, are you?"

"Nope. Been there, done that. I know you're not. That's one of the great things about friends; oh, pardon me, strangers you know, set you up. You feel relatively safe."

"Safe, how?"

"Well, you obviously know Ronnie and his wife wouldn't recommend me to you if they thought I was another Boston strangler or Ted Bundy."

I laughed again, just as Ronnie walked up and shook Roy's hand. "Glad you could make it, buddy. I see you're already met Jackie. What do you think? Did I steer you wrong?"

Roy shook his head and said, "Definitely not, I should never have taken that first 'no' from her. For once you got something right. Now if you could just transfer that to work…"

Now we all three laughed together.

"I was going to ask you to dance," Ronnie said, looking at me.

"Too late," Roy said, I already asked.

"Well, later then," Ronnie said, and left to go back to his seat.

Roy stood up and when I didn't immediately stand, he said, "What? Now you don't want to dance with me?"

"Yes," I said, "Very much, but I was waiting for you to ask. Just because you told Ronnie you had asked, you still needed to ask me."

"Ms. Jackie, would you like to dance?" He was smiling and as we walked to the dance floor he said softly, but loud enough for me alone to hear, "Oh I can see I'm in for a run for my money now. I can anticipate all kinds of wonderful adventures in our path."

I smiled but said nothing.

The rest of that first evening was a blur. When the singer in the band stood and sang Mac Davis' song, "Baby, don't get hooked on me" he whispered, "Should I be listening to the words in this song?"

"You're the only one who can answer that," I said, "Time will tell."

"How long were you married?" he asked.

"Eighteen years."

He kept dancing, but pulled his head back to he could look in my eyes. "Wow, long time. Can't say you didn't try. How many children?"

Now I waited, watching closely to see if he flinched. Most often when I met a guy and admitted I had four children, their interest did one of two things: began to show definite signs of cooling off, or you could read their thought processes as to the possibility of a one- night stand. I think I began to love him right then when he said, "And you don't look as though you have had any. I didn't know Texas grew them so pretty."

Before we all said goodnight, he invited me to go play golf with him the next day. One of the other men from his work who was there that evening was going and he was bringing his girl.

"So, we could make it a foursome," Roy said.

"But I don't play golf. I have never even been on a golf course I my life."

"They're not scary places," he said, "unless someone doesn't yell 'fore! When the hit a ball."

"I have no clubs. Can I rent some there?"

He gave a boisterous laugh. "No, you can't rent golf clubs here like you do roller skates at the rink but you can use mine with me."

"Well, will they fit? Don't they come in different sizes?"

"No, and yes. They won't be the size you get someday if you take golf up, but they will work in a pinch," he said. I loved his grin. I wanted to say lots of silly things to make him laugh.

So, we made the date and he would pick up the other two first and then swing by and get me.

All the way home Ronnie and my friend peppered me with questions, questions, and more questions.

Ronnie said, "How come he didn't volunteer to take you home? Or did he and you turn him down? If so, that was a good move. A good move. Play hard to get."

His wife said, laughing, "What would you know about paying hard to get? You practically camped out on my front doorstep from the moment we met until I finally agreed to marry you."

"Well, he's either lost his touch or he's paying the gentleman."

"Well, don't you agree he's good looking?"

"Very."

"Personable?"

"Yes"

Betty was getting a little exasperated with me.

"Well, why do you think he didn't ask you out?"

"How do you know he didn't?"

"Well, did he at least ask you for your phone number?"

"He has it, you gave it to him, remember?"

"Well, if he didn't ask to drive you home, he might as well at least set up another date."

"He did."

Silence and then Betty laughed and Ronnie said, "I knew it! That sly old fox wouldn't

Let you get away."

"When? Where? What?" Betty asked.

If, just if, this fine specimen and I really did hit it off and become a couple I would never hear the end of it.

"We're going to play golf tomorrow with that Max guy and his girl."

"Golf?" Ronnie sputtered. "How come he invited that idiot Max instead of me?"

Betty said, "You always think you have to be first. With everything and everyone. Maybe Max invited him. You ever think of that? You're not everyone's best or only friend, you know."

"And golf? What kind of a first date is that? And with another couple? No alone time? I could teach Roy a few things."

"And maybe you should concentrate on learning a few things yourself," Betty laughingly told him.

We bantered back and forth and when they reached my house and said goodnight Betty's final words were "Call me tomorrow whenever you get home."

Ronnie gave what he thought was a lecherous look and said, "Or the next day if you don't come home tomorrow…"

Betty said, "You, with the dirty old mind, Shut-up."

I had wonderful dreams, woke early, showered and picked out what to wear. I had a silky, emerald green body suit; like a leotard except with three quarter length silky sleeves. It would be perfect because it would stay tucked in. I selected a slightly darker green pair of shorts which fit me really nicely. I put my hair in a pony-tail and grabbed my new white, bright tennis shoes.

Then, placing them by the front door, I went to the bedroom closet and got my boots and some socks.

I got my eldest two up, gave instructions for the day and said I'd home before dark and I would be at the golf course in Bastrop, Texas, playing golf.

At this, my eldest daughter opened and said, "Golf? Did you say golf?"

"Yes! I'll tell you all about it later."

"Okay. Just be home by 6:30. John and I are going to the movies tonight." Then she said as I closed her door, "Golf?"

I grabbed some breath mints out of my purse but did not take my purse with me, just my driver's license, which I put in my pocket with a folded twenty-dollar bill. It had long become a habit with me. I remembered now how my friend Linda had taught me the importance of always having walk-around-money when going somewhere. I wondered how she was and where she was. We had lost touch, mostly due to her still moving around with her military husband and my divorce, new job and hectic schedule. When the doorbell rang, I put my boots on hurriedly and went to answer it.

I wished I could have had a camera with me to catch the surprised look on his face. I tried to keep my expression serious, but I couldn't help grinning when I said, "What? Texas Tennie's are the right shoes? I have no golf shoes."

"Alright, alright, you've had your fun. Now, grab your real tennis shoes and let's go. I don't want to miss our tee time."

Walking to the car, I said, "Tee time? Is that the same thing as tea time? I like mine with cream and sugar. I thought you were in a hurry and now you say we have time for tea."

"I can see this is going to be a memorable day for a golf game," he said as he opened the door for me, and then closed it after I was safely seated. He got two points from me right then: one for opening my door for me, and one for saying, "Nice shorts."

As I looked over at him and said, "Glad you approve. I wasn't sure what would be appropriate."

"Good choice. I hope Max can keep his eye on the golf ball and off you."

Mentally I thought, Maybe I should give him another point. Even if it's sort of a back-handed compliment, it still made me feel good for him to act like he wanted to keep me to himself.

"I laughed and said, "Is Max a ladies' man?"

"He thinks he is, let's put it like that."

"And what does..." I went on, "What's her name...Stella? Think about it?"

"Who knows? She's just the latest in a long string. I can't keep track of them, much less remember their names."

"That's a little sad, don't you think? How long has he been with this one?"

"Who knows?"

"Well, guess. Two weeks, four?"

I've seen her exactly twice so I would guess less than a month. He goes through them pretty fast."

"And you? You, Mr. Smith, renown bachelor so highly recommended by my closest friends. How fast do you 'go through them'?"

He laughed. "I could ask the same thing of you. How fast do you go through your suitors?"

"Suitors? My, what an old-fashioned term. You must have been raised by a very conscientious mother."

"Yes, she wanted her only son to be a gentleman. Besides there is something a little shady about asking you how quickly you go through *your men*? Don't you think?"

I laughed. "I should get some points for turning you down the first time you called and not acting very interested when Ronnie and Betty kept trying to fix us up, then."

"That, or occurred to me you might be one of those women who think playing hard to get stirs up the interest. I often wondered why women never think a guy uses some of these tricks as well as they do."

Now I really laughed and when he asked, "What's so funny?"

"From that telephone conversation, and then you being the one to ask me to dance right off the bat last night; and sort of monopolizing my time all evening I wouldn't classify that as you playing hard to get. In fact, if memory serves me correctly, I think you paid for my drinks without asking but trying to be rather sneaky about it, didn't you?"

Now he looked a little embarrassed. "Yeah, I did," he said and added, "All two of them. You're certainly not a lush."

"Well, glad to hear that"

"And anyone who orders Black Jack Daniels and then fills the glass up with cola certainly is not a real drinker. That just masks the taste of a good whisky."

"Are you a connoisseur? Should I be worried *you* might be a lush?

He chuckled and glanced over at me. I was sitting there thinking he was just as handsome and charming in the daylight as he had been in the dim lights of the club last night.

Mentally I chided myself for looking for his flaws. He was bound to have some maybe he was just good at hiding them. But then, again, maybe he was "for real? Time would tell.

Right from the start the day was wonderful. The four of us did a lot of laughing and the two guys bravely tried to be patient with Stella and I as we tried our best to hit the ball within a reasonable (at least for a beginner) distance.

Max really teased Roy when he got in back of me and tried to teach me how to grip the club, stand, and swing. A couple of time he told Roy, "Aw, no wonder the poor woman can't get a good hit. You're a lousy teacher. You should let me come show you the right way, Jackie"

I laughed but Roy said, rather briskly, "I got this, Max, but thanks for offering. Stella, excuse me for saying this, but Stella, isn't exactly the top score here today. Maybe she needs a new coach."

Actually, though I was having fun, I took what he was showing and telling me quite seriously and I saw a great deal of progress by the end of the day. I liked it. I vowed to get good enough at (especially if I continued to see Roy) the game to justify getting my own clubs, sized right for me.

We had intended to only play the first nine, but were enjoying it so much we played the entire eighteen.

We stopped at a steak house on the way home and as we pulled into the parking lot, Roy glanced at me and said, "I noticed you took your shoes off as soon as we got in the car at the course. Do your feet hurt?"

I laughed and replied, "No, I'm just a barefoot woman at heart; I love being barefoot."

That's the first thing I take off when I get home from anywhere."

What's the last thing?" Max asked.

"Enough," Roy said to him and then, turning to me he said, Well, you have to put them on now. See the sign on the door: *no shirt, no shoes, no service*? I'm hungry!"

I laughed and put my shoes on and we went in to eat.

Chapter

ELEVEN

⚓

L ater that evening, after our golf date, I called Betty and told her what a great day it had been.

I waited for his call, and was very disappointed when it wasn't immediately the very next day. I wondered if all the joking about playing hard to get was more than a joke to him and he was playing games? I wondered if he didn't like me enough to call for another date?

Maybe he had decided after one date I wasn't his type?

I had really enjoyed the day. There only thing lacking (in my review of the day) was that he didn't attempt at any time even when escorting me to the door when he brought me home was the fact that he didn't kiss me,

I *really* wanted to see how it would be to kiss him. *Hussy,* I told myself, remembering how Betty used this word instead of the more common "bitch" a lot of women used. I never considered myself a "Little Ms. Goody Two-Shoes" but neither did I like unnecessary vulgarity either.

I guess that's one reason I was impressed with

Roy's old-fashioned and courtly manners. He wasn't polished and slick in any kind of sleezy, greasy, gigolo fashion, but he was charming, handsome, and thoughtful. Something else would come to light the next time we spoke.

My lawn-mower had given up the ghost, and when I saw the expense of replacing it, I thought maybe that would be a good excuse for me to call Roy without it seeming so obvious I was chasing after him.

I discussed it with Betty and she immediately gave her approval and opinion that it wouldn't be taken as being too forward.

I got the number from her and called. When the receptionist told me he wasn't there presently, but was expected back before the end of the day, I left my name and my work phone number and asked her to have him call me. All day long I waited nervously for a call,

Bu it was always business related. All day long I thought of the many reasons for him not to return my call and all were very depressing, Obviously, he had not felt the same attraction as I had from our date on the golf course.

Finally, the business day was finished and I went dejectedly to my car and drove home to start preparing dinner. I didn't have a class that night and had left a stew simmering in the slow cooker. All I had to prepare was the cornbread. Just as we sat down to eat, the phone rang. One of the children answered and when they turned and said "It's for you, Mom." I told them I'd take it on the extension in my bedroom.

I sat on the edge of the bed and picked up the receiver I hoped I would be able to speak normally.

"Hello?" I said.

"Hey, hi there! Sorry I didn't get back to your earlier, but I fell asleep on the couch and just now woke up. Did Betty ever tell you what our hours are?"

"No," I said, "She never did. Do you work all night and sleep all day or something?"

Well, you know or I guess you now I am the regional manager for the bread company, the delivery drivers show up here to load their trucks and are out of here on their regular routes by 4:30 am. I have to be here to make sure everyone is here and we're not short a driver, or that we didn't get the bread and other bakery items from the bakers. So, my day begins while you are still snuggled warm in your bed. Then, usually all the trucks are back between two or three-thirty and loads are accounted for and the drivers turn in their delivery sheets and we all go home util the next morning. Sometimes I stay up to do errands or go eat something besides y own cooking, and sometimes I just come home and shower and nap. Sometimes I even go to bed by about five and sleep until my alarm goes off at 3:30 the next morning. So, I didn't get your message until I was already home. I showered and thought I'd just rest a few minutes and I just now woke up. What's up?"

Then, before I could say anything, he interrupted me and said, "I've been meaning to call and tell you what a great time I had on our golf date. We're going to have to do that again."

"Yes, yes we are," I replied and then I took a deep breath and said, "I thought you could help me with something."

"Anything, if I can. What?"

"Well, I'm pretty handy around most things, but my lawnmower just won't start no matter what. I've replaced the spark plug, new points because my son said it might be that; I am at a loss and I don't want to buy a new one, this one is not all that old…"I paused and then I added, "And in exchange I will invite you over for a good home-cooked meal. I imagine you eat out more than you cook."

There was a pause on the other end and then he said in what I thought was a calm, measured, even tone, "I'm not much good with that sort of tinkering," he said, "But I could bring it down here and the guys in the back, like Ronnie, could probably take a look at it and see what they can do."

I teasingly said, "That would be wonderful, how about the dinner invite? What day would be good for you?"

"I appreciate the offer, I really do, but I am going to pass on that. I'm not into making plans where I am committed to being somewhere where someone has put themselves out cooking for me. You work and go to school and are raising four children. You don't need one more to feed. Also, I am so use to eating at such odd hours, or just grabbing something from some drive-in on the way home at 2:00, then getting to bed as quickly as I can. But I appreciate the thought, I really do. I'll come by and pick up the lawn mower soon as I can, or maybe send Ronnie to get it. He might even be able to fix it; he's real handy with these trucks and other things."

I was stunned, truly stunned, I didn't know what to say. I felt like someone had thrown cold water in my face. Immediately flooding back came all my feelings of insecurity. Was he afraid of what and how I would cook? Did he think I ran a dirty house? He had been quite willing to go eat in a restaurant with me; like after the golf day, but this flimsy excuse for not accepting my invitation?

There was a very distinct silence on the phone and then I managed to say, "Oh, hey, sure. I understand. If I had been up since 3:30 a.m. I would be in a hurry to go to bed, too.

"Well, hey, is everybody up for going out Saturday night? I can sleep in on Sunday morning."

"I really don't know," I said, "I haven't talked to Betty for a couple of days"

"Let me know, I'm in."

"Okay, or I'll tell Ronnie to talk to you."

"Sounds good. I really can't wait to see you again. I've been thinking about you a lot."

"That's nice, I've been thinking about you, too," I replied. Mentally I thought, *Yeah, enough so that you couldn't even pick up the phone and just call to say that? And you can sleep in on Sunday morning, but can't make a dinner date on Sunday?*

I thought my last words had been a little cold, and if they were, I was glad. I felt like I had been caught trying to trap him into dinner, and that waited for me to ca him to even tell me had been thinking of me since had last seen me. If I really thought about it, I felt hurt. Then I felt angry. *Who did he think he was? And if he wanted to see me, why did he talk about the entire group going out, and not just invite me individually?*

The next day I called Betty and we discussed the conversation.

"Oh, ho," she said, "There's that old bachelor's nervous twitch."

Puzzled, I looked at her. "Nervous twitch?"

"You know, they always think you are throwing out a net if you invite them to dinner or to do some family thing with your kids included. They think you've already got marriage on your mind and they try pulling back a little. Nobody' going to trap them; or so they think."

"Really? Really, now? Does it ever occur to them that maybe we don't want to be married right now? Maybe we're not looking towards them as marriage material at all."

"No, because even if you told them that, they wouldn't believe you. Men, especially single men, think every woman with just a few exceptions for the work-a-cholic career woman who frightens the hell out of them, seeks marriage above all else."

"Do you really think *men think women* still believe the quickest way to a man's heart is through his stomach?"

Betty laughed. "We know better, don't we? Do you want me to send Ronnie over to get the mower?"

I thought to myself: *Was I really thinking just that when I invited him to dinner? Did I want to show him not only I was a good dancer and good sport about the golf game? Was I trying, instead, to illustrate what I could offer a man? To show him what he was missing in being a bachelor? I had to admit I was sizing him up; physically and how he presented himself to me, as well as what kind of partner he would be. Was that wrong of me? Actually, I didn't like this introspection I was having with myself about my motives. Was I hiding the truth? Was I making too much of this rejected invitation? Maybe so."*

"Actually, I had the boys put it in the trunk and I found a little shop on the way to work where I can drop it off and they will take a look."

"Good for you! Show him what's what and who's who." She looked steadily at me for a few seconds and then she said, "You really like him, don't you? I knew you would, look how long I've been after you to at least just meet him."

I had nodded at her question and now I sighed. "What do I do now, Betty?"

"First of all, you don't want him just showing up at your door to pick up the lawn mower. So, you call and leave a message with the receptionist, before he leaves the office at 2:00 today and you don't talk to him directly besides he will be in the middle reviewing reports, and checking loads in. No, tell her you don't need to have him call you back just be sure and give him the message: 'The mower problem has been solved but thanks anyway."

"Why should I thank him? He didn't do anything."

"I know it, you know it, and he knows it, but it gives you the upper hand on this dinner invite and the whole thing."

"Well, okay," I said doubtfully. "If you say so."

"You like him, right? you still *are* interested in him, right?"

I nodded yes.

"You want to make him think the rejected invite was no big deal and that you totally believed his excuse and that your interest in him has not changed but he will also feel he sent and you received the message he has no interest in more of a commitment than what there is right now right now. In other words, he is a confirmed bachelor and likes it. Of course, it's all bullshit and deep inside he knows it and you know he knows it. It's all a big game. The only thing wrong with his picture of the situation is he doesn't want to admit we might be smarter than he (or any other men) give us credit for."

"But he didn't call me after our golf date; I had to call him under that flimsy pretext. What if that's his way of telling me he's not interested? What if he's giving me the brush off?"

"That's just ridiculous. Of course, he likes you. Why wouldn't he like you?"

"Oh, there could be lots of reasons."

"There's a book you need to get and read. It's all about the games that humans play in different relationships. You'll like it. Some of it is funny, some very interesting, but lots of explanations of why we act like we do in certain situations. It's written by a psychiatrist named Eric Berne (1964). In fact, let me look through some of my books, I may have a copy."

"Meanwhile, since I haven't read the book yet, what do I do about Roy?"

"Don't call him, whatever you do. He's tied up a lot because of his work hours, so pretend you believe that's his reason for not contacting you. I will tell Ronnie not to tell him about our plans for Saturday. In fact, I will threaten him with death if he does. If Roy asks him, I will tell him to say he doesn't know yet, no one has said, he will let him know."

"And will he?" I asked.

"Heck, no. We'll all pretend that we forgot to tell him"

"Like he forgot to call me."

"Exactly, my dear."

"But we will go, right."

"Damn right. And if he shows up, we'll be laughing and dancing and drinking and having a grand old time."

"Yeah," I said, liking the plan.

"And if he asks us why we didn't call him, we'll all say we meant to; we just forgot."

"Yeah, or that we're too busy."

"Yeah, and you will keep dancing with other guys."

I started giggling and said, "Let's not get too carried away, Betty. I don't want to run him off, just pique his interest more and make him more eager for the chase."

As the week wore on, I became more excited about Saturday night. He did call on Thursday night, but I had told my kids no matter who called to say I was out for the evening."

They didn't ask me why, but they did as I asked and then my daughter said, "It was some guy named Roy. Isn't he the one you played golf with?"

"Yes, that's right."

"Why didn't you want to talk to him? I thought you liked him and you had a good time.?"

"I do and I did."

She smiled a conspiratorial smile (between us girls, I thought) and said, "Oh, playing hard to get, Mama?"

"Does it work?" I asked.

"Almost always."

Ronnie couldn't understand why Betty and I were in such silly, happy moods.

"Is something going on that I don't know about?" he asked us more than once. "If so let me in on the secret."

When we got there, Stella and Max were there, and a couple of others. I whispered to Betty, "We forgot about Max. He probably called Roy to tell him we would all be here"

"Maybe, but remember he is not a route driver. It's possible he just came, assuming we would all be here again because most of the time we *do* come here."

Just when I was beginning to think he wasn't coming at all, he walked in. He looked just as good to me as he had the last time, I saw him. I don't know what I had expected, maybe because I had been upset about the dinner invitation, I expected to like him less or see that he wasn't anything different or special; but I acknowledged to myself that I most definitely felt some kind of tingle or shiver, or whatever, but my body was telling me I was glad he had come. I was also very happy that when he walked in,

I was dancing with Max and Stella was dancing with Ronnie. I wanted him to see me having a good me with someone else besides him. Max said something funny and I didn't really even hear it all before I laughed. *Yes, see me? I'm having such a good time I didn't even notice you weren't here.* I had been dying to ask Max where he was or if he was coming, but I stayed strong and didn't even ask about him.

The only thing I had asked Max was if he had been to play golf yet again and if so, how did he do?"

It occurred to me that Roy may have come straight from his office because he was not wearing a suit and tie, but what looked like khaki shirt and slacks. The shirt was open at the top and he looked wonderful to me

When the dance was over and Max and I walked back to the table, Roy was standing still, and he took hold of my hand after we all greeted each other. He pulled me towards the dance floor. Once there, he pulled me close and said, "Hey, how come you didn't call me back about tonight?"

I looked up at him (I could hardly focus, he felt so good) and innocently, and answered, "I guess we all thought you and Ronnie would surely talk during the week, and I wasn't even sure I was going to come."

"Really?" he said, with a funny little smile. All of a sudden, I knew he was seeing through my subterfuge and not only recognized the games but all the rules as well.

Mentally I told myself, *Well, you always said if you ever found the right man, he would have to be smart.* As for this game, it definitely had lost a little of its sparkle.

There was one bit of Betty's advice I realized I had no intention of following: I was going to dance with him every time he asked me. Why? Because, I told myself quite honestly, I enjoyed being held in his arms.

"Hey, I forgot all about the lawn mower," he said earnestly, looking down at me. "Do you still need me to come by and pick it up?"

"Didn't your secretary give you my message?"

When he looked at me, blankly, I realized she probably hadn't because he seemed honestly puzzled

"What message?"

"I called up there one day and left word I got it taken care of."

We were barely moving on the dance floor and he said, "No, I never got the message. I'm glad you got it fixed, though."

My mind was furiously sifting through this information and I realized all this week when I thought I had given him the message that I didn't need his help and that I was sorry I had even asked for it, he had been clueless and gone about is daily life with neither a thought or concern about me. *In fact*, I thought, *didn't this really just prove that he hadn't given a fig about whether or not I got my problem lawn mower fixed; not enough to even ask or call about it?* At that moment, I wanted to yank myself out of his arms and stomp off the dance floor; but the problem was I liked being where I was. *So, what about the stupid lawn mower? Just because I dated a guy didn't mean I could suddenly feel justified in expecting him to do "manly" things (like fix a lawn mower) for me.*

Roy didn't seem taken aback by being left out of the invite for tonight, in fact he got rapidly into the spirit of the evening and in fact, between people coming and going to and from the dance floor or restrooms, he had ended up sitting right next to me and I enjoyed his sneaking one hand under the table to seek and find mine.

There were a couple of real "kickers" (real cowboys) in our crowd and they always wore their western hats everywhere. When they were indoors, they always took them off, unlike some cowboys, and Roy started to reach for one to try on when the owner was dancing and I stopped him.

"Uh-no," I told him. "You don't mess with a real cowboy's hat. That's personal almost as much as his gun might have been in the old west."

Roy laughed and said, "You're kidding me, right?"

"Nope," I said and immediately the guys still sitting at the table agreed with me.

"Hey," Ronnie said to the table at large, "This band is not country enough for me. More jazz and pop than country; besides Roy has not been in Texas long enough to see we Texans for what we really are; or what a true-blue Texas joint or dance hall is. Let's take him over to the Broken Spoke."

The was an immediate agreement.

"Broken Spoke?" Roy asked, "What is that?"

"Only the best Honky-Tonk in town, that's what.

When others from our crowd came back from the dance floor, they were all in for the idea and we began to gather our things.

Roy turned to me and said, "I came straight from work, and would really like to run home and take a quick shower and change before going to the other place. Would you come along and we could join them over there? It won't take me long."

I pretended to be shocked and I replied, "Come along and keep you company in the shower? You think I'm that kind of girl? Second date and you're inviting me to keep you company in your shower?"

I was delighted to see I had embarrassed him at least a tiny bit. He smiled but even in the dim light I may have detected a slight flush on his face.

I spoke up again, almost like poking a sleeping lion to prove your bravery but running like hell if the lion awoke. It was delicious. "Aren't you the one who reassured me you weren't Ted Bundy or the Boston Strangler? Now you want this unconditional trust?"

Betty had overheard some of our conversation and she was trying very hard not to laugh.

Roy said, "Okay, so I didn't put that exactly right. It's not a good idea. I certainly understand your reluctance to go wait and watch T.V. or something. My intentions were completely honorable."

Ronnie said, "Hey, what's going on over there? I want to be in on the joke."

Betty got control of her laughter and said, "Nothing, nosy. Just go get the car and bring it out front, will you?"

Outside I noticed that Roy had walked over to Ronnie and said, "Hey, remember I have never been there. I will follow you in your car so don't lose me."

Hum, I thought to myself. Guess he decided to skip the shower. Something tingled inside me as I credited this to him not wanting me to belong (even temporarily, for the evening) to anyone else. Almost, I mused to myself, like he might be worried about me not being interested in only him, and not caring if he were there or not; I was still going to enjoy myself. My having a good time was not contingent on his presence, either way. At least that's the way I was reading this and I hoped I was right. I also realized I did not want this evening to end.

So, we went on over to the Broken Spoke. Walking from the cars to the door I asked Roy, "Hey, decided not to go get yourself a shower, did you?" Fully in control of the banter now, he said, "Well, when I couldn't get you to volunteer partner-showering with me, I decided I'd just forego the shower and change of clothes. You'll just have to put up with the smell."

When we got there, Roy found out it was a B.Y.O.B. (bring your own bottle) if you wanted hard liquor; they only sold beer and sodas, as well as other mixers. The other men in our party switched over to beer and Roy bemoaned the fact he didn't have any Black Jack Daniels. I noticed the couples at the table next to ours had a couple of men with their Jack Daniels' bottles on the table. When the waitress brought us our beer and mixers, she had brought several extra empty cups. I picked up one and smiling, asked the couples at the other table, "Hey, sorry to bother you, but we've got a Mississippi guy over here who is not familiar with our B.Y.O.B. habits. Think you can spare enough of your bourbon to make a drink for him?"

I handed over the cup and they smilingly said, "Sure, here you go. Let us know when you need a refill. We have plenty. Welcome to Texas, Mississippi."

Roy was horribly embarrassed but tried not to show it. He thanked them. Then he turned to me, and I knew he was going to chastise me at first but then he laughed and said,

"You're something else, you know?"

He split the whiskey in the cup among three different cups and said, "Now, if some of you give me some ice, I'm in business."

In a few minutes of listening to the singer on the bandstand try her hand at an old Patsy Cline favorite, "I fall to pieces", Roy watched the dancers and then he turned to me and asked, "Tell me something. All jokes aside, I really want to know."

"Sure, what?"

"Why do the dancers all move around the floor in a circle?"

I laughed and said, "You mean they don't dance that way in Mississippi?"

"No. A couple sort of stakes out their own little space and boundaries, but they don't continually move with the crowd in this larger circle. I don't understand how they keep from stepping all over each other."

"Well, you did alright at the other club," I said, truthfully.

"Well, maybe, but over there, they weren't as obvious about this circle thing."

"Well, that's the difference in the music which decides how they dance This is true country; the music and the dancing. Over there at the other, they played some jazz and quite a bit off the pop charts. It makes a difference. Tell me the truth, Roy. Who are your favorite artists?"

When he hesitated, I said, "And don't tell me you don't have any, or make up some country star to impress me, either. Truthfully, now."

He grinned and replied, "You'll laugh."

"Probably not, but try me,"

"Most are oldies."

"So what?"

"There is pop, maybe mixed with even a little almost classical, and country."

Now I was intrigued and I said, "Come on, let's have it."

"Well, I could listen to them play "Born Free" over and over, or I'm Always Chasing Rainbows" is another favorite"

"Okay, see I'm not laughing. I like both of those, too. But those are pure instrumental pieces, what about vocalists?"

"Neil Diamond," was his quick response.

"Who else?"

"Ray Charles, Kenny Rogers, Ray Price."

"You realize two things about your choices, don't you?"

"What? That I have wonderful taste in music?"

I laughed and said, "Well, you're dating yourself with a lot of your choices."

"So? I'm an old man."

I laughed again and raised one finger in front of my mouth as though to "shush" him.

"And among your list are some country singers. That's why you can fit in with our crowd. You like other genres too, but you allow yourself to take it all in and not limit your enjoyment to one. Geez, who can ever forget Kenny Rogers' "The Gambler"?"

"Right," Roy said, "or Whitney Houston's "I Will Always Love you"?"

"Let's get up and go in a circle," he said. "I want to hold you and I don't care what song they're playing."

I stood, and with my heart thumping at the words I just heard from him, I led the way to the dance floor. I wish I could remember what song was playing, but music wasn't my focus at that moment, it was his closeness.

That evening we all went out to eat breakfast at a twenty-four-hour restaurant. There was a lot of joking, laughing and conversation but I was only conscious of his leg touching mine under the table and our shoulders touching. I wished I didn't need both hands for my food so he could hold one of them. That would have made it perfect.

When it was time to leave, Roy said, "I'd like to give you a ride home, if it's okay with you."

Ronnie said, "She came with us, we don't mind giving her a ride. You don't even know where she lives."

Betty spoke up before I could and she said, "You ninny Of-course he knows where she lives. He picked her up and returned her safely from their golf date, remember? Besides, who made you king? She can get a ride from whomever she pleases. You're so bossy!"

I spoke up, "Betty, don't be so hard on Ronnie. He means well. Roy offered first and I will ride with him." Then I looked at Ronnie and I asked, "Unless you know something I don't, Ronnie. Does he have a criminal record hidden somewhere...or anything else I should know?"

"He probably does, but I can't *say* if he does because he's my boss and he might fire me. I need that job."

Now we all laughed.

On the way to my home, we discussed some more on our music conversation and he said, "Are you all booked up for Friday evening? There's a movie I've been wanting to see. Maybe we could grab a bite to eat and see a movie?"

"I'd like that," I said simply. "What time?"

"Is five-thirty too early? That way we can eat first and probably make the seven O'clock showing."

"No, five-thirty will be fine." Mentally I was calculating how I could get off a little early so I could go home, bathe and change.

When we got to the house, I was still floating somewhere up on cloud nine, knowing he had asked me by myself and without all our friends out. He had said some very nice things during the evening. As soon as he turned the ignition off, I had expected him to turn towards me and pull me over for a kiss. To my great disappointment, no such luck. He got out of his car, came around to my side in his usual gentlemanly way and opened my door for me He *did* take my hand and walk me to the door I assumed again wrongly, that okay, he was going to enclose me in those strong arms and kiss me goodnight. Wrong again.

Instead, when I turned towards him, giving him every opportunity to scoop me up, I said, "I had such a great time, Roy. I'll look forward to Friday," he put each of his hands on my opposing shoulders, pulled me (not nearly close enough in my mind) and gave me a little "peck" on the forehead. Like he was saying thank you to a child.

"I did, too," he said and he added as he walked to his car, "See you Friday."

As I prepared for bed, I wondered, was *he not physically attracted to me; was this going to be, "I like you, but only as a friend" relationship I had handed out to several men in my past? I didn't want to just be friends, I wanted a sweet, sweep me off my feet kiss which would lead to many others and then? Well, we would see, it might depend on the kiss…if I ever got one.*

Several things he had said over the short time I had known him or things Betty had repeated from Ronnie had already shown me not only did he have perfect manners; he was a traditionalist at heart. He would always open doors for women, he always carried a clean handkerchief; as I found out when I spilled something on my skirt once and he pulled one out for me to use. Of course, I had taken it home, washed and ironed it and then returned it to him, impressed. It didn't matter to him how equal women were treated as long as they were respected and treated fairly. He admitted to being a deacon in his hometown Methodist church for a while. The worst obscenity I had ever heard him say was "Damn!" He insisted on paying for everything whenever he was with me; it didn't matter what it was. He was insistent on it. When I commented on paying my share now and then he actually got offended. Eventually I never carried anything but a folded twenty-dollar bill, a lipstick, and comb. I always would hand these to Roy and he would put them in one of his pockets. During the evening or outing, I could ask him for these when I went to the ladies' room.

The first time I handed him these things he held up the twenty-dollar bill and with raised eyebrows asked "what's this?" I explained about my belief in "Walk-Around-Money".

Then he said, rather wryly, I thought, "You don't have to carry this when I am with you."

"What if you and I have a disagreement and I don't want to have you drive me home?"

Very intently he said, looking right into my eyes. "Anytime I take you somewhere I am responsible for taking you home and I intend to always do just that. If you happen to be mad at me for something, you can just sit in the car and not talk to me, but I *will* take you home. That's a given. Understand? No options."

"Okay, but I still want you to hold on to my twenty-dollar bill; my "walk-around-money.""

The Monday after my Saturday goodnight peck on the forehead, I received a delivery of roses. There were eleven red and in the center was one white one. The card read, *"There is sometimes one special and different from all the others. I think I have found one like that in you. Looking forward to Friday, Roy."*

I was ecstatic! How wonderful! I wanted to dance around my desk. I wanted everyone to ask who they were from (they did). But I would just smile and hold my secret tight to my chest. I didn't want to jinx anything here. The only time I had received delivery flowers before was when Don had sent them to me, along with some for his wife on Valentine's Day that time. Now I felt like young girl, receiving flowers for no holiday, no birthday or anniversary…Just because he wanted to show me, he had *enjoyed* my company.

Of course, I had to call Betty that evening and share this event with but swear her to secrecy about Ronnie because I didn't want Roy to think I was sharing step by step his courting (if that's what this really was).

Friday came and we went to a small Chinese restaurant for dinner. We had a very lively conversation about football (our first). We "play argued" over which teams were best and he was surprised at how much I knew. Of course he had to brag about Mississippi States' team and I bragged on the Longhorns. We even made a bet. We would each choose which college team would win the next week end out of our favorites and which pro team.

"What shall we bet?" I asked.

"Tell you what," he said, "There is nothing I dislike more than doing laundry. If I win, you can pick up my laundry baskets; I usually have two and do my laundry on the week end and I'll pick it upon Monday, after work on my way home."

"And if I win?"

"Hum...How about I'll pick up or have one of the guys pick up your car at work and I'll have it vacuumed out, washed, chammied off and even waxed occasionally."

"You sound like you are giving up already hedging your bets with notice you won't wax it every week end, just occasionally when you lose."

"Nope. Cars don't need to be waxed every week, just occasionally."

So, we shook hands on it and promised we would call each other on Fridays to give each other our bets.

We enjoyed the movie, I especially enjoyed holding his hand when he reached for mine with one, and placed his arm around my shoulders. It was nice, sitting in the darkened theatre, close enough I imagined I could feel and hear him breath. I knew I could feel the warmth radiating from his body, so close and yet not close enough for me.

Again, I allowed myself to get my hopes up for that expected goodnight kiss, but again, it didn't happen.

That night, I lay in bed for a long time with my old doubts rising up. Was he not attracted to me at all? If so, why? And if so, what *was* the attraction? There had to be some reason he continued to want to see me, increasingly more often. What was it, if there were no physical draw? What if he was gay? Immediately I discarded this. There was an aura about him which suggested otherwise. Was he waiting for me to make the first move? I doubted this, too. He was so old-fashioned and traditional about the role men and women played I felt instinctively he would withdraw from any such lead from me. I assumed, (and rightly so) as I later would find out, believed the next step in our relationship would and should come from him. He definitely would feel it was his place.

Chapter

TWELVE

---⁂---

O ver the next few weeks, he did several things that gave every indication that we were becoming a couple; to our friends as well as each other.

He told me there was to be a cocktail party at the home of one of the other district managers and he would like me to go with him. I had been making my own clothes ever since high school and I made me a floor length halter dress. The material was black with tiny, tiny little white dots, and I trimmed the top and hem with white. Since I made my own clothes; it fit really well and I was proud of the way it looked. I made an appointment with another friend who owned and ran a beauty shop, asked for and received the afternoon off and splurged on having her put my hair up. I loved the effect and thought it perfect for the dress.

When he came to pick me up, my reward was the way he looked at me. "Wow," he said, "You look terrific,"

"Thank you, you look very nice as well."

As he walked me to his car and opened my door for me, he said, "I wasn't sure you knew *what* to wear. Did I tell you it was dress-up or not? On the way over here, I was worried you'd decided to finally get out those Texas Tennie's and wear them with jeans or a denim skirt.

"Liar," I said. "You weren't the least bit worried."

He laughed and said, "You're right. If there's one thing I noticed about you from the very beginning is that you've got class."

I was surprised at this compliment. *Maybe he was more observant than I gave him credit for,* I thought.

We had a wonderful time that evening. Anyone could tell he was proud when he introduced me to these people, and he kept lose to me all evening, with his hand on my waist or lightly on my shoulders He tried to hog my attention all night and none of the males there were allowed more than very brief and surface conversations with me. He made it plain I was "his"; not in an assertive way, but proudly as if he was a lucky escort with the perfect woman on his arm. I was thrilled and enjoyed every single minute.

We talked all the way home about some of the different people there. Some he had known for years; some were fairly new to the firm but they seem to genuinely like him.

When we arrived home, I thought sure he was going to enfold me in his arms and I really did anticipate his kiss. He walked me to the door, said, "Thank you for going with me. I really enjoyed the evening. I hope you didn't mind missing Saturday night regulars with the group."

"Oh, no," I said "This was so much fun. Sort of a Cinderella evening. I love having an excuse to dress up."

"Every now and then they throw these little shindigs. They have a bigger Christmas party, and in the spring, there will be an awards dinner where the year's sales figures are announced and bonus checks handed out. You'll have to go to that for sure."

Mentally my mind jumped. This was a sure indicator he held a future for "us" in his mind.

"So, do you usually end up with a bonus check?"

"Always," he said, smiling.

"Well, it's late, I better let you get in to bed. Again, I had a great time." I almost held my breath. Was he going to kiss me?

Again, he put his hands on my shoulders and leaned in to give me that ridiculous substitute for a kiss; a peck on the forehead.

I couldn't help it, I felt cheated.

The introduction of Roy to my children was done gradually, after careful discussion between Roy and I. It was a good way to do it. There was such a difference in their ages at this time; they all needed to be handled differently. We went over what we each considered might be possible hindrances and what might make this a natural progression of the way he and I were beginning to feel about each other.

One week he called and said he had a surprise for me and the kids and could he bring it over after work.

I said he could and then sent the rest of the afternoon trying to guess what it might be.

Especially since he had included my children in his words and this was a first for that.

I told the kids that Roy was bringing us a surprise. My youngest was very surprised, and she patted her chest and said, "For me? A surprise for me?"

"For all of us," I corrected her.

"What is it?" one of them asked.

"How would I know? It's not a surprise I picked out. It's a surprise from him to all of us. At least that's what he said."

The youngest stayed glued to the front window after that. It was almost like when you're on a trip with children and they keep saying "Are we there, yet?"

She kept saying, "When is he coming? It's taking too long."

When he got there, he opened the trunk and brought this big box out with assistance from my eldest son. He then asked for a screwdriver.

He laughed when I handed my pink handled screwdriver from my women's tool box.

"Looks like a toy," he said, "Does it work?"

I ignored his question.

"What is it?" my youngest kept asking.

I could see from the writing on the box that it was a backyard grill; something we had never had, but wanted so we could have our own bar-b-ques in our back yard.

We were all excited and I told him, "You shouldn't have done this, Roy. It's too big a gift. Let me at least pay part of the cost."

He looked up from where he was sitting on the small patio, looking at the directions for assembly and he said quietly, "Don't even go there, Jackie. I wanted to do it. Let me have some fun here, too."

"Now! All we need is some charcoal and lighter starter and we're good to go."

My youngest giggled and said, "Uh-uh. We need something to cook on it, too. Hamburgers and hot dogs and stuff."

Roy laughed and tousled her hair and then said, "All in due time, all in due time, sweetheart."

I was proud of the manners my children exhibited when they each thanked him. He sat down on one of the lawn chairs and grinned at me. "I suppose it's too much to ask, but you wouldn't have a spare Jack Daniels around anywhere? I think I've earned a drink. I'm not at all that good at putting things together. I was worried it might fall right back down."

I laughed with him and answered, "No Jack Daniels, but plenty of Kool-Aid or some sodas."

"Well, that's okay. I just happen to have a brand-new bottle in the car, in case of emergency."

He went to his car and I got out glasses and ice and cola to mix mine with. We sat on the small patio and talked and I felt relaxed and compete. I noticed right off that my youngest, who was a first grader at the time, pulled her lawn chair closer to his and tried to monopolize the conversation with him. He good naturedly accepted this and gave her his full attention when she asked her many questions. It made me feel a little guilty when I saw her obvious delight in his company. I know she missed having a daddy. I remembered how close I had been to mine before he passed. He hadn't been the best parent but he was missed just the same.

As I watched Roy's interaction with my children, asking the right questions to each one, grasping their ages and interests with appropriate and perceptive questions. I knew he had been an only child, and I was surprised at his understanding and the way the children warmed up to him.

He stayed for a little while and then said, "I need to get on home and to bed or I'll never hear that alarm in the morning."

My youngest moaned and with a frown of concentration she said, "Oh, I wanted us to cook something. Why do you have to go so early, Mr. Roy? It's still daylight. It's too early to go to bed. I go to bed at eight o'clock and I'm only six."

The rest of us laughed, and although she thought it made perfect sense for a grownup to stay up later, she accepted it. She jumped up from her chair and said, "So, the next time you come over, can we cook? And can I help?"

He grinned at her as he replied, "Yes and Yes."

I was proud of how the others told him they were glad to have met him, and the other two boys shook his hand as they said it.

He insisted on me keeping the Jack Daniels there for another drink sometime, and I walked him to his car.

"They seem to be real good kids, Jackie. You're doing a great job. They have manners and are very articulate and easy to talk to. I must admit I was a little apprehensive about meeting them. You know, I have been to company picnics and other gatherings when some of the guys bring their families and some of them are so wild and uncontrollable, I wonder why they bother to have children if they can't guide them into being better human beings."

"Thank you. I appreciate that. Of course, you saw them on their good side and you came, bearing gifts."

He chuckled and said, "Is that the key, then?"

He opened the car door and we stood talking for a few minutes. I could see my youngest at the window, curtain pulled back, watching us.

"Hey," Roy said, "What do you think about us christening the grill next Sunday?"

I was taken back for a few seconds and he continued, "I know you all go to church, but we could plan it for the early evening or late afternoon."

I know my excitement must have shown when I said, "That would be perfect. I will plan the menu and you bring a good appetite and how to work the grill."

He laughed, "Still want to go dancing Saturday night with the gang?"

"Sure, if you do," I said, "If we can dance on Saturday night and still get up to play golf at eight in the morning, I think we can manage church and then late afternoon or early evening for a cookout."

"Sounds like a plan," he said getting into his car. "I'll call you before Saturday to go over the menu. Let's keep it very simple the first time on the grill, okay?"

"Like as in hamburgers and hot dogs instead of ribs or steaks?"

He laughed again, "Perfect!"

After he left and I told the kids the plans for the weekend my eldest daughter said, "Can I invite John?"

John was her current steady boyfriend at the time and I not only approved of him, but actually liked him.

"Sure, you can."

Later that night I lay in bed, propped up on the pillows making a list. *I would buy chips, fresh lettuce and tomatoes and onions, pickles and relish, hamburger and hot dog buns, make sure I had plenty of mustard and ketchup. I'd make from scratch my melt in your mouth, fresh apple cake. I added paper plates and plastic silverware and plastic cups and colas, even some olives. Oh, yes! I would make baked beans and my own original potato salad (made with tiny jalapenos) recipe, even the kids liked it). All-beef wieners, and organic ground round (low fat and healthy). Once I added paper napkins sand sliced cheese for those who might want cheeseburgers, I put the list aside. As I lay there, waiting for sleep, I remembered watching his purposeful hands put together the grill, my thought turned to how it might feel to have those hands move to caressing me and holding me close.*

I almost chuckled out loud in the darkened room I asked myself, "If you can't draw a real kiss from him, what makes you think you can get him to make love to you?

When he called later during the week, he kept trying to give him the list so he could pay the expense of the meal and I vehemently refused his efforts.

"There are five of us plus John and we have to eat, anyway. Don't be silly. Now, if were T-bones or ribs or something, I'd let you, but this is merely the old standard hot dogs and hamburgers."

"Well, what can I bring, then?" he asked.

"A grill and yourself."

"If you're sure, I can certainly handle that."

He added after a brief pause, "Can you do me a big favor, then?"

"Sure. What?"

"Don't talk about it to Betty because then Ronnie and her will invite themselves and we can always do it some other time with them, I would like this first time to be with just us."

"Sure," I said, thinking I really wanted it that way. We were all good friends but that didn't mean we had to share every single gathering with them. I also liked being included in the "just us" description.

"I'm afraid my eldest has already asked me if John can come and I granted permission. Is that alright?"

"Sure, he's practically your family, too."

I began cleaning on Friday night. Then got up early Saturday morning and cleaned more. I made all the children help and for once they understood my frenzy and didn't complain. I don't know what made me want to have my hair done that Saturday morning, but I did. I gave strict orders to the kids about not messing anything up, and I showered and wrapped a towel around my hair after I shampooed it. I had no makeup on, and the towel was fastened like a turban. I always had preferred shampooing my own before having it cut or doe professionally, and I would wrap my head in a towel turban to drive to the beauty salon.

I took my youngest with me and told her I'd let her get a manicure and have her nails painted pink. I called Betty who owned the beauty salon, and she said she would work us in. I warned my daughter to not say anything about our "picnic" the next day because it was a secret with just Mr. Roy, myself and her and she crossed her heart and promised.

As we drove towards the salon, my daughter started pointing and excitedly saying, "Look, mama, look! It's Mr. Roy!"

Out of the corner of my eye I could see his car trying to pull up right next to mine. No way was I going to look over there and smile and wave like my daughter wanted me to do. What should I do? I asked myself. Of all the luck! I didn't not want him to see face to face, head on, as it were, with a turban on my head, no makeup and wearing a t-shirt. As I tried to hush my daughter and she kept on waving at him and yelling, "Hi, Mr. Roy; Hi Mr. Roy."

I decided my best choice was to pretend to be so deeply concentrating on my driving, I was unaware of him in the next car lane. I took the first chance to change lanes, turn off somewhere and go another way, pretending I never saw him.

So, that's what I did; his car went straight on, I turned (several times, to make sure he couldn't come back and find me. Later I realized the humor behind this entire episode but at this time in our relationship I was still in what they call "the Honeymoon Stage" where I wanted him to think I always was pretty and well put together. I guess I wanted him to think I woke up every morning looking just like I looked when we said goodnight the evening before. In other words, I wanted to pretend (and have him believe) that I was perfect. What foolishness, I told myself but it was too late now. The die had been cast. My best hope was to completely stick to my story that I hadn't (indeed, regardless of the little blabbermouth beside me) even been aware of him driving beside us. That was my story and I was sticking to it, by gosh, I didn't care how unbelievable it was.

"Mama," she said to "Didn't you see Mr. Roy? Why didn't you wave at him?"

"Mr. Roy? Where was he? I didn't even see him. Are you sure it was him?"

She nodded her head and said, "It's okay, Mama, I saw him and I waved and he waved back at me."

Later when he came to pick me up for Saturday night with the gang, he asked me, "Hey, I saw you two driving down Congress Avenue this morning and I did everything except crash into you and never got you to even acknowledge me."

"I know, I know," I said sheepishly. "She told me I missed you. I guess I am sort of tunnel-visioned when it comes to driving. I honestly really am one of those people who realizes the need to drive but acknowledges truthfully, I don't enjoy driving and traffic now days gives me a headache. I'm sorry I didn't see you."

"You had this white thing around your head…" he paused then and grinning he said, "For a minute or so I thought you were deliberately ignoring me."

"You're crazy! Why would I do that?"

Then, God bless the little children, my young daughter said, "Probably 'cause you had a towel wrapped around your head and you thought he wouldn't recognize you, Mama."

That night when he picked me up, he chuckled again as he opened the car door for me to get in and said, "If we go on seeing each other, Jackie, even if it is at a swimming pool or amusement park or some other place, chances are someday I am going to see you with a towel around your head. And you are probably going to see me when I need a shave, or a haircut or not wearing a suit."

"Can we just quit talking about this?"

He laughed one more time and said, "Yes, however that brings up another subject I'd like to talk with you about when we have more time."

Though immediately my curiosity was up, he didn't continue and I waited, thinking he would get to it later that evening.

We had arrived at the club and I could see Betty and Ronnie entering the door.

"Well, no time like the present," I said with sweaty palms and dry mouth. "We could sit here and talk before we go in."

"No, I don't want to feel under pressure and I want to think how I'm going to say it. We'll do it later."

A swift pain went through me. *Was he breaking up with me and just looking for the best way to tell me?*

He looked over at me, pointed to the console between our seats. It was pulled down and he opened it to reveal a bag of peppermint candies. "Look what I have for you. I noticed how much you like peppermints so I have them in my car, and…" he paused and dipped in his pocket to show me some he had stashed in there and said, "In my pockets; even in my apartment."

"Is this leading up to you offering to show me, instead of your etchings or paintings, your peppermints?" *I was trying to keep the conversation light and cheerful but where was he going with this?*

"No, but that's not a bad idea."

All that evening I kept wondering about this little talk he wanted to have with me. What was that about? Did he want to verbally warn me (remembering what Betty had said about bachelors with their guards up) that he was a life- long bachelor and was never going to commit to more? I grew more and more curious as the evening wore on and I could barely concentrate on any of the conversations flowing around me. I remembered the song by Mac Davis "Baby, Don't Get Hooked on Me" that I had teasingly asked him once if that were his theme song. Perhaps he now felt he was getting into this relationship over his head, and wanted to clarify where he stood on the commitment ledge.

I tried to plan what my strategy should be…should I be cheerful and reassure him I wanted nothing more than this friendship? Because basically on so many levels, that is all we were at this point in time…

friends. Not that I didn't want to move forward, but until I sensed he did, too, we stayed on this plateau. I thought to myself, Somewhere, long ago and in the past, it would be at this point where a young woman's father would ask about a suitor's intentions.

I wondered if this had something to do with a planned visit his mother was making the next week. During her forty-five year to his father they had never spent one singe night apart. His father had died from an unexpected and sudden heart attack the summer before and he still found it difficult to even talk about him in any depth.

He tried to take a few days each holiday season to spend some time in Mississippi with her, but she was in her eighties and did not enjoy flying. He had scheduled her flight this time, and she was coming to town the following week, probably to stay a week. It would be my first time to meet her and while I was a little anxious about her approval, I was also encouraged by Roy's desire to have us meet.

All kind of thoughts swam around and around in my head but I did not really know what prompted a request for this "talk".

We were both quiet on the drive home; me, because I had allowed a sort of dread build up in me, anticipating nothing good, and Roy, because I imagined him preparing to give me bad news. We had declined an invitation to go to breakfast with the rest of our friends, claiming a difficult preceding week.

When we arrived, he shut the ignition off and I asked him, "Would you like to come in and I could fix some coffee while we talk?"

"Let's just sit here and talk. I don't want to take a chance on waking any of the kids up."

That added another notch to my apprehension.

"Are you comfortable?" he asked. "If you were any further over there, you'd be out of the car. Come on over here, close to me."

Now my apprehension lessoned somewhat. This didn't sound like goodbye…

I slid over and settled (gratefully) into him, my head on his chest. I took a couple of deep breaths and tried to relax as much as possible.

He began, "This is difficult for me to talk about, but it's also something I feel strong about so I'm going to be very honest with you."

"I want you to be," I felt like I had to force the words out.

"Remember when Ronnie and Betty were trying to fix us up?"

"Yes, of course I do."

"And you told me you had a quasi-serious relationship going on with 'what's his name?' I don't think I ever knew his name. I thought you were dating someone else and I didn't know how serious it was so I didn't pursue you until I felt you had stopped dating him. I knew I had no right to tell you who to see at that point."

"Right, I guess," I said.

"However, with each passing day I have grown crazier about you. Crazy is the right word, too, because it's been years since I have felt even close to what I feel about you."

My heart began to soar with his words.

"I have genuinely tried to curb my feelings because I am afraid of how they will be received by you. I am worried at the depth of feeling I have for you. I am also worried that the feeling you have for me is not as deep or sincere as my own feelings for you."

I started to respond to him but he shushed me with a finger to my lips and said, "Wait. Let me finish while I have the nerve."

"Before I let myself go into any further with whatever it is, we have, I need to know you feel the same, or at least there's a possibility you are heading down that same path. I have never been one to be playing the field, as they say. I am not seeing anyone else but you, and have no desire to do so. I guess I want some reassurance you feel the same. I don't think you are still dating 'what's his name', Mr. Serious..." he paused here and tilting my chin up so our eyes met he said, "Are you?"

I started laughing I couldn't help it, I laughed at the surprised look on his face and when I finally got control of the laughter I said, "I can't decide if you are asking me if I'm sleeping with anyone right now or if you are telling me we might be moving that way ourselves, if I am so inclined."

I started laughing again and he said, "Well, what's so funny? I don't know what you might be doing on the nights we aren't together."

"I'm laughing," I said, a little breathlessly, "Because you said something my youngest says to me all the time; maybe in different words. When I tell her, I love her she always says, "I love you more and we will try to argue each other on who cares the most for the other; she or me?" I paused her and then went on, "and I'm laughing because I have been worried you weren't attracted to me in a physical way. Am I now to believe you have been having a hard time holding yourself in check because you want me as badly as I want you? Or because you want to make sure it will be a one woman-one-man relationship and I'm not sleeping with someone else and neither are you? *Of-course,* I'm not seeing anyone else besides you. I don't know how in the world I would juggle my job, my children, our relationship, and finish my final degree. Who do you think I am, Wonder-Woman?"

"Yes," he said, and he enfolded me into his arms and I got my long-awaited kiss…In fact I got more than one and they were everything I had imagined, and more.

I never got a "down on one knee with a little ring box proposal" from Roy. What I did get was Roy running into my house one day, a brown paper bag clutched in one hand and a pencil in the other. "Look," he said, sitting me down at the dining room table, spreading the sack out to show me some figures and pencil calculations on the bag "This is how much I earn after taxes each payday. This is what I think you probably make. These are a list of any bills I have. Add yours to it. What do you think? Should we go ahead and get married?"

In the pleasant aftermath of the first time Roy and I ever made love, I lay in his arms and I said softly, "Did you see them?"

"See what?"

"The fireworks," I said.

Of-course," he said softly.

Then I added, "Did you hear them?"

"Hear what?" he asked holding me close to him.

"The bells and whistles?"

"Of-course I did," he said.

"*I* did, too," I said softly.

EPILOGUE

Time passed, I walked across the stage and received my M.S. in Psychology. I walked across the auditorium stage and received my Ph.D. in Psychology and Education with Roy and my children in the audience. President Bill Clinton was the Keynote speaker. Not bad for a sixteen-year-old high-school drop-out to travel. My eldest daughter married her John and moved to New Mexico where she got her education degree and became a teacher. My eldest son finished high-school and (against my pleading) joined the Navy. The next one down joined the Marines. My baby considered "Mr. Roy" her father and called him Dad. I have grandchildren, and even great-grandchildren. I have faced many difficult times, but enjoyed many more blessings.

…But that's another story for another time.